THE
CORN BRIDE

Mark Stay got a part-time Christmas job at Waterstone's in the Nineties (back when it still had an apostrophe) and, despite being working class and quite lippy, somehow ended up working in publishing for over 25 years. He would write in his spare time and sometimes those writings would get turned into books and films, including the Witches of Woodville series from Simon & Schuster, and the 2023 Warner Bros. horror movie *Unwelcome*. *Nautilus*, the #1 Amazon Prime TV series, was based on his treatment. Mark was also co-presenter of the award-winning Bestseller Experiment podcast, which has inspired writers all over the world to finish and publish their books. Born in London, he lives in Kent with YouTube gardener and writer Claire Burgess and a declining assortment of retired chickens.

@markstay
markstaywrites.com
witchesofwoodville.com

Also by Mark Stay

Robot Overlords
Back to Reality (with Mark Oliver)
The End of Magic
The End of Dragons

The Witches of Woodville series

The Crow Folk
Babes in the Wood
The Ghost of Ivy Barn
The Holly King

THE CORN BRIDE

The Witches of Woodville V

Mark Stay

**SIMON &
SCHUSTER**

London · New York · Amsterdam/Antwerp · Sydney · Toronto · New Delhi

First published in Great Britain by Simon & Schuster UK Ltd, 2025

Copyright © Unusually Tall Stories, Ltd 2025

The right of Mark Stay to be identified as author
of this work has been asserted in accordance with the
Copyright, Designs and Patents Act, 1988.

1 3 5 7 9 10 8 6 4 2

Simon & Schuster UK Ltd
1st Floor
222 Gray's Inn Road
London WC1X 8HB

Simon & Schuster Australia, Sydney
Simon & Schuster India, New Delhi

www.simonandschuster.co.uk
www.simonandschuster.com.au
www.simonandschuster.co.in

The authorised representative in the EEA is Simon & Schuster Netherlands BV,
Herculesplein 96, 3584 AA Utrecht, Netherlands. info@simonandschuster.nl

A CIP catalogue record for this book
is available from the British Library

Paperback ISBN: 978-1-3985-2082-0
eBook ISBN: 978-1-3985-2083-7
Audio ISBN: 978-1-3985-2084-4

This book is a work of fiction. Names, characters, places
and incidents are either a product of the author's imagination or
are used fictitiously. Any resemblance to actual people living or
dead, events or locales is entirely coincidental.

Typeset in Sabon by M Rules
Printed and Bound in the UK using 100% Renewable Electricity
at CPI Group (UK) Ltd

MIX
Paper | Supporting
responsible forestry
FSC® C171272

To Emily & Kai.
May your wedding day be slightly less
chaotic than this one ...

April, 1941

War has spread to North Africa, Yugoslavia and Greece as more nations fall to Axis powers. The United States offers aid in the form of its Lend-Lease Act, but Britain still endures nightly bombing campaigns and terrible losses in its cities. Meanwhile, a small village in Kent awaits the arrival of Faye Bright, due to return home on leave after some months of intense and secret training. And there is going to be a wedding! But before we join the impending nuptials, let's begin our story with a night in London ...

A Blitz Lullaby

Faye Bright lay on a platform of the Oxford Circus underground station as the city above took a hammering from the Luftwaffe.

Sleep came and went in brief, delirious shifts. Every time she fell into a deep slumber, another salvo of bombs rolled like thunder, the floor trembled, dust trickled from the ceiling and Faye jolted awake. Again.

For the Londoners snoozing around her, it was just another raid. Perhaps they were used to it by now? Or maybe those who couldn't cope had fled to the countryside, leaving only the hardy town mouse types who were able to endure this kind of nerve-shredding hell night after night? 'We can take it!' was a familiar refrain, though Faye had to wonder when they might start dishing it out for a change.

She checked her wristwatch – the one her commanding officer Bellamy Dumonde had insisted on giving her after she was late for *one* session of training at Beaulieu – and was astonished to see that it was ten to five in the morning. The raid had started a little after nine o'clock last night. This was a punishing one by any standard.

Faye had been caught out after a pleasant dinner with Vera Fivetrees, Head Witch of the British Empire, at Duck Island Cottage, her official residence in Saint James's Park. Bellamy had been there, too, and they had spent the evening discussing anything but the war. Faye was due a few days' leave and was looking forward to going home and being back in Bertie's arms for their wedding.

This would be her first trip to Woodville since the strange events of last Christmas, which had culminated in her beloved Bertie proposing to her. Faye had said yes without hesitation. She had known Bertie all her life, and in the last year had fallen head over heels for this sweet and brave boy. It all made sense. Apart from the fact that she had to leave the morning after the wedding to begin her training with Bellamy's Special Operations Executive: Paranormal Division.

But tomorrow she would be going home.

Woodville was where Faye had been born. She knew its every nook and cranny, and greeted everybody by name. But now, as she lay on the dusty platform in the heart of London, the village felt as distant as the moon.

For the past few months, her every waking moment had been dedicated to applying her witchcraft skills to cryptology, weapons training, martial arts, orienteering, fitness and sabotage. It was exhausting, but there was never a dull moment. And she was good at it.

Bellamy was quick to praise her interrogation skills and her swift right hook. Would Bertie notice the change in her? Would it scare him off?

After dinner with Vera and Bellamy, she had decided to take an evening walk back to her lodgings above a pub in Oxford Street. She'd been close to the Oxford Circus underground station when the siren sounded, and had ducked inside.

The Londoners' famed Blitz spirit was alive and kicking to start with, and there had been music, singing and laughter. But around midnight, folks had become more subdued. As it became clear this was going to be a long raid, they all hunkered down for the duration.

And now, some eight hours or so later, Faye sat up and stretched. The sun would rise soon and the raid would end as the Luftwaffe returned home from their deadly mission.

A handful of people were already awake, reading newspapers or solving crosswords – one man was clearing his lungs a little too enthusiastically for Faye's liking – but most were still asleep. Faye considered nodding off again.

Then she heard the singing. Eerie, distant and childish.

'Golden slumbers kiss your eyes,
Smiles awake you when you rise;
Sleep, pretty wantons, do not cry,
And I will sing a lullaby.
Rock them, rock them, lullaby.'

Faye stood slowly and glanced around. The folks nearby were rubbing their eyes, yawning and scruffing their hair as they woke. One woman was knitting a pair of socks. No one else reacted to the echoing voices. There had been children playing and singing when she had first arrived, but she looked about and found them piled asleep on top of their parents further down the platform.

Treading carefully, Faye walked silently past the snoring children. As she approached the darkness of the underground train tunnel, something in the air changed. An electric sensation that left a metallic taste in her mouth.

Magic.

She reached the empty maw of the tunnel and glanced back along the platform. She couldn't see the moon down here, of course, but could still draw on its energy. She created a glamour so that no one saw her hopping from the platform and onto the rails. Faye was fairly certain the power had been turned off during the raid, but she kept away from the electrified third rail nevertheless. The tingling sensation of the glamour comforted her, giving her what she felt might be a mis-placed sense of invincibility, but one she welcomed all the same as she stepped further into the dark.

> '*Golden slumbers kiss your eyes,*
> *Smiles awake you when you rise.*'

A chill brushed at her cheeks, a trickle of cold sweat snaking down her spine. The air was laced with smoke and dust and something that made Faye think of when the pub's outdoor lavvy was blocked.

The singing continued, echoing off the curved walls of the tunnel.

> *'Sleep, pretty wantons, do not cry,*
> *And I will sing a lullaby.*
> *Rock them, rock them, lullaby.'*

Faye wondered if she was dreaming – after all, it wouldn't be the first time that eerie singing had haunted her dreams – but as her eyes adjusted to the gloom, she saw them.

> *'Care is heavy, therefore sleep you.*
> *You are care, and care must keep you.'*

They were holding hands, dancing in a circle.

> *'Sleep, pretty wantons, do not cry,*
> *And I will sing you a lullaby.'*

Three boys and three girls, dressed in school uniforms. The boys wore caps. One had broken specs. The girls all wore their hair differently. The mousy one had a ponytail, the blonde had pigtails and the littlest one wore hers with a blue clip. Their parents had gone to some effort to make them presentable for school, yet—

'Bloody hell,' Faye muttered as she moved closer to the children. Their glistening faces were blistered, blackened and burned. Light curled around them, and she thought of the magic lantern shows she had seen as a child. How the colours blended and swirled hypnotically. These children were ghosts. Victims of another raid, perhaps. Their lives cut short by this hideous war.

The all-clear siren sounded. A long drone, no rise or fall in pitch. Faye instinctively looked up at the sound and the children stopped singing. When she looked down again, they were all staring at her.

Faye's bowels loosened and she nearly had an unfortunate incident but managed to keep it together.

The children began to sing again, their voices creating a forsaken harmony with the siren.

> 'Huffity, puffity, Ringstone Round,
> If you lose your hat it will never be found,
> So pull your britches right up to your chin,
> And fasten your cloak with a bright new pin,
> And when you are ready, then we can begin,
> Huffity, puffity, puff!'

The singing ceased with the siren, the children vanished in a burst of light and Faye's ears popped. Something fluttered in her chest, her breath coming in short rasps.

She took a moment to gather herself in the dark of the tunnel before turning on her heel to make her way back to the platform.

Silhouetted in the arch of light, another figure blocked her path. Still and silent.

Inhuman.

It was a corn dolly, but one as tall as Faye, wearing a white wedding dress. The corn dolly's head was a cluster of wheat shafts, like an exploding star. Her fingers were broken stems poking from her sleeves.

Faye's mouth was dry. A ringing began in her ears, growing louder and louder.

Creaking like wicker, the Corn Bride slowly raised her makeshift hand and pointed at her.

Faye tried to speak, but no words would come. Her chest heaved; her limbs were paralysed.

The Corn Bride tilted her head back and rushed at Faye, hands raised as if to shove her deeper into the dark.

Faye's training kicked in as she bunched her fists and took a defensive stance, but the Corn Bride whisked straight through her, turning into swirls of vapour and vanishing on the dusty breeze.

Faye blinked. The ringing in her ears subsided. She was alone once more.

As her heart slowed, she found her voice again. 'Blimmin' 'eck.'

It was time to go home.

FLIGHT TO BAVARIA

Otto Kopp – Bavarian Druid, founder of the Thule Society, leader of the Black Sun; a man the mere mention of whose name was enough to cause a panicked exodus from Bratislava two centuries ago – was flying back to the place of his birth in pitiful shackles and rags. He was a prisoner and traitor to the Reich, flanked by his former subordinates in the Black Sun.

While they were dressed in their crimson robes, Otto was barefoot, in oversized trousers held up by braces over an off-white shirt with no collar. Hardly fitting for a Druid of his stature, but this was all an exercise in his ongoing humiliation. The Bavarian had endured more than his fill since that fateful day last summer on the White Cliffs of Dover. Defeated by a novice witch and a gaggle of tea-slurping hags, he'd had little choice but to use the blue flame of the aether to escape. As far as they were concerned, he would have vanished into thin air before their very eyes. For Otto, the journey had been a stomach-churning leap through a void between worlds. One that had ended with him landing with a slap on the rough concrete of a secret hangar at the airfield in Juvincourt, Northern France. Only a few hours earlier, he had left aboard a Dornier Do 17 bomber with promises to wipe out Britain's magical defences. He had returned vanquished and in agony as the blue flames burned his left arm. His Black Sun siblings were waiting like hyenas. They unleashed their pathetic curses on him, taking advantage of his weakened state and binding him in chains.

Himmler had appointed Otto as leader of the Black Sun one chilly January morning in 1940. The secret occult organisation had grown rapidly from the ranks of the pre-war Thule Society and was answerable only to Himmler and the Führer. But how could one wrangle such a gaggle of mewling kittens? Each would eat their own young for the opportunity to rule, and that's exactly how Himmler wanted it. Otto's reign was doomed from the start.

That first night in the cell had been the worst. Writhing in pain, the skin on his arm blistering as he waited for word to come of his inevitable execution. The mighty Otto Kopp, bested by a girl from Kent, of all places. Not only had his failure made the Black Sun a laughing stock in the upper echelons of the Third Reich, but Göring's Luftwaffe had been sent packing by the RAF. The Battle of Britain had been lost, Operation Sealion had been postponed and Hitler had turned his sights to Russia. Otto would have warned the Führer that if Napoleon could not conquer the

Russians, then his odds were pretty grim, but Hitler had stopped listening to good advice a long time ago. For as much as Otto had foreseen the rise of the Nazis, he could now also smell the rot of their demise. The infighting, the corruption, the fanatical demagogue. The head was already eating the tail. He gave them four years at the very most.

The Focke-Wulf Fw 200 banked to starboard and rectangles of moonlight crawled across the deck. The pitch of the propellors fell to a drone as they slowed. A low hum resonated through Otto's boots as the landing gear lowered into place.

Himmler had wanted Otto shot, but Hitler felt the Druid might still prove useful and so there had been a stay of execution. They had imprisoned him in some chateau in France, but after three escape attempts – each ending in recapture by his Black Sun minions – Otto was being taken home. He was to be kept in the dungeons of Hohenzollern Castle. No witch or Druid could escape its walls. Otto knew this because he had designed the secret dungeons himself in the nineteenth century. He had thought he was so clever back then, and many of his former adversaries had met their fate thanks to his thoroughness and attention to detail when it came to magical suppression curses, oubliettes with no light whatsoever and walls that screamed. It truly was hell on Earth.

But Otto would never need to plan an escape because he had no intention of going there in the first place. He would flee soon after they landed at

Augsburg-Haunstetten airfield. And they would not recapture him this time.

Because they had given him a mirror, the fools.

For all their precautions and boasts of cunning, they had made one fatal mistake and he would make them pay for it. Otto Kopp toyed with the fragment of glass hidden in his palm as the plane began its descent. It shook violently, rattling like the proverbial bucket of bolts, before dipping suddenly and levelling out. The whole flight had been like this, and Otto suspected their pilot was either inebriated or trying to intimidate his cargo.

Mirrors, of course, were powerful tools of magic, and Otto had been forbidden any access to them, along with candles, salt, volcanic stone, mushrooms or wine. However, as the SS guards had escorted him through the French chateau's grand halls he had made one last attempt at escape, shoulder-barging them to one side. In the struggle, he had crashed into a four-hundred-year-old mirror. It had been pathetic and humiliating when his Black Sun siblings had laughed at his feeble attempt, but in their arrogance, they hadn't noticed that he had snatched up a tiny fragment of glass. They had searched him, of course, but they had not thought to look beneath his tongue. A couple of unremarkable coughs mid-flight helped him move the shard to his palm, where it was now ready for use. As much as Otto loathed sleight-of-hand sideshow conjurors for denigrating the art of magic, he had studied and mastered the fundamentals some time ago, and none of his captors were any the wiser.

The plane landed without fuss, and as it taxied along the runway to the hangar, Otto pressed the glass into his palm, drawing blood. He would need quite a bit if this was going to work, and so he dug deeper, until the thick burgundy liquid spread in rivulets. He opened his palm slightly and angled the mirror until he found the face of one of his Black Sun brothers. Gunther was a dim oaf from Austria whose family connections to old magic were the only reason he had been able to join this exclusive order. He was, however, built like a brick outhouse and perfect for Otto's needs.

The blood from Otto's palm oozed across the reflection of Gunther's face and seeped into the young Druid's largely empty mind. With a shudder, Otto knew that he had him.

Otto closed his eyes and, with his mind, spoke three words to Gunther: *Kill them all.*

Gunther blinked and scrunched his nose in confusion.

Kill them all, Otto repeated, more insistently this time.

The big lump wriggled a finger into his ear.

Otto sighed. The man might be dense, but ironically that was making him more difficult to control. He gazed directly at the reflection of Gunther in his palm. *Gunther, kill them.*

The sibling opposite Gunther, a thin strip of a thing with an ambitious Hitler moustache, leaned forwards, no doubt wondering what was wrong with him. 'Gunther?'

Gunther's body began to spasm. He was putting up an admirable fight. One he would lose. Foam flecked his lips. The brother with the Hitler moustache recoiled and was about to cry out when, without warning, Gunther drew his obsidian dagger and plunged it into his chest.

Hitler-moustache screamed, gargled and died. The six other Black Sun acolytes were momentarily baffled and looked to one another for some indication of how to react. It was only when Gunther stabbed a second of their number in the head that they finally sprang into action. But there was no stopping Gunther, who slashed the throat of one brother and gouged out the eye of another.

Otto sat quietly as they fought. One by one, the remaining Black Sun members were slaughtered with deadly efficiency. The pair of SS guards drew their weapons, but before they could fire Gunther broke their wrists, then their necks. The pilots tried to get involved, but had been told little of their passengers and were not prepared for the vicious and merciless assault. Their blood and brain matter decorated the windows of the cockpit. After only ninety seconds of mayhem, the job was done, and Otto released Gunther from his spell.

The young Druid stood panting, staring at his black and bloody blade, wondering what he had done. He turned to find Otto standing, but still in his shackles. Gunther gasped, his mind his own once more, and rushed at his former master, but he had barely taken two steps before Otto raised his palms, the mirrored glass embedded in the centre of his left hand. Gunther caught sight of his own reflection and faltered.

'No, Otto, please.'

Otto simply smiled and nodded. Gunther fell to his knees, lips quivering as he tried to resist Otto's power. Slowly and deliberately, he raised the point of his knife to the soft flesh under his own chin and slid it upwards.

'Black Sun will find you,' he said, trembling, but with one final snarl of defiance. The blade continued its slow progress into his body. 'There is nowhere you can hide. If it takes us till the end of time, we will—' Gunther choked. His eyes rolled back and he fell to the deck with a thud.

Otto took a ring of keys from the belt of the sibling lying closest to him and unlocked his manacles. He tossed them away, rubbing life back into his wrists as he moved to the cockpit. Sadly, there wasn't enough fuel for his purposes – he would need a new plane. He peeked out at the handful of SS officers and guards waiting impatiently in the hangar for the Black Sun siblings to disembark with their prisoner. Steps had been wheeled to the door at the rear.

Otto took a moment to conjure a glamour before opening the door. He did not dare descend the steps. Not yet. Instead, he waited. The SS called out the names of the Black Sun members. When no reply came, they drew their Lugers and hurried aboard. Otto retreated into the shadows. Two officers looked directly at him but saw only darkness, protected as he was by the glamour. Orders were given and they rushed out again, calling for help and raising the alarm.

In the chaos that followed, Otto calmly walked down the steps unnoticed and onto the windswept airfield. He found an isolated Messerschmitt Bf 110 aircraft that suited his purposes. The crew had just finished fuelling it.

Otto conjured a different form of glamour. He cheerfully thanked them for their help. They thought they were addressing a pilot of the Luftwaffe and wished him luck on his mission as they helped him take to the air. Once airborne, he turned north-west. His destination was the Kentish coast of England.

His mission, one of vengeance.

Home Again, Home Again, Jiggety-Jig

The army truck's brakes squeaked as it pulled up by Saint Irene's Church. The bell tower was gone, but the main church building stood as solid as ever in the moonlight. Just as well, as that's where Faye and Bertie were getting married. Faye's heart swelled with an odd combination of pride, love and abject terror whenever she thought of her impending nuptials.

A soldier lowered the flap at the rear of the truck, then extended a hand to help her out. Faye shouldered her kitbag, took his hand and jumped down onto the familiar cobbles of the Wode Road. She wore scuffed regulation army boots, her comfiest dungarees and her flight jacket to ward off the spring night chill.

'Thanks for the lift, Jack.' She nudged her specs up her nose and pointed along the road past the church. 'Keep going that way for about a mile and a half. Look for the long drive with all the silver birch trees.

19

Hayward Lodge is the big house with turrets and what-not. Can't miss it.'

'Ta, Faye.' Jack tipped back his steel helmet and gave her a wink. 'Stay lucky, eh?'

'You too,' she said as he jumped into the cab of the truck and crunched it into gear. It chugged away, leaving Faye alone.

Even the air in Woodville smelled sweeter. None of the soot or fumes of London, and definitely less chance of being run down by a tram or bus. She had nearly come a cropper twice in Piccadilly Circus.

The next few days were going to be barmy, for sure. Not a minute's rest. So it was important that she enjoy this gift of a moment of precious solitude and—

'Faye!'

Bertie Butterworth, the love of Faye's life and the young man she was to marry, was coming towards her with his arms wide. Having been born with one leg shorter than the other, his limp and the slippery cobbles meant that he couldn't come rushing into her arms like they did in those soppy movies, so Faye decided to rush into his instead. She dropped her kitbag and ran full pelt at Bertie, nearly flattening him. Their embrace was clumsy, and their kiss was more a meeting of teeth and noses than of lips, but Faye had longed for his touch for months. Her breathing quickened, her blood rushed and she warmed all over as they kissed.

Bertie came up for air and his cheeks could barely contain his smile. Then his eyes raked up and down Faye's face, and he bit his lip. 'Are you all right?'

Faye knew what he must be seeing. She had changed, and in so many ways she didn't know where to start, but this was not the time.

'I am now,' she said, kissing him again.

'How was it? Tell me everything, er ...' The tendons in Bertie's neck tensed and he looked around furtively. The Wode Road was completely empty of people and blackout dark, but you never knew who might be listening. 'How's your Aunty Doreen?' he asked in a loud and stilted voice.

Bertie had come up with Faye's cover story just before she'd left. As far as the other villagers were concerned, Faye had suddenly rushed away to care for her ailing Aunt Doreen in Dorset.

'I'm sorry to say that poor Aunt Doreen is still unwell, and I'll need to return to her in a week or so, but she's being looked after while I'm here.'

'Oh, poor thing.' Bertie's smile rather undermined his consoling words.

'You don't have to look so happy about it, Bertie,' Faye whispered, pecking him on the cheek.

'But I am. This is it.' Bertie's voice was light and bubbly, so happy he sounded fit to burst. 'This is all I've dreamed of. Not weddings and all that frippery. Just ... being with you is everything.' His hand slipped into hers and their fingers tangled together.

'Oh, Bertie.' Faye pulled him closer and kissed him again.

It was some time before they surfaced, and it took an additional minute for Bertie to get his breath back.

'Your dad's just put the kettle on. Come on,' he said, once he had. Hand in hand and smiling, they strolled in the direction of the Green Man pub.

⌀

Little had changed in the Green Man since Faye had left. The Christmas decorations had been packed away, of course, and it looked like the floor of the saloon bar had finally been varnished. Her father was whistling 'She'll be Coming 'Round the Mountain' as he turned the chairs over and rested them on the tabletops. So engrossed was he in his jolly tune that he hadn't noticed Faye and Bertie's arrival.

'Evenin', Dad.' Faye dropped her kitbag on the floor. 'No chance of a cuppa, is there?'

Terrence – with his big cheeky grin and hair like puffy white clouds cresting over a balding hill – often looked like he was about to break into a cheer. But as soon as he saw his daughter framed in the doorway, he threw his arms so wide they almost flew off. He didn't so much speak as blend words together with chuckles and whoops as he scooped Faye up in his arms.

'Nice to see you, too, Dad,' she wheezed. And it was. As much as Bertie gave her a romantic thrill, seeing her father again was truly like coming home.

'What you been up to, then?' Terrence held her by the shoulders and looked her up and down, a wry smile on his face. 'Witchy stuff?'

'Witchy stuff.' Faye smiled back, wishing she could tell both of them what she'd really been up to these past few months, training at Beaulieu with the other new magical agents.

How lonely she had been as the only girl.

The officers there weren't keen to have a young woman in their ranks, but Bellamy Dumonde – second-in-command of all the witches of the British Empire – had dismissed their complaints and dealt with Faye's magical training regime personally. He kept hinting that he was readying her for 'something big' but wouldn't tell her what. Still, he was good company, patient and encouraging. Faye had learned so much while she'd been away, but she couldn't tell Bertie or her father any of it, and they knew better than to ask.

Terrence squeezed her firm biceps and pursed his lips in appreciation. 'You taken up boxing, girl?'

'A bit. I could probably show you pair a thing or two when it comes to an arm wrestle. And you should see my pins.' Faye extended one of her booted legs. 'I've done so much cross-country running, I've got the calves of a Grand National winner.'

'So you can do a runner with this one?' Terrence nodded to Bertie, who flashed the same nervous smile he always gave when his prospective father-in-law made a cheeky comment. Terrence turned serious for a moment. 'How long are you back for?'

'A week's leave,' Faye said. 'And that includes the honeymoon. Not that we've got two pennies to rub together for anything like that. Then there's the dress, the cake—'

'Don't you worry about any of that now.' Terrence patted the air with his palms. 'Me and Bertie and Mrs Teach have it all under control.'

'Mrs Teach?' Faye flinched. The thought of either of the village witches – the ebullient Mrs Teach and the calculating Miss Charlotte – getting involved with the wedding planning gave her the collywobbles. 'We didn't ask for her help.'

'I don't think anyone ever does,' Bertie said.

'You won't have to worry about a thing, Faye,' Terrence insisted. 'We've got it all planned like a military operation.'

'Dad, the Charge of the Light Brigade was a military operation.'

'I thought you were happy to leave it all to us,' her father said, glancing at Bertie with a slightly hurt pout.

Faye's heart clenched. It was true. When she'd been called up by Bellamy, she had been happy to absolve herself of all responsibility for the wedding and leave it to them. Unlike most of the girls she knew, Faye hadn't dreamed of a white wedding when she was little. She'd been happier playing in the mud and marvelling at butterflies, bumblebees and ladybirds. But she loved Bertie and a wedding was the right thing to do.

'I am happy, Dad, I am, but what was the last thing I said to you before I left?'

'Don't rent out my room.'

'Before that.'

'Ooh!' Bertie raised a hand like an eager schoolboy, then rolled his eyes about as he recalled Faye's words.

'"This wedding is not to be a bleedin' palaver, Father. No fancy twaddle. Keep it plain and simple."'

Faye snapped her fingers at Bertie. 'Bingo. And what's the very definition of a walking, talking palaver?'

Bertie nudged Terrence with his elbow. 'I know this one, too: Mrs Teach.'

'How wrong you are. She's been very helpful,' Terrence said, folding his arms. 'It's amazing what she can rustle up at short notice.'

Faye sighed. 'I know. I'm sure she's been marvellous. You all have. It's just, it's been a long day and I'm cream crackered. I just need to get some kip and I'll be—'

> *'To market, to market, to buy a fat pig.*
> *Home again, home again, jiggety-jig.'*

Faye's head snapped up. She turned to her father to check if he'd heard the singing, too. He had, cocking his ear. It was coming from outside.

'What the blazes is that?' he asked, his brow wrinkling as he headed for the door.

'Sounds like children,' Bertie said, sounding puzzled as he trailed after him.

A shiver of anxiety rippled through Faye. Bertie was right. She had hoped last night's encounter in the underground had been a one-off.

> *'To market, to market, to buy a fat hog.*
> *Home again, home again, jiggety-jog.'*

With a growing sense of dread, Faye followed her father and Bertie as they stepped outside into the spring night. It was chilly, and somewhere a nightingale greeted them with an energetic trill before flying off. They didn't have to go far to find the source of the song.

> *'To market, to market, to buy a plum cake.*
> *Home again, home again, market is late.'*

Bertie and Terrence stared agog as six children danced in a circle in the middle of the Wode Road. They left little swirls of rainbow light in their wake and Faye could see the street's cobbles through their spectral forms. They wore school uniforms with satchels on their backs and cardboard gas mask boxes on strings over their shoulders. It was the same three boys and three girls as before, their faces dreadfully bloody and burned, holding hands as they skipped and sang around the Corn Bride, resplendent in her white dress.

> *'To market, to market, to buy a plum bun.*
> *Home again, home again, market is done!'*

The children all turned and pointed at the Corn Bride, who promptly burst into flames. Faye recoiled as the heat pressed against her face.

'What the bloody hell is going on?' Terrence asked, not unreasonably.

Faye tried to keep a calm front so as not to panic Bertie and her father. 'I'm not sure what the fire's about.' She gestured to the burning Corn Bride. 'But I met the Corn Bride and her spooky nippers during an air raid in London last night.'

The children continued to dance around the burning bride, singing a new rhyme.

'*Here we go round the mulberry bush,*
The mulberry bush, the mulberry bush,
Here we go round the mulberry bush
On a cold and frosty morning.'

'London?' Bertie frowned. 'You were in London? I thought you were in the countryside somewhere?'

'I've probably said too much already, Bertie, but yes, I was in London for a bit and there was an air raid last night. A big one. I came across these ghosts in the underground tunnel at Oxford Circus.'

'The ghost of a bride? And ghostly schoolchildren?' Bertie shivered and tucked his hands into his armpits as he tried to make light of a very strange situation. 'Do you think they'll come to the wedding?'

'Well, we are short of pageboys and bridesmaids.'

Bertie chuckled, though he was unable to completely suppress his unease. 'Not sure the vicar would approve, but it would be fitting for a witch's wedding, I suppose.'

'Reverend Jacobs would completely lose his nut.' Faye snorted a little laugh. 'So I'm all for it. In the meantime, there's a fire in the middle of the road, and I reckon we should do something about it.'

The children changed their tune.

'*Oranges and lemons,*
Say the bells of Saint Clement's.'

'I'll get a bucket!' Terrence declared, rushing back into the pub.

'*You owe me five farthings,*
Say the bells of Saint Martin's.'

'You don't reckon it's some sort of . . . omen, do you?' Bertie took Faye's hand as they watched the Corn Bride burn. 'I hope this hasn't put you off,' he said, giving her fingers a little squeeze.

''Course not,' she told him, almost believing it herself.

'*When will you pay me?*
Say the bells at Old Bailey.'

'A lovely evening for burning an effigy,' came an imperious voice from behind them.

Faye and Bertie turned to find Mrs Teach marching towards them in her bottle-green Women's Voluntary Service coat and hat. Always an impressive woman, her robust form threw long, dancing shadows on the cobbles as the flames intensified. Faye's heart swelled to see her.

'*When I grow rich,*
Say the bells at Shoreditch.'

'Welcome home, Faye.' Mrs Teach pecked Faye on the cheek. 'I see you've not been back five minutes and already there's chaos.'

> *'When will that be?*
> *Say the bells of Stepney.'*

'A fine little inferno,' said another voice, cutting off Faye's protests.

> *'I do not know,*
> *Says the great bell at Bow.'*

She spun to find Miss Charlotte somehow standing immediately behind them, her white hair glowing in the light of the fire. She had a new patch over her right eye, scarlet and trimmed with gold to match her dress. Faye felt safer than ever. The village hecate was complete once more.

> *'Here comes a candle to light you to bed.'*

The willowy witch arched a brow as she continued, 'But then I would expect nothing else. Don't take this the wrong way, Faye darling, but your return could only mean trouble.'

> *'And here comes a chopper to chop off your head!'*

The children all turned on Faye, pointing at her and grimacing madly. Their mouths were contorted, their eyes wide and staring as they all drew their fingers across their throats and made grisly, gurgling death-throe noises.

Faye tensed, wondering if the Corn Bride would rush her again as she had done in the tunnel. She was about to warn the other witches to be ready when the Corn Bride's smouldering face was doused with water. She vanished in wisps of vapour before the splash hit the cobbles. The children cavorting around her melted into the smoke.

Faye twisted her head round to find her father wielding an empty bucket, a curious look on his face.

'You know what?' Terrence pursed his lips in solemn contemplation. 'That really looked like your mother's wedding dress.'

OMENS AND PORTENTS OF DOOM

Ten minutes later they were all sat in the Green Man's saloon bar, reeking of smoke and burned straw. The fire had been easy enough to put out but had inevitably drawn the attention of the village Air Raid Precautions volunteers, Mr Paine and Mr Motspur. Both took their duties seriously and would not be fobbed off with excuses; they had even threatened to alert Constable Muldoon. Fortunately, Miss Charlotte had a wide selection of special powders in the pockets of her dress. A quick puff of a glittery grey dust into each of the ARP men's faces had them wandering off into the night with no memory of burning bridal effigies whatsoever.

Faye was still rattled by her father's vague assertion that the Corn Bride's wedding dress might be her mother's. She tapped her foot impatiently as she sat by the dartboard, watching him approach with a tray of tea things.

'So, if that straw lass in the dress was a ghost,' Terrence began as he lowered the tray, 'how come I could smell it burning?'

'Never mind that,' Faye snapped. 'Was it Mum's wedding dress or not?'

Terrence shrugged as he passed around cups and saucers. 'I can't be completely sure. From my soppy old memory, I would say yes. But we don't have any photographs of the day.' He rested a hand on her shoulder, noticing how upset she was. 'I'm sorry I even mentioned it, Faye.'

'Where's the dress now?' Faye asked, patting his hand and calming down.

Terrence frowned as he sat. 'Went back to Kathryn's cousin Mary in Stepney. It was her "something borrowed". Most likely eaten by moths by now.'

Faye turned to her witchy colleagues. 'Were any of you at the wedding? Did you see Mum's dress?'

'I was ... elsewhere,' Miss Charlotte replied enigmatically.

'As was I,' Mrs Teach said, waving a dismissive hand. 'Darling, all wedding dresses look the same to men. I wouldn't get too hung up on what is almost certainly a case of mistaken identity. And as for your suggestion that this Corn Bride is a ghost, Terrence ... I suspect you might be incorrect about that, too.' She took control of the teapot from him and began to gently swish it in circles. 'Corn dollies have an important role to play in folklore and magic. I suspect this could be an omen of some kind.'

Bertie stiffened at the mention of omens. Faye gently squeezed his hand.

Terrence scrunched his nose. 'We used to make corn

dollies at school at harvest time when I was a nipper. Weren't no omens back then.'

Miss Charlotte stuffed tobacco into her clay pipe. 'And what were you told of these corn dolls? What was their purpose?'

'If you made a good 'un, you got a prize at the village harvest festival. Candy apples, if I recall. I never won. Mine looked more like corn soldiers, all stiff and upright.'

'Good grief,' Miss Charlotte muttered, before striking a match and lighting her pipe.

'What?' Terrence straightened in his seat, wondering what he had done wrong.

'It's not you, Terrence.' Mrs Teach poured him a cup of tea. 'Miss Charlotte does get upset when ordinary folk practise old rituals with little to no idea of why they do them.'

'I thought it was just a bit of fun?' he said.

The tobacco in Miss Charlotte's pipe burned red. 'There is an ancient belief that the spirit of the corn lives within the crop,' she said, as if that explained everything.

She was met with blank faces.

Mrs Teach took over as she continued making everyone a cuppa. 'It was the duty of the farmer to make a doll from the last sheaf of the wheat crop. In this doll, the crop's spirit would reside through the winter. Then, come the spring, the doll would be ploughed into the first furrow and the corn's spirit would be released.'

'Like it'd been hibernating?' Faye suggested.

'In a way,' Miss Charlotte said, before sucking on her pipe again.

Bertie leaned closer. 'You said it was a spirit. So it *is* a ghost?'

Miss Charlotte exhaled slowly, wreathing herself in smoke as she looked down her nose at Bertie. 'I find such definitions to be childish.'

Bertie shrank back.

Faye leaned forwards and waved the air clear. 'And I think smoking's a filthy habit. Look, why have these poor burned and bloody children followed me all the way from London? And why do they keep bursting into song-and-dance routines?'

'As I said – omens, warnings.' Mrs Teach rested the teapot on the table. 'Much like banshees, only in school uniform.'

Faye shrugged and turned up her palms. 'Then why don't they just tell us what they're warning us about?'

Mrs Teach sat and stirred her tea. 'Few ghosts can make a noise, let alone speak.'

'These ones can sing. And Leo could speak,' Faye said, reminding her of the ghostly pilot who had haunted Larry Dell's barn last summer.

'Yes, but if I recall, your pilot friend wasn't actually aware that he was dead for some time. That can make a difference to the recently deceased's state of mind. These children are victims of the Blitz and have taken to their roles as portents of doom like ducks to water.'

'Portents of doom.' Bertie's shoulders quivered. 'What doom do you think they're ... portenting?'

'They seemed rather focused on you, Faye,' Miss

Charlotte said. 'Any thoughts on what they could be warning you about?'

Faye found herself instinctively glancing at Bertie before she could stop herself. He saw it and stiffened again.

'Not a clue,' Faye declared, leaning back and trying to look relaxed. 'But I'll be jiggered if I'm going to let a bunch of spectral ankle biters and an oversized corn dolly give me the willies. I've got a wedding to sort out.' She brushed a hand over Bertie's thigh and his face brightened into a smile.

'Speaking of which, you need to see Reverend Jacobs tomorrow,' Terrence said, slurping his tea.

Faye narrowed her eyes. 'Why? What's up?'

Bertie squeezed her hand gently. 'It's about the banns. They've been read here three times and no objections—'

'I should bloody hope not.'

'But he needs to know if the banns have been read at the parish where you've been training.'

''Course they have.'

Bertie's head twitched in apology. 'He wants proof.'

'Bertie, I've been training in a top-secret location that I can't even tell you about, so I'm not going to blurt it out to the village reverend.'

'That's not all.' Mrs Teach's voice rose in volume and authority. 'We must discuss the dress, the cake, the guest list, the reception, the food, the drink, the rings and the flowers.'

'Please, Mrs Teach,' Faye said, taking off her glasses and rubbing her eyes. 'Can we start this in the morning? I really need a proper kip.'

Miss Charlotte removed her pipe from her lips and poked the stem at Faye. 'Ever thought of running off to Gretna Green? Young lovers have been absconding to Scotland for centuries. They don't need the permission of their parents to wed. No banns are read. No food. No guests. No ... palaver.'

Faye winced at the word, but Gretna Green wasn't a half-bad idea and she entertained it for all of three seconds. Then she blinked and shook her head. 'I don't think so, do you, Bertie?'

'A little palaver goes a long way,' he said. 'Besides, I think we're overdue a bit of a knees-up.'

'That's all well and good.' Mrs Teach stood, clasping her red handbag. 'But I would remind you of how little time we have to organise this wedding. Tomorrow is Tuesday. You are to be wed on Thursday.'

'May the first,' Miss Charlotte added approvingly. 'Good day for a wedding. Not that any of you would know why.'

'Beltane,' Faye snapped. 'The old pagan festival to celebrate the beginning of summer. It's why we chose it. Happy?'

'Delirious,' Miss Charlotte replied.

'Get some rest, Faye,' Mrs Teach said. 'But we start tomorrow. There's not a moment to lose.'

'First thing after breakfast, I promise.' Faye pecked Bertie on the cheek. 'Right. Bed. Sleep. Rest, and forget any talk of omens, portents and corn dolls. For tomorrow, the palaver begins.'

DARK MATTER

Otto flew the Bf 110 low over the glistening dawn waters. He wasn't very experienced as a pilot, but he knew enough to fly in a straight and level line, and he had spent the night navigating by the stars. Of course, he could have used his magic to fly. He was one of a handful of those powerful enough to do so, but it was exhausting – not to mention extremely dangerous over the seas around England – and he needed every ounce of his magical power for what was to come.

The vast expanse of the North Sea lay to his right, the rolling patchwork of the fields and farms of Kent to his left. The Chain Home detectors would surely have spotted him by now, and it was only a matter of time before the Royal Air Force sent fighters to intercept him. He hoped they wouldn't be too long. Ideally, Otto wanted to be shot down somewhere around Margate.

The RAF did not disappoint. If anything, they came too soon. A pair of patrolling Spitfires banked behind him, hot on his tail.

Otto didn't want to make his goal too obvious, so he made some vague efforts at evasive manoeuvres, veering languidly from side to side. But the Spitfires lived up to their name. Tracer bullets flashed by and shattered the Bf 110's starboard engine. Black smoke billowed from the cowling and flames licked along the wing as the enemy fighters roared past.

Otto calmly raised the cockpit's canopy and cast a glamour.

The Spitfires circled around for another pass. He would need to time this perfectly. He clambered out of the cockpit, no parachute on his back. As the Spitfires' guns blazed again, he leapt clear of the Messerschmitt.

The starboard wing broke free, spiralling off madly as the rest of the plane plunged into the sea, exploding on impact.

The Spitfires peeled away, one pilot having the nerve to do a victory roll, as if shooting down an unarmed craft was any kind of triumph.

Flying was a matter of releasing one's self from the bounds of Earth's gravitational pull. Landing was a trickier negotiation between magic and gravity, and had been the undoing of many a foolhardy witch or Druid. Otto was experienced enough to descend gently, landing barefoot on the shingle beach just north of Deal Pier. No one noticed him. Not the fishermen working on their nets, nor the ARP lookouts who cheered the Spitfires' victory.

His bones ached. Sustaining a glamour after flight would have sent any other Druid or witch into a stupor, but Otto pushed through the weight of fatigue and kept going.

His glamour made him look like an odd light reflecting off the sea's shimmering surface. A couple of the fishermen's dogs barked at him, but he ignored them as he headed into town. He would have preferred to have arrived a little closer to Woodville, but he still had time. His first priority was to find Faye Bright. Find her, then destroy her and everyone she loved. That would go some way to making amends for his humiliation at the hands of the Black Sun, all a result of Bright's meddling last summer. Otto had made the mistake of underestimating her once – actually, twice, now that he thought about it – and he wouldn't be fool enough to make that same mistake again. If his plan was to work, he needed an ally. Someone in the village who could be his ears and eyes.

On aching legs he walked for a little over an hour until he found what he needed. A secluded pond in a small country park west of Deal. The pond was shallow enough for him to lie back in and was surrounded by long grass and bullrushes. Perfect for performing his ritual undisturbed. As the water soaked his clothes and trickled into his ears, Otto closed his eyes and drew on the energy around him. Invisible particles from the birth of the universe, still beyond the understanding of so-called scientists. While they blundered along with their theorems, Otto embraced the unknowable darkness. He recalled the ritual from a grimoire he had studied in Berlin before the war. Bound in human flesh, it was rumoured to have been unearthed in Assyria during the reign of Manasseh of Judah, changing hands several times over the centuries before ending up in Hitler's personal collection. Otto had stolen it and digested the whole thing in a weekend. A mostly dull series of stories about long-forgotten demons, he had nearly given up on it, but then on page 751 he had stumbled upon this spell. It was new to him, but older than the written word. It promised breathtaking power that drew on the very energy that would eventually consume the universe. When he mentioned it to his contemporaries in the Thule Society, they warned him off such dark magic with childish tales of madness. Later, when he brought it up with his siblings in the Black Sun, they forbade him from mentioning it again. He realised now more than ever that they were fools.

As Otto recited the verboten words, he found his foggy mind blossoming, his weary muscles flexing and his heart kicking as if he was a newborn. He welcomed the strange energy as it crept under his skin, filling him like oil soaks a rag. It opened his mind to the eternal song of the universe.

Borne aloft on the gentle hiss of the ur-particles, Otto coasted on the swell and lull of radio waves. He stretched out with his mind, combing through frequencies until he at last found Woodville. Many homes there had a wireless of some kind, and across the village various devices malfunctioned, the voices of droning BBC presenters crackling and fading as Otto searched for an ally among their number. Someone weak, someone disaffected. It wasn't long before he found exactly who he was looking for. Oh yes, they were perfect in every way.

Otto spoke to his new friend, sending him into a hypnotic stupor. This was going to be easier than he had thought. His new, pliable comrade was all too eager to help him plan his invasion of the village and wreak his vengeance on Faye. As they discussed preparations, Otto's patsy let something slip. Something that made his heart soar.

Faye Bright was making preparations for her wedding day!

This was delicious. Not only would Otto have his revenge, but it would be all the sweeter coming on the girl's special day.

Otto gave his little puppet a set of tasks to complete before they spoke again later that evening. Blinking his eyes open, he sat upright. Steam rose in idle spirals around him. All the water in the pond had evaporated in the intense heat of his magic, and his backside was wet with mud, but he didn't care. He had never felt so alive. The ritual had invigorated him, but there was so much to do in so little time. To begin with, Otto would need a change of clothes.

After all, he had a wedding to attend.

A Rummage in
Terrence's Drawers

Since starting her training at the beginning of the year, Faye had slept in tents, bunks, hammocks, the backs of various army trucks, a ditch and – for one night only – a three-hundred-year-old four-poster bed. But nothing could beat the familiar lumps and dips of her own mattress and the comforting *tick-tock* of the longcase clock from downstairs. It had been the best night's kip she'd had since Christmas, and she all but sprang from her blankets with a to-do list fully formed in her mind. First, she would track down Reverend Jacobs and sort out all this banns nonsense, then she would find Mrs Teach for, well, everything else. But first, she needed a cuppa and a proper breakfast.

As Faye skipped down the stairs, she heard voices from the kitchen. Light and familiar and sprinkled with delighted chuckles. Faye was curious. Her father was many things, but he was not what you'd call a chuckler.

A cackler, definitely. He loved nothing more than a hearty guffaw at a filthy joke, but this was a warmer form of laughter, flirtatious even.

Faye had to know more. Slowing to a cautious tiptoe, she swung the kitchen door open to find her father chatting with the milk lady, Doris Finch. They both leaned forwards over the tiny kitchen table as they spoke, clutching their teacups like holy chalices. Between them, freshly brewed tea steamed in the little brown pot.

Doris, always a handsome woman, looked particularly radiant this morning, her eyes bright and her ready smile framed with red lipstick. She was the first to see Faye standing in the doorway, and jolted upright like she'd just been on the receiving end of Harry Newton's cattle prod.

Terrence twisted in his seat to greet his daughter. 'Morning, Trouble,' he said, his eyes briefly glancing at the woman seated opposite him. 'There's enough in the pot for one more if you want a cuppa? Fancy another?' He asked this last of Doris.

'Actually, Terrence,' she said, placing her teacup down, red lipstick on the rim, 'I'd better get back to the dairy.' She stood, flexing her fingers and nodding at Faye. 'Lovely to see you, Faye. Good luck with the wedding.'

'Ta, Doris. Hope everything's all right with you—' Faye began, but the woman was gone and already the *clip-clop* of her delivery horse's hooves could be heard hurrying down the Wode Road outside.

Faye had received plenty of instruction on interrogation techniques during her training, and while she and her father endured a short and awkward silence, she wondered if any of them were applicable here. Faye reckoned that if Terrence had survived all that hoo-ha with the Holly King over Christmas, then he should be able to resist even the most intense inquisition.

She decided to keep it simple and get to the point. 'So, you and Doris Finch, eh?'

Terrence straightened his back. 'What's that supposed to mean?'

'Is she moving back in?' Faye asked. Doris had lodged with them for a few days last summer after her cottage burned down. The poor woman had suffered a hell of a time, losing her home to a fire and her son to the sea when he went down with all hands after his battleship was torpedoed by a U-boat in the North Atlantic.

'I don't know what you're insinuating, Faye.' Terrence raised his chin as he tidied away the tea things. 'Doris pops in for a cuppa and a chinwag at the end of her round, that's all.'

Faye's cheeks reddened. She didn't want to embarrass her father, so she got busy pouring herself a cup of tea. 'Sorry, just being cheeky.'

'Yes, well, we'll have less of that, thank you.'

'How is Doris these days?'

'She's fine.' Terrence verged on the wistful as he spoke. 'Just ... fine.' He blinked and snapped his fingers. 'Actually, Faye, before you start your breakfast, I have something to show you.'

Moments later, Faye found herself standing in the least-visited room in the whole pub. Her father's bedroom.

The bed was made neatly. The teak wardrobe with the door that wouldn't quite close properly was present and correct. An alarm clock ticked on a little bedside cabinet. And a small window criss-crossed with anti-blast tape cast a ghostly, pale light on the rug before the bed.

Faye's father made for the chest of drawers. Its surface was bare except for a small black-and-white photograph tucked into a silver frame angled towards the bed's pillows. Terrence tugged on the handle of the sticky top drawer, rocking the picture back and forth. Faye snatched it up before it toppled over.

'I do love this photograph,' she said, gently brushing her thumb along the edge of the frame. The picture showed her mother, Kathryn Wynter, posing with a young Doris Finch and a gaggle of friends. The carefree-looking women were wearing gingham dresses and laughing together at a lemonade stand at the Woodville Village Fair. 'And look at you, Dad.' Faye pointed him out in the ensemble. A younger and less wrinkly Terrence Bright was gazing adoringly at Kathryn in the background. 'Didn't you ask her to get married that day?'

The tendons in Terrence's neck were taut as he continued to struggle with the sticky top drawer. 'We'd been stepping out since we were your age, or thereabouts. And it was always a bit on and off for one reason or another. But yes, that's when I finally summoned the courage to ask your mother to marry me.' The drawer surrendered, groaning as it opened. 'There!' Terrence exclaimed, rummaging through a lifetime of knick-knacks. Chewed pencils, rubber bands, two balls of string, a Philips screwdriver and more were swept aside as he searched. 'Sit down, sit down,' he urged Faye.

'You're still not sure if that was Mum's wedding dress?' Faye said as she replaced the frame on the chest of drawers and perched on the end of the bed. Her right knee bounced and she bit her lip before asking, 'What if she's trying to tell me something? Don't you have any wedding photographs at all?'

Terrence continued to rummage, his back to Faye. His shoulders fell, and she decided not to push her luck. She understood how unsettling it must be for him to know that she had, on rare occasions, made some kind of tenuous contact with her late mother. It wasn't like Faye and her mum could sit and chat and gossip. It was more like a comforting feeling, as if Kathryn had just left the room. Faye dreamed of her often, more so when she was away training, but though her mother's voice came to her in these dreams, when she woke the words always melted away.

Terrence finally shook his head, opening another sticky drawer. 'Don't think anyone I knew had a camera back then.'

'It wasn't *that* long ago. When was it? Nineteen twenty?'

'Twenty-two. We didn't want a fuss. We were both a bit old to be married compared to most.'

Faye did the sums in her head. 'So you'd've been thirty-seven?'

'Hmm. We decided we needed to get a move on. Aha! Gotcha.' Terrence retrieved a little black wooden box from the drawer. It sat snug in his palm and he clutched it to his chest. 'Budge up, budge up,' he said as he sat next to Faye at the end of the bed. 'I know you and Bertie have got more legs than pennies at the moment . . .'

'That's putting it mildly. We're skint.'

'And I heard tell that you weren't bothering with rings and such.'

'Nah. Bertie proposed on the spur of the moment and hadn't even thought about an engagement ring. See, his mother never bothered with rings, either, what with her always mucking out the horses and pigs on the farm. And his gran lost her wedding ring birthing a calf.' Faye mimed a hand stuck up a cow's private parts. 'Poor old LuluBelle was never the same after that.'

'LuluBelle?'

'That was the cow.' Faye chuckled, all jolly and light, but she had some inkling of where this conversation was headed, and a little well of apprehension opened up in her belly.

Terrence lowered his hand, revealing the little black box and its brass hinge. Carefully, he lifted the lid. Sitting inside, nestled in blue velvet, was a ring.

'It was your mother's,' he said.

Faye's skin tingled. It was a simple gold band, but she had never seen anything more beautiful.

'Actually, it was my mother's before that. When me and your mum got married, we didn't have much, either. Didn't bother with fancy stuff like an engagement ring, but my mum had passed away a few years before and it seemed only right. I was really nervous when I offered this to your mother. She could have had her pick of anyone in the village. Anyone in the world, for that matter. But she chose this poor landlord's son.' Terrence sniffed and puffed his lips. 'Anyway, that's by the by. I've spoken to Bertie about this. I didn't want to tread on his toes or insult him with this gift, but he's a fine lad and he accepted it with good grace, and he insisted that I be the one to show you the ring.'

Faye's mouth was dry, and she took a couple of attempts to speak. 'You ... you're offering me Mum's wedding ring?'

Terrence's lashes fluttered. 'If ... if you want it. I know you're not one for girly stuff, but I just have this feeling it's what she would have wanted.'

He offered the box to Faye. She hesitated.

'Something wrong?' he asked.

Faye's eyes remained on the ring as she spoke. 'When I was little, we'd go for walks and Mum would take my hand and I would feel that ring. It was always warm. Like it was a part of her. Oh, Dad, what if I lose it?'

Terrence frowned. 'Don't be daft. How would you lose it?'

Faye thought back to her training. Bellamy had told

her there would be times when she might need to go undercover and pretend to be someone else. To be single. She hadn't thought much of it at the time, but she realised now that the last thing she needed would be the indentation of a wedding band. Any ring she owned would be more off her finger than on, so what would be the point? She glanced up at her father's glistening eyes.

'Sorry, Dad. I'm . . . a little overcome.' She fanned her face before taking the ring from the box. It felt heavy in her palm. 'It's beautiful,' she whispered.

Faye would wear the ring. Of course she would. For the wedding. It wouldn't be a wedding without rings. Until then, she would keep it in a pocket. The little pocket in her dungarees that snapped shut with a popper. Then, after the wedding, she'd put it in the pub safe or something. Till the war was over. Then she would wear it every day.

'Try it on,' Terrence said, then added hastily, 'Of course, we'll almost certainly have to get it adjusted to fit your— Oh!'

Faye had slipped the ring onto her wedding finger. Fourth finger, left hand. Closest to the heart. It was a perfect fit. She glanced down and could have been looking at her mother's hand. Too frightened to speak in case she burst into tears, Faye felt any such trepidation melt away as she hugged her father.

LOSING ONE'S MIND
ON A BENCH

Edith Palmer, the village postie and occasional volunteer ambulance driver, was cycling up the Wode Road, having finished her first round for the day, when she saw him. Timothy, or Reverend Jacobs to the rest of the village, was sitting alone on a bench by the birch tree at the bottom of the road. The tree's roots had risen up sometime over the last year and dislodged a few paving slabs, including those underneath the bench. It tilted at an odd angle, giving the impression that the Reverend was patiently waiting on a slowly sinking ship. He was staring unblinkingly at the telegraph pole outside the police station. A pair of army trucks thundered up the cobbled street, and the villagers went about their day claiming rations at the butcher's and baker's, but Reverend Jacobs noticed none of them. His hands rested on his thighs, his breathing deep and slow as if he was asleep.

Edith hopped off her bicycle and approached with caution. She noticed flakes of dried mud around the soles of the Reverend's shoes. Usually, his Oxfords were immaculately polished, with the laces tied in neat, matching rabbit-ear bows. This morning the laces were undone and riddled with clinging burdock burrs.

'Timothy?' She spoke softly. 'Are you all right, duck?'

Edith hadn't spoken to Timothy properly for some time. There were polite greetings at church, and when she dropped off his post, but they'd not had a decent conversation since they'd broken up at Christmas. As far as Edith was concerned, the parting had been amicable. After the initial infatuation and the rather saucy thrill of stepping out with a vicar, she'd realised they had little in common. He was a gentle soul, kind and patient, but there were times when he would withdraw into himself and not speak for hours. Whenever Edith dared to break the silence, he would get irritated with her. She had hoped for arguments that might clear the air, but Timothy had simply bottled everything up and let it simmer for days on end. Edith had seen enough repressed rage in her own parents to understand the relationship was doomed. She'd let the Reverend know it was over on Twelfth Night as they'd taken the decorations down in the vicarage, leaving him weeping, draped in tinsel and paper chains.

And now here he was again, lonely and lost on a bench.

Edith leaned her bicycle against the birch tree, edged closer and tentatively reached for his shoulder.

'Do you remember Christmas, Edith?' he asked suddenly.

Edith jolted back, half expecting angry rebukes for how she'd left him that night. But his voice remained calm as he stared at the telegraph pole.

'I have it in my head that we all took part in some sort of debauched street party,' he said, frowning. 'All of us, all the villagers, here, in the Wode Road, in the snow. Everyone was in some kind of fancy dress. At least, I think they were. I recall crowns and ... antlers. Yes, antlers. How odd. Does any of that ring any bells?' He turned to her, his eyes drifting from side to side as he struggled to focus.

Edith was ready to call him a silly thing. Who would have a street party in the snow? She cast her mind back to Christmas but found only hazy glimpses of villagers staggering about in grey slush, and a vague memory of her slapping Timothy for some minor indiscretion.

'Now you mention it,' she said, 'I do recall a bit of a knees-up. I thought it was in the Green Man, but I confess I had a bit too much to drink that night, so my memory's fuzzy to say the least. May I?' She gestured to the empty space next to him. 'I think we all had a little too much that night, didn't we?'

'It was the same night the bell tower was bombed.'

'Was it? Oh yes, of course.'

'So why don't I remember it?' Timothy's voice became tense as more army trucks rattled by. 'Why don't I remember *any* of it? I'm the village Reverend. I should remember Christmas! I should remember the night my bloody church bell tower was destroyed by the Luftwaffe, but none of it's there.' He was tapping his temple furiously. The trucks passed by, leaving dust swirling in their wake. He bunched his fists in an effort to calm down, and Edith noticed his knuckles were criss-crossed with scratches, like he'd just crawled through a thorny thicket. 'Edith, may I tell you something in confidence?' he asked, his voice settling into a more even tenor. 'I know we've had our ups and downs, but I trust you.'

'Of course, ducks.' Edith thought about patting his hand, but she knew how confused he could get by such gestures. Instead, she nodded sympathetically. 'You can tell me anything.'

'It must go no further. Do you promise?'

'I promise,' she said, and she meant it. Since taking over the village postal round, Edith had become privy to all kinds of secrets, and she was duty-bound to keep them all.

'I have these odd memories,' the Reverend began, 'or they might be dreams. I cannot be sure. Half-formed visions of scarecrows, ghosts, strange hairy creatures … antlers again. I think … I think I might be losing my mind.'

'Don't be silly, those are just bad dreams,' Edith reassured him, though she'd had some very odd dreams about scarecrows herself. A tall one with a pumpkin for a head, lording it over them all. And a few dog walkers she knew had reported seeing a hairy man stalking about in the woods … but she decided it wouldn't be helpful to bring all that up now. 'I wonder if you've been overdoing it, Timothy,' she said, looking into his watery eyes, the skin beneath them dark as a bruise. 'You're always so busy, I don't know how you manage, I really don't.'

He beckoned her closer, his voice a whisper. 'Do you know where the name Woodville comes from?'

Edith shook her head.

'You were born here, Edith. Have you never given it any thought?'

Edith shrugged. 'Is it because we're next to a wood?'

Timothy chuckled. 'Ah, such guilelessness, Edith. That's what I love about you.'

Edith pressed her lips together. She didn't know what 'guilelessness' meant, but she didn't much like the sound of it and would be looking it up in her dictionary as soon as she got home.

'Like many newcomers to the village, I assumed there was some connection to Elizabeth of Woodville, Edward IV's queen, but I was wrong. I looked it up in the parish records. The village was originally called Wodeville. "Wode" being the old word for "mad". We ...' Reverend Jacobs began to chuckle. 'We are literally ...' His chest and shoulders heaved. 'We are literally living in Mad-ville!' Belly laughs rocked his body as he started to lose control. 'Mad-town!' He was hooting now, slapping his thighs and kicking his legs. 'Mad!'

The people in the queues outside the butcher's and baker's had started to stare as the Reverend gasped for breath. Edith noticed Milly Baxter and Betty Marshall – the terrible twosome – covering their mouths as they exchanged catty comments. Mr Paine stepped out from his newsagent's, a puzzled expression on his face as he wondered who was making such a hullaballoo.

Edith inched away from him. 'Timothy, please, you're scaring me.'

The Reverend's breaths were short, hoarse, panicked. He made a choking noise. His eyes bulged and he clutched at his own neck.

'Help!' Edith cried. 'Someone help!'

'How do, Edith.' Faye Bright hurried over to the bench and crouched before Timothy, her voice calm and in control. It was as though she had appeared from nowhere, but Edith didn't have time to question her good fortune. 'Reverend Jacobs, it's me, Faye.'

His panic intensified, his hands flapping about, a deathly whistle emerging from his mouth.

Faye turned to Edith. 'Brace yourself, Edith. This might look a little strange.'

'Strange? How—?'

Faye leaned forwards, resting her forehead against the Reverend's. She closed her eyes, gripping his temples, and began to whisper something in the same register as birdsong and with about as much sense.

Timothy's head jolted up, his eyes rolled back and he slumped forwards, silent.

'Oh my good gawd.' Edith pressed a hand to her chest. 'Is he dead?'

Faye chuckled. 'Nah, just kipping.' She glanced over at the queues outside the butcher's and baker's. The villagers had lost interest. 'It's something I learned from a friend in London.'

Edith, who fancied herself a bit of an expert on London, having visited twice, nodded sagely. 'Hypnosis?'

'Something like that,' Faye said, inspecting the catatonic Reverend and noticing the mud on his shoes. 'He's been for a hike. No wonder he looks so knackered. Shall we get the poor fella home?'

THE DRUMMING OF
THE WOODPECKERS

Faye and Edith roused the poor Reverend and guided him back to the vicarage, one on either side and each with an arm over their shoulders. Once inside, they got him up to his bedroom and lowered him onto the bed. Faye rested a hand on the vicar's forehead. There was no fever to account for his delirium, which only worried her all the more.

Edith had taken the Reverend's black jacket, and was about to hang it up when a small spiral-bound notebook fell from one of its pockets.

'Whoopsie,' she said as she crouched to pick it up.

Faye instinctively extended her hand. 'Edie, let's have a look,' she said, lowering her voice.

Edith hesitated. 'It's private, Faye.'

If Faye had learned anything from Mrs Teach and Miss Charlotte, it was to only ask for something once, and in such a way that would brook no argument. She fixed her eyes on Edith until she handed the notebook over with a shamefaced shuffle.

Faye flicked through to the last written page. Edith, despite her protestation of privacy, was quick to perch herself behind Faye as she read aloud.

'Well, well, our Rev has been doing the rounds this morning,' Faye said, tracing a finger down a list written in pencil. 'Corner of Harry Newton's Farm on Bogshole Road. Postbox at Pillory Lane. Outside the police station at the bottom of the Wode Road . . .'

'That's where I found him,' Edith said. 'Why's he listed the other places?'

Faye looked over at the Reverend, lying on his side, fast asleep. A troubling thought was stirring at the back of her mind. She gently took Edith by the elbow and steered her to the landing outside the bedroom.

'I think I know what they are,' Faye whispered. She chewed her lip, wondering if she was just imagining things or if her training had made her paranoid.

Edith was vibrating with expectation. 'Come along, Faye, spill the beans. What are they?'

Faye glanced back inside to make sure the Reverend was still asleep. 'Telegraph poles,' she said, and Edith's excitement crumbled into confusion.

'Are you sure?'

Faye nodded. 'There's definitely one outside the police station, and by the postbox on Pillory Lane, and do you remember when they plonked a whole row of them next to Harry Newton's farm and he complained they were putting his cows off milking?'

Edith shrugged. 'So why would Timothy write a list of telegraph poles?'

Faye tensed. Why, indeed. Thanks to Bellamy's training, Faye knew that before an action of attack, any invaders would cut all lines of communication. And to do that they would need someone to make a note of all the locations of telegraph and telephone lines. Faye looked at Edith's expectant face, wondering how she might react if told that her former beau, the village vicar, just might be a fifth-columnist spy.

'Green woodpeckers!' The Reverend's voice came from within the bedroom.

Faye and Edith peered inside to find him sitting up, looking dazed.

'Green woodpeckers?' Faye repeated, puzzled.

'You're quite right, Faye. Those are all telegraph poles. I've noticed that green woodpeckers are using them to drum.'

Faye and Edith continued to look baffled.

'That is, they peck on them at this time of year in order to, uhm . . .' He trailed off, trying not to look at Edith. 'In order to attract a mate.'

Faye could feel the heat from Edith's cheeks blushing.

'I'm something of an amateur ornithologist, you see.' He gestured at the notebook in Faye's hand.

She flicked through the pages and there were indeed notes and sketches of bullfinches, cranes, sparrows and magpies.

'You went birdwatching at the crack of dawn in your best shoes?' Faye asked, not looking up from the book.

She had noticed the state of his shoes back at the bench. That, and the whiff of manure from the soles.

'Edith will attest that I can get rather excited at the prospect of catching a woodpecker at first light.' He flashed a weak smile. 'They are rather the percussion section of the dawn chorus. They're my favourite bird.'

Faye glanced at Edith, who scrunched her nose and nodded. 'He does get a bit doolally when it comes to peculiar birds.'

A wave of relief flushed through Faye, and she cursed her paranoia.

'Sorry about that, Rev.' She shuffled back into the bedroom and handed him the notebook. 'How are you feeling?'

'I should be the one to apologise,' he said, brushing a hand down his face. 'Especially to you, Edith. I made such a spectacle of myself. I dread to contemplate what you thought of such an embarrassing display.'

'I'm the village postie,' Edith said with a wink. 'I've seen worse.'

'Nevertheless, I am dreadfully sorry. I must blame a severe lack of sleep for my part.'

'Then we'll let you get some rest, Reverend,' Faye said, before raising a finger. 'Though there is just one quick thing. The reason I came looking for you was my dad said there was a problem with the banns.'

Reverend Jacobs dismissed her worries with a wave. 'All taken care of, Faye. Once your father explained your unique situation to me, I decided to make an exception. I've written to the diocese and I look forward to marrying you and Bertie on Thursday, when I shall be bright-eyed and bushy-tailed.'

Another weight lifted from Faye. 'That's very good of you, Reverend, thank you. And you're sure you're all tickety-boo? Can we make you a cuppa?'

✶

Reassured that the Reverend had hot tea and could look after himself, Faye and Edith strolled from the vicarage back towards the Wode Road. Faye's belly did a flip when she took in Saint Irene's Church. Last night, it had been a shadow in the blackout. In the daylight, it was a wounded giant slumbering among gravestones. The rubble had been cleared and the church's north wall was propped up with lean-to ironworks, but it didn't look right without its bell tower.

'They say they're going to rebuild it, ducks.' Edith rested a sympathetic hand on Faye's shoulder as she noticed the direction of her gaze. 'But not till after the war, they reckon. When all the men are back.'

With uncanny timing, and a grim sense of irony, an army ambulance rattled up the road towards Hayward Lodge.

Faye pushed her specs up her nose, stuffed her hands in her jacket pockets and resumed walking back to the slanting bench. 'What do you think about the Rev? How worried should we be?'

Edith thinned her lips and looked around surreptitiously. 'As I'm sure all the gossips will tell you, Timothy and I were stepping out for a short while.'

Faye tried to look surprised, but Edith and the Reverend had hardly made it a secret over Christmas. Then again, Faye was one of the few who remembered those terrifying days of the Holly King with clarity.

Edith shrugged. 'He's a lovely chap, don't get me wrong, but blimey he was hard work.'

'How so?'

'After all that kerfuffle over Christmas, he changed. All quiet. Staring off at who-knows-what half the time. You'd have to ask him something twice before he snapped out of it. I'm a busy girl, Faye, I don't have time to be asking the same questions again and again.' Edith retrieved her bicycle from where she had left it leaning against the birch tree. 'I suggested that we spend some time apart. And then I suggested it again, because he hadn't heard me the first time.'

'Has he ever been as bad as just now?'

Edith shook her head. 'No, that was new to me, ducks. I worry the poor chap might have lost his marbles.'

'Let's not condemn the man quite yet, eh?'

Edith swung her leg over the bicycle's saddle. 'Sorry, Faye, I need to get back to the post office. I've another round to sort.'

'Of course, just ...' Faye leaned closer and lowered her voice. 'Keep an eye on him for me, will ya? Let me know if he does anything else that's ... peculiar.'

'Course I will, ducks. And good luck with the wedding. You excited?'

Faye pasted on a smile. 'Cock-a-hoop. Lots to do. I

have a meeting with Mrs Teach that, try as I might, I can't put off any longer.'

Edith pecked Faye on the cheek. 'Don't let her boss you around.'

'That's like asking the sun not to shine, Edith. Take care.'

✄

Reverend Jacobs remained standing in his cottage doorway. Only moments ago, he had been waving Edith and Faye farewell. Then he'd blinked and they were gone. A grey cloud passed over the sun and he found himself chilly and confused. He stepped back inside to find that his tea was cold. His heart kicked so hard at his sternum that he feared he might pass out again.

What a fool he had been. What did he think he was doing? Enough was enough. No more nonsense. He would pray for strength. Pray for guidance. Pray for silence from the voice in his head.

FRIPPERY

Few people realised that Mrs Teach's simple terraced house halfway up the Wode Road was in fact the dead centre of Woodville. All the road signs had been removed in case of invasion, but there were still a few ancient stone remnants nestling in nettles by the side of the road declaring 'Woodville: 5 Miles' and so on, and those five miles would lead you directly to Mrs Teach's doorstep. Her house was also on the spot of the home of a Filí who had once negotiated with Caesar in 54 BC, but the only remnants of their conversation were a triskelion door knocker wrought in iron and a lingering sense of Britannic defiance. The house also had a cavernous cellar filled with poisons and remedies, and Mrs Teach enjoyed the best radio reception in the village by far.

Faye did not need to use the triskelion knocker of number thirteen as the door opened of its own accord as she approached. Mrs Teach, resplendent in a floral pinafore dress, waved her in. As she made tea,

Faye brought her up to speed on the encounter with Reverend Jacobs.

'Poor man,' Mrs Teach said as the kettle began to whistle. 'Though I'm surprised it took this long.'

Faye arched a brow. 'You didn't have anything to do with it, did you?'

'Certainly not! The man and I rarely see eye to eye, but I would never wish him any permanent harm.' The kettle's whistling reached a shrill crescendo and she turned off the gas. 'There are some who struggle to absorb the goings-on in this village, and he's the worst of the lot.'

Mrs Teach poured the steaming water into a hand-painted teapot showing a cheery scarecrow with a pumpkin for a head standing in a field. Faye shuddered at the sight of it.

'If one tries to hold back the tide,' Mrs Teach continued, 'then one should not be surprised when one is swept out to sea.'

'Are you the tide in that analogy, Mrs Teach?'

'Young lady, when one is a witch, she is all the oceans combined,' Mrs Teach said, shrouded in the kettle's vapour. 'A force of nature, and not something that people like the good Reverend should dare to challenge. Never forget that.' With a blink, her cheery smile returned. 'Come through, come through. We have much to discuss.'

Mrs Teach carried the tea things into the living room, a veritable museum of doilies and chintz, and Faye followed behind with the biscuit barrel like a drummer boy off to battle.

'Speaking of "goings-on",' Mrs Teach began as she lowered the tea tray onto the occasional table, 'you've not seen any more of those ghostly schoolchildren, have you?'

'Not since last night,' Faye said. 'Any thoughts on how to get rid of them?'

'Miss Charlotte is looking into that as we speak. She has requested that you pop along to see her once we're done here.'

Faye slumped into an armchair. 'Typical. I've not been back a day and already you two are bouncing me from pillar to post. I reckon I've got enough on my plate, Mrs Teach.'

'Do you want to be rid of these ghosts or not?' Mrs Teach poured the tea, a pinched look on her face.

'Of course I do,' Faye said, taking her cup and stirring the milk in more vigorously than was entirely necessary. 'Just remember that I ain't a little girl anymore, and I won't be pushed around.'

'I don't recall pushing you around even when you were a little girl.' Mrs Teach sat back and rested her hands on her thighs. 'Faye, darling, you've changed considerably since this war started, and your powers are nothing short of extraordinary. Please know that Miss Charlotte and I have a fierce appreciation of your talent and the things you have achieved.'

Faye blushed, but she knew that any praise from Mrs Teach was merely the sucker punch before the knock-out blow.

'But you're gravely mistaken if you think we're going

to let you get too big for your boots after a few months' training with that wet lettuce Bellamy Dumonde. First and foremost, you are a witch of Woodville Village. One of three who have a duty to protect these poor wretches from dangers of all kinds, including and not least themselves. We work together, agreed?'

Faye sat up straight. 'Yes.'

'Good, so do as I say and go and see Miss Charlotte when we're done.'

Faye chuckled as Mrs Teach sipped her tea. It was good to be back. 'Right, let's get this over with.' She put her cup down with a clatter of china on china. 'You wanted a chinwag about the wedding?'

'Oh dear.' Mrs Teach lowered her cup. 'This impatience and the frivolous use of words like "chinwag" have me alarmed, girl. You are approaching this wedding with a reckless disregard for preparation. I am here to ensure the day is not a complete disaster. Let us begin with the rings.'

'Got one.' Faye patted the little pocket with the popper on the trouser leg of her dungarees. The ring was still there. 'Dad let me have Mum's.'

'Very touching. And Bertie's?'

'Er. No idea.'

Mrs Teach tutted. 'We shall speak to the boy in due course.'

Faye shuddered and wondered how she could protect poor Bertie.

'The reception?' Mrs Teach asked.

'All back to the pub.'

70

'Most fitting. The catering?'

'The menu is roast chicken, spuds, green beans and gravy. And we're serving it on smaller plates so the portions look bigger.'

'Your father's idea, no doubt. The cake?'

'Ah, well, the bell-ringers – who in peacetime would have rung the bells for free – have instead pooled their rations to make us a fruit cake. There should be plenty for everyone.'

'And how many is "everyone"? How many have you invited? I've yet to receive my invitation, by the way.'

'Oh, we're not bothering with invitations. All are welcome.'

The wheeze of horrified shock from Mrs Teach's windpipe rivalled the kettle for shrillness. 'Darling,' she said, coughing away the blockage, 'I would remind you that we live in a time of rationing and austerity. If people hear there is free fruit cake and roast chicken up for grabs, they'll be arriving by the busload from as far as . . .' Mrs Teach winced. 'Margate.'

'Don't be daft, it's just the villagers.'

'This isn't some ad hoc knees-up, Faye. You'll be telling me you don't even have a dress next.'

Faye bit her lip.

'Oh, good grief.' Mrs Teach slapped her palms down on her thighs.

'I've been meaning to, Mrs Teach, but I've been a bit busy and never quite got around to it. Besides, I never looked much cop in a frock, anyway.'

Mrs Teach stared aghast at Faye's dungarees and

flight jacket. 'Don't tell me you're getting married looking like some . . . Land Girl?'

'Nah, I'm sure I'll find a nice frock at the clothing
exchange or something.'

'Don't you dare.' Mrs Teach patted at the air to al-
leviate her distress. 'Never fear. I have a dress you may
borrow. Up, girl, up.'

She got to her feet, taking Faye's hand and moving
her to the centre of the room. From a pocket in her
pinafore, she produced a tailor's measuring tape and
began wrapping it around Faye's waist.

'It will need a few adjustments, of course.'

Mrs Teach darted around Faye, who stood patiently
as she was prodded in some very personal places by the
tip of Mrs Teach's tape measure.

'Have you at least given any thought to bridesmaids?'
the older witch asked as she tightened the tape around
Faye's chest.

'I have, actually,' Faye said, 'and I was hoping that
you and Miss Charlotte would do me the honour. That
is, you would be the Matron of Honour and Miss
Charlotte would be, well, whatever she wants to be.'

Mrs Teach's head rose slowly from her measuring.
Her eyes met Faye's.

'Oh, Faye, darling, I'm touched.' She took Faye's
hand. 'The honour is all mine. And on Beltane, too.'

'If Bertie'd had his way, we would've been wed on
Boxing Day, but something about May Day felt right.'
Faye squeezed Mrs Teach's hand. 'I know you think
I'm being all frivolous and such, but the truth is I ain't

too keen on weddings. Old men giving away their daughters to young men like heifers at an auction. I want this day to be about me and Bertie. I don't care if it's in a church without a bell tower, or a pub or in a ditch. All that matters is that Bertie and me make a promise in front of all the people we love. The rest is all ... frippery.'

Mrs Teach smiled and brushed a hand on Faye's arm. 'I shall be honest with you, Faye, I was concerned that you were too young to be wed. That you weren't ready for the responsibility and were doing it for all the wrong reasons. I see now that I was greatly mistaken. I think that this will be a wonderful wedding. But may I make a request?'

'Of course.'

'I'm rather fond of frippery. Can we have just a little?'

'Mrs Philomena Teach, Matron of Honour, do you accept the role of Commanding Officer of Frippery for this wedding?'

Mrs Teach beamed and clapped her hands together. 'I do!'

A Change of Clothes

Otto found what he was looking for after following the River Stour inland for a few miles. Sustaining a glamour for this length of time would normally sap all of his strength, but thanks to the dark energy flowing through his body he had a skip in his step. He avoided the town and its shops. Too many barking dogs, and impossible to find any decent attire in these days of clothes coupons, exchanges and utility wear. No, if Otto was to crash a wedding, he wanted to do it in style.

He stepped through a stone arch into a once-impressive walled garden dotted with imposing topiary. Raised beds were peppered with wooden signs for onions, carrots and lettuces. Looming over the greenery, framed by sycamore trees, was a Georgian red-brick mansion with more rooms than any one family could possibly need. Obscured by his glamour, Otto strolled past oblivious gardeners onto a gravel drive. His bare feet were sore but silent as he walked by a chauffeur polishing a rather splendid Rolls-Royce

Phantom II. The man didn't even look up as Otto took the stone steps two at a time then slipped through the open front doors.

Most houses this size had been requisitioned by the military, but not this one. The fusty air that swirled around the corkscrew columns in the reception hall reeked of old money and greed. Oil portraits of moustachioed men in uniform lined the stairs. Empire builders, conquerors, slavers. Otto had no issue stealing from these inbred degenerates.

As he hurried up the steps, he gave a passing maid such a chill that she dropped her tray of tea things with an almighty crash. A gruff cry came from the drawing room, the lord of the manor's cigar-smoke-filled nest.

Otto left their squawking behind and stepped onto the landing, finding the master bedroom at the end of a narrow hall. The bed was neatly made and faced a large wardrobe. Next to that was a full-length mirror. He winced at the sight of his muddy trousers and shirt. This simply wouldn't do at all. He opened the wardrobe doors and was not disappointed. A row of suits, shirts and trousers all awaited his inspection. Time was pressing, and after some short deliberation he chose a Brook Taverner three-piece green suit with blue and merlot overcheck tweed. The pink shirt was an extravagance, to be sure, but it would be splendid with the navy knitted tie. The tan brogues and argyle socks looked like a perfect fit, and through the window he spotted pink roses blossoming in the garden that would make a delightful addition to the ensemble. Otto found a pack of cigarettes and a book of matches in the jacket pocket, then wondered if he dared find time to bathe and shave. Perhaps that was too risky to—

'Who are you?' a child's voice demanded.

Otto froze. His glamour was still in place. Despite the great effort it took to sustain, there were always those who could see through it. Dogs, cats, the more alert witches and Druids, parrots for some reason, and small, annoying children.

Otto continued to inspect the knitted navy tie as he calmly turned to face the child.

She wore a nightgown and slippers, and looked perhaps eight years old, though she might well have been older. Her hair was blonde, neatly brushed, and fell down the length of her back. Her skin was pale and waxy, and her forehead glistened with sweat. Clearly ill, which explained why she wasn't in school. No, she was more than ill. She grasped a handkerchief in her right hand and Otto noted there were dull spots of blood spread across both the fabric and her fingers. The girl's hazel eyes were surrounded by shadows, but they fixed him to the spot as she asked again, 'Who are you?'

'I'm a friend of your father's,' Otto said with a smile, smoothing off the edges of his Bavarian accent.

'Father doesn't have any friends,' she countered, resting her hands on her hips.

'We were at school together.' Otto laid the tie on the bed next to the tweed suit. 'I've known him since I was your age. He kindly agreed to lend me some clothes for a very important meeting.'

'Father isn't kind,' the girl said, coughing and bringing the handkerchief to her mouth. 'He's selfish and cruel.'

Otto's smile broadened, appreciating how lucky he was to be found by a child who loathed her father so much. Any other brat would have raised the alarm by now, but this one was curious and defiant. A dangerous combination, but one he was sure he could use to his advantage.

'And you must be . . .' He tailed off, expecting her to offer her name as so many others would.

The girl scrunched her nose and folded her arms. 'If you know my father, you will know my name.'

Otto crouched down to meet her eyes. 'You're a very clever young lady, aren't you? There are few who truly understand the value of names.'

'You don't have any eyebrows,' she observed with a morbid curiosity.

Otto chuckled. 'This is true.'

'Your voice is strange.' She frowned at him. 'Are you a Nazi?'

Otto thought for a moment. 'Not anymore.'

The girl crinkled her brow, puzzled by his reply. 'You don't know my name, and you don't know my father, but you're stealing his clothes. So, who are you? And tell the truth. I always know when people are lying.'

'Oh, really? How?'

She glanced about before whispering, 'The light around them changes colour.'

Otto pursed his lips. 'You see a light around people?'

She nodded.

'That is a very special gift,' Otto said, meaning it. 'Some call the light an aura. What aura do you see around me, child?'

She breathed loudly through her nostrils as her eyes took in the air around Otto's head and shoulders. 'It's black. But not like at night. It's like there was never any light there to begin with.'

Otto nodded slowly. He looked into her eyes and she was strong enough to look directly back without so much as a blink. They had an understanding.

'Young lady, you are wise and gifted, and because of that I am going to tell you my name and the truth about me. Then you can tell me yours, yes?'

The girl bit on her handkerchief as she nodded.

'My name is Otto Kopp. You are correct. I don't know your father, and I'm stealing his clothes because I am travelling to a place called Woodville to kill a witch.'

The girl still didn't blink as she took this in.

'Now your turn,' Otto said.

The girl unclogged her nose with a loud sniff. 'My name is Petunia Gertrude Parker. I'm ten-and-a-half years old, and are witches really real?'

'They are,' Otto told her. 'And they are as cruel and wicked as in the fairy stories. The one I'm visiting tried to murder me. Twice.' He gestured at the air around him. 'Am I lying, Petunia?'

She narrowed her eyes. 'I don't know. The darkness hasn't changed, so I suppose not. Perhaps. You're not like normal people.'

'Neither of us is, Petunia. Tell me, do you see things

that others do not? Shapes and shadows and lights where there should be none?'

She nodded.

'And when you tell normal people, do they call you a liar?'

A more emphatic nod.

'I was the same, Petunia. They drove me away from the village where I was born. My own parents tried to kill me. Have your parents tried to kill you?'

'Mother died when I was born,' Petunia said flatly. 'Father said it was my fault and he calls me his burden.'

'Because of your gift?'

'Because I'm so poorly all the time.'

Otto glanced at the handkerchief in her hand.

'He doesn't say it out loud,' Petunia continued, 'but I hear the words in his head and he says he wishes I would just get on with it and die.' She shivered before asking, 'Am I dying?'

'Petunia, I shall let you into a secret that no one else will have the courage to tell you, least of all your wicked father. We are all dying. From the day we are born, the sands of time trickle through the necks of our hourglasses. Some of us have fewer grains of sand than others. And you, Petunia, have so very few left.'

Petunia's eyes glistened. 'How few?' she asked, her voice a sliver of fear.

'I could count them on one hand,' Otto said.

Petunia took a breath to scream. It would be her last.

✄

Otto loitered unseen in the reception hall, sitting patiently in a burgundy Chesterfield Queen Anne chair, brushing lint from the trouser legs of the tweed suit. It was a shame about the girl. If he wasn't in such a hurry, he might have taken her under his wing. She had talent, wisdom and power. A rare combination these days. Alas, time was of the essence, so she had to go.

He watched as the maid carried a silver tray bearing carrot soup and a glass of water up the stairs. He waited as she bustled to the child's room at the end of the hall.

A horrified scream sounded moments later, accompanied by the clang of the tray and the crash of the glass. The butler came running, as did the chauffeur. Petunia's father, a gaunt man with half-moon spectacles perched on his nose, shuffled from the drawing room, gripping a copy of *The Times*, the crossword half-finished. He spent the entire journey from there to the upper floor grumbling to himself. Otto waited until the man reached his daughter's room. There was a moment of silence before a bellowing wail of grief reverberated through the house.

Otto smiled. He had lingered for too long. The coast was clear, and he sauntered swiftly out to the drive and into the Rolls-Royce. He drove calmly past the still-oblivious gardeners, in the knowledge that he had at least ended one person's suffering today.

THE TENANT

Mrs Teach had brought Faye up to speed with Miss Charlotte's new situation. The brouhaha with the Holly King last Christmas had wrought many changes in the village, the most notable among them being the destruction of the church bell tower – though the official explanation of a Luftwaffe bombing was widely accepted – along with a surplus of tree roots sprouting up through the pavements and a lingering sense that many villagers had behaved quite disgracefully and would never speak of it again. Less well known was that the wood's lone resident had lost her home. Miss Charlotte's cobwood cottage had been smashed to splinters by the demigod and she had found herself homeless at Christmas. Never one to beg, Miss Charlotte had simply moved in with Mrs Teach on Boxing Day. This arrangement lasted less than twenty-four hours before the two women were threatening to kill one another. Mrs Teach made speedy arrangements with Mr Gilbert and Mr Brewer, who had a spare room to rent above their antiques shop on the corner of the Wode Road and Rood Lane. The gents hadn't been aware that their spare room was available to rent until Mrs Teach had convinced them otherwise, and that was how they ended up with a three-hundred-and-eighty-six-year-old witch living above their shop.

Mr Gilbert and Mr Brewer were excellent sources of gossip and always cheery company, so Faye was looking forward to catching up with them. A bell tinkled above the door as she stepped inside, and she savoured the familiar tang of freshly applied furniture polish.

Mr Gilbert was behind the counter, immaculate in his pinstripe suit. His reading glasses were perched on his impressive Roman nose as he inspected a black ledger, ticking lines with a pencil. Mr Brewer busied himself dusting the frame of an oil portrait depicting a pale-faced couple bedecked with powdered wigs standing hand in hand by an oak tree. The shop was brimming with knick-knacks. Clocks, all showing different times, were dotted along the walls between paintings, hanging rugs and tapestries. Georgian tables competed for floor space with Victorian chairs and ancient naval trunks. Mirrors bounced light onto brass candelabra, pewter jugs, crystal decanters and an ivory chess set. A globe was flipped open by the counter near Mr Gilbert. The bottles of gin, rum and vodka within were not only for display purposes.

'Darling Faye!' Mr Gilbert's nasal voice might be considered a bit snooty by those who didn't know him, but there was always a warmth in his words. 'How delightful to see you again.'

'Yes, we'd heard you were back.' Mr Brewer peered out from behind the portrait frame, waving away motes of dust. He adjusted his specs, their thick lenses giving him an owl-like demeanour. He wore a brighter, candy-striped suit with a pink tie. 'Are you excited for the wedding?'

'Cock-a-hoop,' Faye said, giving one of her standard replies. 'You'll have to forgive me, gents, but I'm here to see your paying guest.'

Mr Gilbert's head twitched. There followed a brief and silent conversation between the two men as they urged each other to be the first to speak up.

Faye put them out of their misery. 'Is she being a pain in the arse?'

Mr Brewer puffed his cheeks. 'We don't want to be rude, but—'

A low moan reverberated through the ceiling, making the chandelier shimmy and sprinkling the air with flakes of paint and plaster. Soon every trinket in the shop was tinkling in sympathy, and even the windows, shored up with anti-blast tape, vibrated to the verge of smashing.

The sound ceased after only a few seconds, but it was enough to have Mr Gilbert reaching for the gin in his globe.

'How often does she do that?' Faye asked.

'Oh, that's relatively new,' Mr Brewer said. 'It started last night and twice again this morning. But it is, I'm saddened to say, the latest in a long line of ... idiosyncrasies from Miss Charlotte that have us a little, well, vexed.'

Mr Gilbert was more direct. 'She never sleeps, never pays her rent, and she's driving me up the bloody wall. She has to go!' He took a swig of his gin, straight from the bottle.

Mr Brewer's eyes scanned the ceiling. 'Keep it down.'

'Keep it down?' Mr Gilbert screeched. 'This is my store. My *home*. Faye, she's a catastrophe, I tell you. She scares off the customers with her racket, she leaves the kitchen and the bathroom a complete tip, she drinks tea from my best china, and more than once she's walked in on us at night completely in the nude!'

Faye bit her lip. 'Just to be clear – who was in the nude? You, or her?'

'Her!' The corner of Mr Gilbert's mouth twitched. 'All she had on was her eyepatch. It's giving me nightmares, Faye.'

The low moan resumed, and something crashed in the far corner of the shop.

'My Toby jugs!' Mr Gilbert cried, dashing to save them.

Faye gave Mr Brewer a sympathetic smile. 'Want me to have a word?'

Mr Brewer's big eyes glistened. 'Would you, please? Before this one has a nervous breakdown.' He glanced over to where Mr Gilbert was curled up on the floor, clutching a family of Toby jugs to his bosom.

⌀

Miss Charlotte's room was at the very top of a flight of melodramatically creaky stairs. Mr Brewer pointed out that they had never made a sound until Miss Charlotte's arrival, and now each step groaned as if it had been condemned to eternal damnation.

Faye readied her knuckles to rap on the door – 'Enter, Faye!' – but, of course, never got around to knocking as the woman on the other side knew she was coming.

The door swung open to reveal Miss Charlotte, fully clothed in her siren suit, much to Faye's relief.

'I'd offer you a chair,' she said, gesturing about the room, 'but you'll be lucky to find one.'

Faye crossed the threshold into the kind of scene one might find after a particularly intense Luftwaffe bombing raid. Dust sheets covered furniture piled in the corners, and clothes had been flung far and wide. A pair of scarlet knickers hung from the handle of the room's only window like a kinky pirate's flag. The bed had been casually introduced to some bed-sheets, but they lay wrinkled in a heap next to a scrying mirror, assorted Rider-Waite Tarot cards, an ivory-handled hairbrush and a red lipstick. A black kettle sat on a cold stove, and on the mantel were six clay pipes, all with broken stems. Above the fireplace, a pentagram had been drawn in charcoal, surrounded by a dozen runes.

'Cosy,' Faye said, nodding and rocking back and forth on her heels.

In the middle of the room sat a green baize card table, but instead of playing cards, three silver coins were arranged in a neat triangle at its centre. Faye picked one up. It was heavier than any coin in circulation, and instead of the usual heads and tails there was a crudely drawn smiling face on one side and an owl on the other.

'Obulus,' Miss Charlotte said by way of explanation as she attempted to close the door. It was a sticky thing and took three hefty shoves to wedge into place.

Faye frowned with incomprehension as she turned the coin over.

Miss Charlotte placed her hands on her hips and smiled. 'Corpse coins,' she said.

Faye grimaced as she placed the coin back on the baize and brushed the tips of her fingers clean on the front pocket of her dungarees.

'You mean like the pennies they put on the eyes of the dead to pay the ferryman into the afterlife?'

'Yes, though these particular oboli are from Ancient Greece and would have been placed on the tongue.'

Faye shuddered. 'Normal people collect nice things like stamps or cigarette cards.'

'Normal people die of boredom. And this isn't some idle hobby, Faye. I've been using these oboli to see what normal people cannot.'

'My ghosts?'

'Not yet, but now that you are here ...' Miss Charlotte arched a brow. 'Have you seen them since your last encounter?'

'No, and I can't for the life of me figure out why they've come to me.'

'Tell me where you first met these children.'

Faye jabbed a thumb in the vague direction of London. 'Like I said, in Oxford Circus underground station after an air raid the night before last.'

'Very good. We shall begin there.' Miss Charlotte snapped up two of the coins. 'Palms, please.'

Faye turned over her palms for inspection.

Miss Charlotte slapped a coin onto each one. 'Lie back on the bed and put these on your eyes.'

Faye grimaced. 'You ain't sending me to the under-world, are you?'

Miss Charlotte took Faye's hand and led her to the bed. 'Did you ever hear of the Phorcides? Also known as the Grey Sisters?'

'Are they the witches who shared an eye?'

'And one tooth,' Miss Charlotte added.

'Wonder how that worked? Think they had a rota?'

'Quite possibly.' Miss Charlotte made a small effort to spread the sheets out before lying Faye down and tucking a pillow under her head. 'They used the eye to see the past and the future. Only it wasn't a real eye.'

'It was an obolus!' Faye said as Miss Charlotte lay beside her. A wicked thrill coursed through her as she imagined what anyone walking in on them might think. The young bride-to-be and the scarlet witch on a bed together. The thought of the scandal made Faye give an involuntary chuckle. She waved away the curious look she got from her bedmate.

'Of course, there is a catch,' Miss Charlotte said as she briefly fidgeted to get comfortable. 'To see such visions, one must be blind in at least one eye.' She raised the flap of her eyepatch, placed an obolus over her missing eye, then lowered the patch again. Her fingers twined with Faye's until they were holding hands. 'Pop your coins over your eyes, Faye. And mind – this might be a little bit terrifying.'

GHOSTS OF THE BLITZ

Duck Island Cottage might well have been Faye's favourite spot in all of London. Not simply because it was handy for Whitehall, where she had been completing the latest part of her training, but because it always made her chuckle to see a witch's cottage plonked right on the edge of Saint James's Park for all to see. And, of course, there was the food. Duck Island Cottage was the residence of Vera Fivetrees, High Witch of the British Empire, and not only was she a virtuoso of every kind of magic, but she could also cook the most astonishing meals from the most unpromising ingredients. Quite the knack in times of rationing. Tonight's supper was shredded cabbage and carrots – from her cottage garden, of course – and steamed dumplings. Faye knew that if she had prepared this meal herself, it would have been filling. In the same way that ingesting a rock is filling. What Vera served up to Faye and Bellamy that night was something that Faye's palate was still getting used to. Flavour.

Bellamy Dumonde, now Head of Operations and Training for the SOE's Paranormal Division – informally known as SOEPD and scornfully referred to as the Soap Dish – was the first to tuck in. They sat around the cottage dining table, the one with the pentangle carved into it, and made for an odd trio. The landlord's daughter from Kent in her disguise of an Auxiliary Territorial Service uniform, the witch from the Caribbean in her bright red dress and Bellamy in his RAF blues.

Bellamy shoved another forkful into his mouth. 'Is this the best meal I've had since the war began?' he asked between chomps. 'I rather fancy it is.'

Faye took a bite. The dumplings had a heat to them that gently bloomed in her mouth, followed by a brief bitterness, then a lingering sweetness.

'That's magic,' she declared, helping herself to more.

'Actually, it's nutmeg,' Vera said from her high-backed chair at the head of the table. 'My sister sends me some every month or so. Don't ask how,' she added with a wink.

Where are the schoolchildren? Miss Charlotte's voice burst into Faye's psyche.

Faye's mind whirled as she reconciled the continuing conversation with Vera and Bellamy over supper in London with the fact that she was lying on a bed in an antiques shop in Woodville.

I asked, where are the schoolchildren? This is Vera and that blatherer Bellamy. You're in the wrong memory, girl.

'This is how it started,' Faye told her. 'I had a bit of grub at Vera's after training and then . . . Ah, here we go.'

The cottage melted away and Faye found herself

strolling up Oxford Street at night. The waxing sliver of a crescent moon was bright and, despite the blackout, there were plenty of people about, going to restaurants, hailing taxis, window shopping, skipping into nightclubs and generally acting like there wasn't a war on at all.

Why are we here?

'I had my lodgings in a room above a pub off Oxford Circus. I used to walk back from Whitehall every night. There was so much to see. I loved it.'

You are the proverbial country mouse, Faye.

Air-raid sirens sang their dreadful harmony. Even in memory, Faye could feel her heart racing. It was odd how differently people reacted. One woman bolted into the street, panting as if she might burst, and was almost hit by a taxi that honked its horn as it screeched to a halt. A clutch of elderly women on the corner of Regent Street stood around chatting, as if they had all the time in the world. Searchlights swept across the night sky, revealing barrage balloons tethered in place, and ARP volunteers began to herd people into the shelter in the Oxford Circus underground station.

The vision melted again.

Faye sat on the hard platform of the station with dozens of others as the bombs thundered above. Some slept on steel bunks, a few children laughed as they chased one another up and down the still escalators. A man played a fiddle as volunteers came around with tea. Faye recalled how calm everyone had seemed, happily chatting as the Luftwaffe rained down hell on the city above.

Is that them? Miss Charlotte asked as the children ran by giggling.

'No,' Faye said, her gaze drawn to the darkness of the underground station's tunnel. 'They came later when ... Yes. This is it.'

The vision swirled around them, and suddenly Faye was lying on the hard platform. A handful of people were awake, reading newspapers or solving crosswords, but most were asleep.

'The raid went on till five a.m.,' Faye told Miss Charlotte, 'and I was woken up not long before that by the singing.'

> *'Golden slumbers kiss your eyes,*
> *Smiles awake you when you rise;*
> *Sleep, pretty wantons, do not cry,*
> *And I will sing a lullaby.*
> *Rock them, rock them, lullaby.'*

Faye walked along the platform past snoring Londoners.

'I knew it was something magical,' she said, drawn to the underground train tunnel. 'You know when the air feels alive?'

> *'Golden slumbers kiss your eyes,*
> *Smiles awake you when you rise.'*

The vision swirled again. Faye stood in the musty shadows of the tunnel.

'Sleep, pretty wantons, do not cry,
And I will sing a lullaby.
Rock them, rock them, lullaby.'

As Faye's eyes adjusted to the gloom, she could see the children.

'Care is heavy, therefore sleep you.
You are care, and care must keep you.'

They were holding hands, dancing in a circle.

'Sleep, pretty wantons, do not cry,
And I will sing you a lullaby.'

Three boys and three girls, dressed in school uniforms. Much as Faye recalled, yet—

Good Lord, Miss Charlotte said as Faye moved closer to the children with their glistening faces blistered, blackened and burned. *Is it me, or do their wounds look worse here than last night?*

'Yes,' said Faye, leaning closer for a better look. 'I think you might be right. Are they healing, do you think?'

The all-clear siren sounded. The children stopped singing and stared directly at Faye.

That's interesting, Miss Charlotte observed.

'Interesting?' Faye said. 'I nearly widdled myself.'

'Huffity, puffity, Ringstone Round,
If you lose your hat it will never be found,

So pull your britches right up to your chin,
And fasten your cloak with a bright
*   new pin,*
And when you are ready, then we can begin,
Huffity, puffity, puff!'

The singing ceased with the siren; the children vanished.

'This is it,' Faye said as her heart picked up its pace. 'I turned around and this is when the Corn Bride appeared and . . . hang on.'

A flickering light came rushing up from the depths of the tunnel. Faye listened for the familiar rattle of an underground train, but this thing was moving too fast to be any locomotive.

'Now, that's new,' she said, trying to stay calm as the tunnel was filled with the roar of an engine. One that was all too familiar to anyone who had lived through the Battle of Britain.

A spectral Messerschmitt Bf 110 aircraft thundered through the tunnel, its cockpit in flames. A cloud of black dust billowed before it, rails bent and buckled, sleepers were tossed into the air like twigs. In the pilot's seat was the Corn Bride, her flaming eyes bearing down on Faye as the girl was swept away with the aircraft like a leaf in a tornado.

ɤ

Faye groaned as she slowly sat upright on Miss Charlotte's bed, the oboli falling from her eyes. She caught them without thinking.

Miss Charlotte also woke, though with a great deal more poise. 'The ghostly aircraft was not present at your encounter in Oxford Circus?' she asked as she removed the obolus from beneath her eyepatch.

'I think I would have remembered *that*.' Faye puffed out her cheeks and took a moment to reorientate herself in the real world. It was good to feel the floorboards beneath her feet, even if the room continued to sway like a ship at sea. 'What can it mean? If it's a warning, then what should I be wary of? It's not like I go around thinking: Ooh, look, a Luftwaffe fighter, I wonder if it will be my friend?'

'Indeed.' Miss Charlotte paced about. 'Did anyone else see these spectres?'

Faye shook her head. 'Not till you lot last night, which makes me think that's significant.'

Miss Charlotte raised her chin as she thought. 'Quite possible. Did you mention this to Vera or Bellamy?'

'No, that night was the last I saw of them before I left. Tell me straight, Miss Charlotte, have I lost my marbles?'

'Nothing wrong with your marbles, Faye. They're all present and correct.'

Faye took her specs off and rubbed the backs of her hands across her eyes. 'Then what the blimmin' 'eck do they want?' She put her glasses back on and looked at Miss Charlotte. 'Is it about the wedding?'

Miss Charlotte pursed her lips. 'I think you and I and Mrs Teach should meet tonight to lure and observe these children and this Corn Bride in the ... I was about to say "flesh", though I suspect "ectoplasm" might be more appropriate.'

'Where? Dad won't much appreciate having any ghostly nippers in the pub – he has very firm views on ectoplasm in the workplace.'

'The standing stones. We'll meet there at sunset. A little after eight.'

'The standing stones are in the wood, and from what I hear a certain guardian of the wood ain't too keen on folk wandering in without his say-so.'

'The woodwose.' Miss Charlotte nodded. 'He has been somewhat uncooperative of late.' She smiled and slapped Faye playfully on the thigh. 'We shall have to convince him that our cause is just.'

A low moan reverberated through the floor and walls, the same eerie sound that had shaken the chandeliers earlier. It grew to an unsettling crescendo for almost a minute, rattling the little window and making the broken clay pipes on the mantel perform a jolly jig, before coming to an abrupt end.

Faye turned to Miss Charlotte, who looked as perplexed as she did.

'Wait, that sound ... that wasn't you?'

Miss Charlotte straightened her back. 'Certainly not. It happens whenever next door flushes the loo. Indoor plumbing. Can't trust it. Probably trapped air or a loose washer somewhere. I've been meaning to tell the boys about it.'

Faye chuckled. 'Leave that to me,' she said, hopping off the bed. 'Meet you at sunset.'

HAROLD THE BUDGIE

Mrs Jessica Wallace was done for the day. Herne Bay had been her home since she had chosen to retire here five years ago. She had visited with her friend Edna at Easter in 1933 and had quite fallen in love with the place, especially its many tea rooms and the splendid Grand Pier Pavilion. Although these days the pier was covered in barbed wire and camouflage netting, having been commandeered by the Army. They had even blown up two sections to prevent 'enemy landings'. What foolishness. Why would any enemy land on a pier when there was a wide-open stretch of beach? Such an act of reckless vandalism. Mrs Wallace hoped that this cursed war would be over soon. She passed the pier now as she made her way down the Central Parade to her home overlooking the sea.

'Good afternoon, Mrs Wallace.' A bobby on the beat smiled as he tapped the peak of his helmet.

'Good afternoon, Constable Croft,' she replied sweetly.

'I see we have some very important visitors.'

For a moment, Mrs Wallace had no idea what Constable Croft was talking about, then he gestured to the rather smart Rolls-Royce parked outside her house.

'Having His Majesty the King over for tea, are we?' he said with a chuckle.

'Oh, I say. That is rather posh, isn't it?' Mrs Wallace smiled. 'I'm afraid I don't know His Majesty, or anyone with such a splendid motor car. Perhaps they've come for the sea air?'

'Indeed.' The constable opened his mouth to say more, but Mrs Wallace kept moving.

'Have a splendid evening,' she told him as she bustled away.

Mrs Wallace had no time for idle chit-chat. After the death of her beloved Albert and her decision to move to the seafront, she had been concerned that her life might be one long, drawn-out moment as she waited for death's embrace. But Herne Bay offered all kinds of clubs, societies and recreational activities for a lady of Jessica's age. Her days were full to the brim. Today had been non-stop with volunteering at the church clothing exchange. She had been on her feet all afternoon. And she had left her most important task till last. Every Monday, without fail, Jessica would make a pilgrimage to the post office to see the delightful Mr Shepherd behind the counter. She would hand him her weekly missive to her sister Peggy in Dublin. Mr Shepherd would ensure that the letter had the correct postage and reassure Mrs Wallace that her sister would receive the letter within days. Once that important task was done, Mrs Wallace could finally return home, feed Harold, her budgerigar, and enjoy a pink gin while listening to the wireless. The *Radio Times* had promised a selection of Schubert songs this afternoon on the Home Service, and she did not want to miss it.

Mrs Wallace took the steps to her door one at a time, turned the key and stepped inside.

'Coo-ee, Harold!' she called to her faithful budgie as she gathered up a few postcards and letters strewn on the doormat – she would deal with those in a moment. 'Mummy's home. I've got you some lovely cucumber.'

Silence.

Mrs Wallace paused in the hallway. Harold always greeted her with a series of enthusiastic chirps. This wasn't like him at all.

'Harold?'

She shuffled down the hall, not even stopping to take off her coat and boots. 'Harold, darling, you're unusually ... Oh.'

There was a man sitting in Mrs Wallace's living room. A bald man with no eyebrows. He lounged in her favourite armchair by the fireplace, drinking tea from her best china, if you please. On the arm of the chair was the little bell from Harold's cage.

Mrs Wallace feared the worst, but looking around she quickly saw that Harold was safely in his cage by the bay window, though he shuffled anxiously on his perch. Mrs Wallace imagined that he was looking guilty for letting this man in. She would have words with that naughty budgie later.

'Ah, Mrs Wallace, how thrilling to finally meet you.' The man spoke with a breathy Bavarian accent. As he did, he rang Harold's bell. Just once. It baffled Mrs Wallace and sent poor Harold into a frenzy. He began to chirp with great urgency.

'Harold!' she snapped at him. 'Pipe down!'

The man replaced the bell on the arm of the chair and leaned forwards. 'Allow me.'

He poured Mrs Wallace a cup of Earl Grey, milky with one sugar, just how she liked it. He wore an expensive-looking tweed suit, and she wondered if that was his Rolls-Royce parked outside.

'Who are you?' she demanded. 'And how did you get in here? There's a constable just down the road. I shall call for him, you see if I don't.' She turned on her heels and made for the door.

'I think that would be a mistake, Fräulein, don't you?'

The bald man rang the little bell once more and she froze, her hand gripping the frame of the living room door.

'After all, you wouldn't want to blow your cover, would you, Agent Siskin?'

Jessica's training kept her silent and cool, though her belly turned to ice and her mind reeled as she slowly spun back to face him, trying to recall if the Luger she had hidden in the larder behind the suet pudding was still loaded.

'Neither of us wants that, do we?' the man said,

brushing crumbs from his trouser legs. Even in the midst of her rising tension she saw he'd helped himself to her shortbread, too, the bloody cheek. 'I assure you, we're both on the same side.'

'So what *do* you want?' she asked when she eventually found her voice once more.

'We'll get to that in a moment, but first I must convey my sincere admiration for your work here. As I understand it, you receive intelligence from our agents in the United States, encoded in letters and postcards ...' He glanced at the day's post gripped in Jessica's hands. She hid the letters and postcards behind her back. 'Then you assess the reports and forward the best leads to our contact in Dublin, who then transmits them to Berlin. Virtually untraceable, with you as the least likely spy anyone on this pitiful island could imagine. Quite remarkable.'

He slid the cup and saucer towards her, then rang the little bell again. Harold resumed his panicked cheeps.

'Harold, silence!' Mrs Wallace ordered, and the bird did as he was told.

The German smiled at the budgie. 'Delightful little fellow.'

Mrs Wallace calmly placed her post on the mantel, then sat in a chair opposite the man. She picked up the cup and saucer, but she was no fool. She wasn't about to drink any tea offered to her by someone who had invaded her home. Though she wasn't about to give off any signs of panic or suspicion, either.

'Mrs Wallace,' the bald man began. 'May I call you Jessica?'

'You may not.'

'Forgive me,' he said, ringing the little bell again.

Mrs Wallace scowled. 'Why the blazes do you keep ringing that—'

'Our cause has suffered setbacks regarding the Führer's plans for the invasion of this island. Things have changed, and we must ask more of our agents in the field.'

Mrs Wallace did not like the sound of that. She put down the cup and saucer with a defiant clink. 'What do you ask of me? Have I not given enough?'

'Are you refusing to co-operate, Mrs Wallace?' The man frowned. He rang the bell again. 'There are others like you, I suppose. But Jennifer Gentle is in prison awaiting execution. Lady Morgana has gone to ground. Mrs Barham is being watched by the Secret Service. No, you are ideal, Mrs Wallace. There can be no other.'

Mrs Wallace blinked. Her head felt light. There were sparkles at the edge of her vision. How was this possible? She hadn't drunk the tea.

'I would remind you of your oath,' the man said. 'You swore—'

'I know what I did.' Mrs Wallace sat up straight, trying to focus. 'I swore my obedience to Adolf Hitler. Not to some bald stranger.'

'Indeed.' The man rang the bell, a growing intensity in his eyes.

Was it her imagination, or did the room seem larger than it had been a moment ago? Harold's chirps sounded as if they were coming from inside her head.

Mrs Wallace wanted to tell him to be quiet again, but she couldn't find the words.

'What was the final line? Do you recall?' The man tapped his chin as he thought. 'Oh, *ja*! "I shall at all times be prepared to give my life for this oath."'

Jessica found herself face down on the carpet. She did not recall falling.

The man was kneeling by her side, his eyes staring into hers.

'The good news, Mrs Wallace, is that I don't need your life. Not now. For the moment, all I need is a body. Your body. One that is compliant. One that won't be missed. One that will fulfil its pledge to the Fatherland. However, I see that your reputation for insolence and insubordination is well deserved, so I have taken a simple precaution. I am trying something new, you see. Well, actually, something very ancient and powerful. It has enabled me to put your mind ... elsewhere.'

He held up the little budgie bell before Mrs Wallace and rang it one last time.

Jessica blinked. Everything was a blue haze. She blinked again, and slowly the world came into sharp focus with dazzling new colours and dimensions. She could see the bald man leading her from the living room. She looked old, her back bent as he steered her into the hall.

Mrs Wallace had been invited by Mrs Delany to a psychic medium show on the pier a few months ago. The whole thing was complete bunkum, of course, but there had been a brief discussion of something called an out-of-body experience. The medium had recounted a story about a soldier in the Great War who saw himself having his leg amputated as if he were suspended from the ceiling of the surgeon's tent.

That sounded an awful lot like what Mrs Wallace was experiencing now. The bald chap had somehow hypnotised her with Harold's bell and she was dreaming. And what a peculiar dream. It was almost as if she was seeing all of this from the inside of Harold's cage.

His incessant chirping was getting most annoying now.

'Oh, do be quiet, Harold!' was what she wanted to say, but all that came out was a series of whistles. 'What's happening?' she asked in a blind panic, but her question was rendered in high-pitched squawks.

Mrs Wallace caught a glimpse of something out of the corner of her eye. She turned for a better look – though for some reason she felt compelled to hop – and there, through the bay window's net curtains and blast tape, she could see herself being helped into the Rolls-Royce by the bald man. Her eyes were glassy, her mouth open as if yawning.

The man took a moment to ensure she was comfortable in the back seat before shutting the door. He bid good afternoon to a passer-by before getting in and driving away.

'No! Come back!' Mrs Wallace cried. 'That's my body you've got. Bring it back!'

Jessica Wallace was talking nonsense, of course, and not least because her words all came out of her beak as birdlike tweets. How could she possibly be here and there at the same time?

It had to be a dream. She spun about, only to find herself looking at the tiny mirror in Harold's cage. And Harold's blue, green and yellow-feathered face staring back at her in its reflection.

From somewhere inside her head, his voice came to her. 'I tried to warn you, ya silly old bat!'

CHILDISH THINGS

Bertie had a little routine before he set off for the evening shift at the Green Man. He would scrub his face with carbolic soap and hot water from the kettle until his cheeks shone. Then he would brush his teeth with a pea-sized blob of Euthymol toothpaste on his Bakelite toothbrush, because fresh breath was important when serving the public. And finally, he would run a comb through his hair until it was all neatly in place. Bertie felt it was important that the pub's customers have their pints pulled by someone well-turned-out, but this little routine was also Bertie's own thinking time.

Bertie did a lot of thinking. On long walks, when milking the cows or mucking out Delilah's stable, but these few minutes before setting off to work he dedicated to the really important stuff, namely Faye Bright, getting married to Faye Bright and living happily ever after with Faye Bright.

Reverend Jacobs had read out something in church on Sunday that had engaged Bertie's interest, for a change. He couldn't remember which bit of the Bible it was from, but it went on about how when you were a child, you spoke like a child and thought like a child. But if you were to become a man, well then, you would need to put away childish things. If Bertie Butterworth was going to be married, then he definitely needed to put away his youthful knick-knacks.

Which is why, this afternoon, Bertie took down his model aeroplanes from the ceiling, then gathered up his collection of *Beano* comics and chucked them all in the bin.

He couldn't honestly say that he felt any more manly – if anything, it made him more sulky – but if that's what it took to be worthy of marriage, then so be it.

Bertie was peering into his little shaving mirror, trying and failing to pin down an unruly coil of hair springing up from the back of his head, when there was a knock on his bedroom door.

Angling the mirror, he saw his father step into the room.

'Bertie, son, can I have a word?'

Robert Butterworth – always Robert, never Bob or Bobby – was a man of few words. 'Morning' and 'Night' were the ones he used most with Bertie, to bookend each day. Any other communication came via grunts and gestures. He wasn't an unfriendly man. He simply never saw the point in talking about something when it would be far quicker just to get on with it.

Bertie glanced at the alarm clock by his bed. He'd

spent far too long on his hair, and there was a good chance he would be late for work if he didn't leave soon, but if his father wanted a word with him, then it must be important.

Bertie remained rooted to the spot as his dad stepped further into the room, somehow making it shrink around him. He was tall and broad, and the floorboards harmonised with his every measured and slow step. He looked at Bertie's simple bed and dresser as if seeing them for the first time, and frowned when he saw a copy of *The Land of Mist* by Sir Arthur Conan Doyle on the pillow. Bertie liked to read a chapter each night before going to sleep, though this one wasn't as good as the Sherlock Holmes books, and it got all sorts of stuff wrong about the supernatural. But Bertie wasn't going to bother his father with that.

'Everything all right, Dad?' he asked.

His father pursed his lips and thought hard before speaking.

'This ... wedding,' he said finally. There followed another long pause, during which any normal person might feel the need to interject and gee things along, but Bertie knew his father well enough to wait. 'What I want to know is, Bertie ...' Robert Butterworth looked up at the bare bulb hanging in the centre of the ceiling. There were little holes in the plaster where Bertie had pinned the strings for his model planes. 'What I want to know is, Bertie,' he repeated, 'have you thought this through?'

Bertie had thought of little else since Christmas Day,

when he had proposed to Faye. Some folk had said he'd been rash, that he was too young, but Bertie had never been more sure of anything in his life. He drew in a breath to say as much, but his father raised a finger.

'What I'm meaning is, Bertie, is you're a young man. You might want to, you know . . .'

Bertie did not know, and it pained him to see his father looking so anguished. The man hadn't said this many words in such a short space of time in years.

'Might want to . . . ?' he prompted.

Robert set his jaw before speaking. 'Sow your oats, boy.'

Bertie's head went numb. Firstly, he was shocked that his father even knew such an expression, one that Bertie had encountered many times from patrons in the pub after he'd announced that he and Faye were to be wed. It seemed to Bertie that every randy old goat in the village – and countless servicemen – wanted him to get his end away before getting hitched. And secondly, he was stunned that his father had just used that same expression in the very room where Bertie's mind had conjured up fantasies of what his wedding night with Faye might be like. It was all he could do to keep breathing. His father recognised that perhaps he had gone too far and raised his palms.

'Forget I said that.' He turned his attention to a framed photograph on the dresser. It was of the three of them: Bertie was just a toddler, sitting on Delilah's back with his mother and father holding her reins. Bertie had thought long and hard about whether this photograph was a childish thing to be discarded, but in the end, he couldn't bear to be parted from it.

'Think of the fuss your mother would have made of this wedding, eh, Bertie?' Robert picked up the frame, and Bertie warmed to see a smile on his father's face. 'She'd be proud of you, lad.' Robert put the frame down. He turned to face his son and stuck his hands into the pockets of his boiler suit. 'From the day I met your mother, the poor love was often ill. She had pains that no doctor could ever explain, and headaches that made her proper sick. Some people ...' Robert sniffed and looked to the window, the dusk light catching his eyes. 'Some uncharitable people dismissed your mother as weak, or they thought she was putting it on to get attention.'

Bertie's mind reeled with anger and questions, but he kept silent. His father had more to say.

'I can tell you, son, that your mother had no truck with wanting sympathy. She was up at the crack of dawn with me. She milked the cows, shod Delilah. She was a fine farmer's wife and did whatever needed to be done, whatever the weather. I could not have asked for a more ...' Robert's chest swelled as he took a breath. 'Your mother and I, we ... We didn't have as long as most, but all that time we had together was worth it. Even at the end. All I'm asking is ...' He stepped forwards, his hands emerging from his pockets, grasping at the air as if it was an idea. 'When the vicar says in sickness and in health, he means it, Bertie. All that lovey-dovey stuff you're going through is all well and good, but what I suppose I'm asking is . . . Do you love this girl Faye enough to stick by her when all the lovey-dovey stuff is done? When she's suffering? Those are the hardest times of all. When the person you love is in pain and there's nothing you can do. Are you ready for that?'

Bertie couldn't find the words, and there was a sudden swelling behind his eyes, so he nodded.

'You're certain, Bertie? Because what it might mean – and I hope to God it doesn't – but what it meant for me was that I had to love your mother enough to let her go. Can you do that?'

Bertie nodded emphatically, though he had questions about what his father meant about letting his mother go. He would save them for another time.

'Good lad.' Robert raised his chin in pride. 'In that case, I have something for you.' He rummaged in his pockets. 'I made this.'

He handed Bertie a ring. A simple silver band.

'I know you can't afford one yourself, so I made you one.'

Bertie gasped as he turned the ring over, holding it up to the light. 'But . . . how?'

'Remember that Spitfire that crashed in the onions in March?'

Of course Bertie remembered. The pilot had bailed out and landed in the garden. It had been the most exciting day of the year. Apart from the wedding. Maybe.

'After they took it away, there were some scraps still lying about,' Robert said. 'I reckoned I could have a go at making a ring. Bit of caustic soda, battery acid. Fairly straightforward.'

Bertie was struck with a sudden patriotic guilt. 'Dad, we're supposed to hand over all scrap metal. This is hoarding.'

Robert shrugged. 'If they wanted it, they would have taken it.'

'But ... but ...' Bertie was hypnotised by the ring. A ring made from an actual Spitfire. It was the most wonderful thing he had ever seen. And it was made from forbidden metals needed for the war effort. 'But for want of a nail, the kingdom was lost, Dad. What about that?'

Robert slapped a hand on Bertie's shoulder and looked his son in the eye. 'Nails? There's plenty of nails,' he said. 'But there's only one of you, Bertie Butterworth.'

SLIVERS OF HUMANITY

As the sun began to set, the three witches of Woodville crossed over the old Roman bridge and headed into the wood. Faye was lumbered with a wicker picnic basket, Mrs Teach had a blanket draped over her arm and an unencumbered Miss Charlotte led the way.

The wood was throbbing with spring's unstoppable new life. A woodpecker darted before them, squeaking for a mate. Butterflies danced about, yellow wings fluttering excitedly. A cock pheasant swaggered along the path like a bored tourist guide. In a larch, Faye spotted a pair of wood pigeons necking with such erotic ferocity that she blushed and had to look away.

The trees were up to their usual tricks, playing silly buggers to baffle the visitors. Shadows shifted, false paths tried to lure them into taking shortcuts and the sun and the moon occasionally switched places, but it would take more than age-old shenanigans to fool these women.

Faye could sense something else besides the

mischievous trees. She caught a hint of masculine sweat, damp hair and suppressed rage in the air. The woodwose was following them, tracking their every move. Faye didn't bother trying to look for him. She knew they would only ever see him when he wanted to be seen.

Their first port of call was the hollow oak at the centre of the wood. Its roots spread across the whole clearing now – a consequence of its sudden growth spurt last Christmas – and it bore the charcoal scar of a lightning strike, but the tree stood as strong and proud as ever.

Faye lowered the wicker picnic basket and flexed her fingers as she stood before the oak. Mrs Teach and Miss Charlotte glanced around the clearing.

'How does one summon the guardian of the wood?' Mrs Teach asked. 'Is there some kind of ritual?'

Faye cupped a hand to her mouth and hollered, 'Oi! Sidney!'

'Ah, yes.' Miss Charlotte nodded in appreciation. 'The ancient Druid method of yelling into the dark. Very good. I count myself lucky that I was here to witness such a—'

'Sidney Birdwhistle!' Faye called, hoping that the woodwose would remember his human name. 'It's me, Faye Bright. I'm back for a short while. Don't worry, we're not moving into the wood. This isn't permanent.' She crouched to the basket and unbuckled its straps. 'But we'd like to ask your permission to work a little magic up at the standing stones tonight. No idea how long we're going to be. Could be all night, but I promise you we won't be making a habit out of it. We offer you this . . .' Faye stood, bearing a suet-based pudding on a plate. 'It's jam roly-poly. Mrs Teach made it especially today. It's all yours.'

They waited as the leaves hissed in the evening breeze. A blackbird sang its nightly report.

Mrs Teach gave a hum of disappointment before speaking. 'I wonder if he's even listening?'

'Oh, he is,' Miss Charlotte said, looking over Mrs Teach's shoulder. They all spun to find the woodwose standing behind them, in the centre of the clearing.

He was over eight feet tall, covered head to toe in coarse hair, topped off by his crown of holly. His hooded brow cast shadows over his eyes, and his chest rose and fell, slow and fulsome. He gripped a club carved from heavy oak, and the menace in his stance made Faye begin to question the wisdom of asking a favour. Poor Sidney Birdwhistle had been transformed into a woodwose last Christmas in a final desperate bid to save the village. Faye had promised to change the lad back, but had needed to make the choice to leave him as a woodwose in order to defeat the Holly King. It was a decision that haunted her darker moments. If the big, hairy fellow was pissed off, he had every right to be.

She took a slow, deliberate step forwards and lowered the plate holding the jam roly-poly to the ground.

Mrs Teach cleared her throat. 'Sidney, I have news of your parents.'

Faye's neck tensed. They had debated long and hard

about this. Miss Charlotte was dead against it, but Faye and Mrs Teach thought it only fair to tell the boy.

'They've moved to Eastbourne,' Mrs Teach told him. 'Your father was not fit to work after all that business with the Holly King, and so he took early retirement. Your mother works in the sorting office down there. She sends me letters, and I know they think of you every day. But they couldn't bear to stay. Too many memories. I hope you understand.'

For a moment the woodwose did nothing but breathe.

'We thank you for your steadfast work here in the wood, guardian,' Miss Charlotte said, her voice solemn. 'And our offering is sincere.'

The woodwose stared at her for some time. Then he raised his club, took one step back and pointed it in the direction of the standing stones.

'Most generous of you, guardian,' Miss Charlotte said, bowing her head.

Mrs Teach and Faye bowed, too. As they made to leave, Faye caught the woodwose's eyes. They were shiny black marbles, inhuman, but there was something else deep inside. A hint of the boy he used to be.

Faye smiled. 'Good to see you again, Sid.'

ɤ

It was another half an hour before they arrived at the standing stones. Faye recalled being disappointed when the witches had first brought her here. She had expected Stonehenge-sized magnificence, but in the end these knee-high, nettle-covered stumps had saved lives, and she had a much better appreciation of their power now. They nestled on a rise overlooking the village, which she could just make out in the gloom of twilight.

Mrs Teach laid the tartan picnic blanket on the slaughter stone while Faye unpacked the food and drink. Miss Charlotte lit her pipe as she watched distant searchlights probe the skies.

'Quiet tonight,' she said.

'The Luftwaffe have shifted to bombing the cities now,' Faye said. 'That's what Bellamy told me, anyway. They couldn't beat the RAF in a fair fight, so now they want to bomb ordinary folk into submission.'

''Twas ever thus,' Miss Charlotte mused. 'There are two sides in every war. Those with the weapons, and the poor, innocent bastards who end up dead because of them.'

'Language!' Mrs Teach snapped, before speaking sweetly to Faye. 'And how is Bellamy?'

Faye wagged a finger. 'Now, now, Mrs Teach, you know I can't say anything about my training.'

'Did I ask anything about your blessed training? I asked about Bellamy.'

'I hear he conscripted you,' Miss Charlotte said, through a cloud of pipe smoke.

'No ... well, not exactly.' Faye scrunched her nose. 'I was training, it was ... hard, and I was having second thoughts about the whole thing. I mentioned it to Bellamy, who wasn't too happy about that. Then in February, when women were told to register for government work, Bellamy didn't have to beg anymore. He said I could work for him, or he could send me to a Spitfire factory in Coventry.'

'Crafty sod,' Miss Charlotte said with an appreciative chuckle.

'Why were you having second thoughts?' Mrs Teach asked.

Faye took off her specs and cleaned them with a cloth she took from her flight jacket pocket. 'It's tough work, for sure. I mean, I don't mind a bit of a challenge, you know that, but I worry about what it's doing to me.'

Mrs Teach knelt to open the Thermos flask. 'Too much running about, dear?'

Faye slid her glasses back on and shook her head. 'I can cope with the physical stuff. It's ... I've always tried to be the forgiving type. I've tried to understand why people do the things they do, but this training is trying to knock that out of me.'

'They want you to be cold, analytical,' Miss Charlotte said. 'Deadly.'

'Exactly.'

Mrs Teach passed a mug of tea to Faye. 'And you can't do it?'

'I can. That's the problem. I'm too bloody good at it, if you ask me. I ain't one to brag, but Bellamy says I'm the best in his class. But it's changing me and I'm not sure I like it.'

'Of course you're changing,' Mrs Teach said, pressing a hand to her chest. 'Why, I'm not the same as eighteen-year-old Philomena Cranberry, and I very much doubt that the Miss Charlotte you see before you is anything like the one from, what, the 1570s?'

'No, you're wrong.' Miss Charlotte smiled. 'I've always been like this.'

Mrs Teach rolled her eyes. 'Change is inevitable, Faye, though I share your concern that Bellamy's training might infect you with a cold, heartless streak. But take a tip from someone with a little experience in *espionage*.' As always when she said this word, Mrs Teach gave it a little French flourish. 'Never forget what it is that you're fighting for. The freedoms we cherish that would be taken by the Nazis should they win.' Mrs Teach leaned closer. 'Personally, I found it helpful to personify that sense of freedom in a young man I was rather keen on at the time.'

Faye gasped. 'Wait up. There was another before your Ernie?'

'*Others*.' Miss Charlotte arched a brow. 'Young Philomena Cranberry was quite the floozy.'

'Quiet, you!' Mrs Teach snapped. 'My point is that during this war it will be our duty to do unthinkable things, and do them we must, while at the same time clinging to some vestige of our humanity. Think of your betrothed, Faye. Young Bertie is courageous and pure of heart. Think of how your actions will save him and other innocents in this madness.' She rested her hands on her hips. 'Enough of this wittering. Shall we begin?'

While Faye and Miss Charlotte stood in position on either side of the slaughter stone, Mrs Teach took a beeswax candle and a box of matches from the wicker picnic basket. Placing the candle in its holder on the tartan blanket, she lit the wick and then plucked a silver coin from a pocket of her coat. She placed the coin before the candle, face down, then shrugged off the coat and rested it on the basket. The trio stood around the candle and closed their eyes.

'*Moon penny, bright as silver*,' Mrs Teach recited, '*come and play with the little childer*.'

She extended her hands to Miss Charlotte and Faye, and the three witches began a circle dance around the slaughter stone as they sang.

> '*Wallflowers, wallflowers, growing up so high,*
> *We are all young maidens, and we shall all die.*
> *Except for Faye, she's youngest of all,*
> *She can dance, she can sing,*
> *And she can dance the wedding ring.*
> *Fie! Fie! For shame! For shame!*
> *Turn your back to the wall again.*'

When Faye had last made contact with a ghost, it had been Leo, a Hurricane pilot who initially spoke to her through the microphone and headphones of an RAF helmet. Faye didn't think that would work with these spectral schoolchildren who only sang in rhymes.

> '*Wallflowers, wallflowers, growing up so high,*
> *We are all young maidens, and we shall all die.*'

Around and around the witches went, singing and dancing until the candlelight became a golden streak in their vision, the words no longer made sense and the melody blended into a breathless chord.

> *'Fie! Fie! For shame! For shame!*
> *Turn your back to the wall again.'*

Faye did not know how long they danced, but her knees buckled, sweat crawled down her back and her thoughts were lost in a fug of delirium.

Mrs Teach trailed off, distracted by the sound of young voices. They were singing.

> *'My Mother said, I never should*
> *Play with the witches in the wood.*
> *If I did, she would say,*
> *"Naughty girl to disobey!"'*

Faye's hair stood on end. The singing was coming from the darkness between the trees. 'That's them,' she said. 'They're here.'

MY MOTHER SAID I
NEVER SHOULD . . .

The witches turned to face the wood as the owners of
the unseen voices drew closer.

> *'Your hair shan't curl, your shoes shan't shine,*
> *You witchy girl, you shan't be mine!*
> *And my father said that if I did,*
> *He'd rap my head with a teapot lid.'*

Faye caught a glimpse of one, then another. Spectral
lights darting from tree to tree.

> *'My mother said, I never should*
> *Play with the witches in the wood.*
> *The wood was dark, the grass was green;*
> *By came Faye with a tambourine.'*

Faye's neck tingled at the mention of her name. The children were dashing between the trees, faster and faster, hands waving, smiles flashing as they giggled with glee.

> 'I went to sea, no ship to get across;
> I paid ten shillings for a blind white horse.'

As one, the children stepped out from their hiding places, all staring at Faye. Miss Charlotte had been correct. Their faces were still burned and blistered, but not as badly as before.

> 'I upped on his back and was off in a crack.
> Faye, tell my mother I shall never come back!'

They began to run away, ducking behind bushes, leaping into ditches, climbing up trees.

'No, wait! Come back!' Faye was about to give chase.

'They like it here.'

This new voice came from behind the witches.

They spun to find a blonde girl in a nightgown and slippers, gripping a handkerchief. She looked around nine or ten and had bright hazel eyes. She stood at the head of the slaughter stone, and Faye noticed that even though the crescent moon was bright, the girl cast no shadow.

'They like it here,' the girl repeated. 'And they want to stay.'

'Do they indeed?' Mrs Teach simply couldn't help

the patronising tone in her voice. 'And who might you be, little girl?'

'You give me your name, madam, and I might give you mine.' The girl folded her arms.

Mrs Teach stiffened and emitted a series of shocked and appalled blusterings. 'Well, of all the ... impudent child ... no manners whatsoever.'

Miss Charlotte chuckled, dabbing the tip of her pipe's mouthpiece at the girl. 'I like her.'

Faye stepped forwards. 'I'm Faye Bright,' she said to the girl. 'These are my friends, Mrs Teach and Miss Charlotte. Pleased to make your acquaintance.'

The girl narrowed her eyes at Faye's companions, but she gave a brief curtsey to Faye. 'I'm Petunia Gertrude Parker, and I'm ten-and-a-half years old. At least, I was until I died this afternoon.'

'Oh.' Faye shared a glance with the other witches. How do you cope with a recently deceased ten-year-old who's returned as a ghost? Mrs Teach had decided to clam up, and Miss Charlotte was having too much fun as an observer to help. 'Sorry to hear that, Petunia. So you're not with the other children?'

'Oh no, I was lost in a great and empty darkness, and then I heard their singing and I followed them here to this wood. Where are we?'

'Near Woodville. North Kent.'

Petunia squinted as she made a quick estimate. 'Not too far from home, then.'

'You said they like it here, Petunia. So you can speak with them?'

'Not exactly.' Petunia brought the hankie up to her nose and gave it a wipe. She inspected it briefly. 'No more blood. And I'm not coughing all the time. Well, that's something, I suppose.'

'That's nice.' Faye struggled to stay on track. 'How do you know they all want to play here, Petunia?'

The girl scrunched her nose. 'This is going to sound rather odd.'

'Believe me, we're used to that round here,' Faye assured her.

'I can hear their thoughts,' Petunia said, looking into Faye's eyes as if searching for any sign of mockery.

'Go on,' Faye urged her.

'They feel safe playing in the wood. Even at night. Can they?'

Faye looked back into the depths of the trees, wondering just who might be watching. 'That's not up to us, Petunia, but I can put a good word in with the landlord, so to speak. Warn the kiddies that he can be a bit reluctant to share.'

Petunia's face hardened.

Faye raised her palms. 'But I'll do everything I can. I promise. Now, Petunia, can you help me first, please? Can you ask the children why they've been following me?'

Petunia thought for a moment. 'I'm not entirely sure. They keep saying the same name over and over, and . . .' She faltered, biting her lip. 'And it's the same name as the beastly man who murdered me today.'

Faye felt a shadow weigh down on her. She knew the

answer to her next question with such dread certainty that she didn't want to ask. 'What man? What's his name?'

Petunia looked up, her eyes darting between the witches. 'He said he was coming here to kill a witch. A cruel witch who had tried to kill *him* twice. Are you . . . ?' Petunia took a step back. 'Are you witches? You can see me and talk to me, and you don't seem that shocked about it. You don't look like witches. Though actually . . .' She pointed at Miss Charlotte. 'That one does.'

'Flattered,' Miss Charlotte replied.

Faye took a breath. 'Yes, we are witches, Petunia. But we're not cruel, I promise.'

'That's exactly what a cruel witch would say.'

'Very probably, but if this man is who I think he is, then he is the most cruel and dangerous man I know.'

'I'll say,' Petunia said, raising a hand to her throat. 'The rotter throttled me to death.'

Faye's heart flipped. 'What's his name, Petunia?'

'Otto,' the girl said, and the moon hid itself behind a cloud. 'Otto Kopp.'

⚶

On a secluded beach looking out to the North Sea, Otto Kopp completed the preparations for his ritual. Searchlights probed the night sky, revealing barrage balloons dotted about as part of Churchill's 'Coastal Crust' to protect against invasion. The beach was littered with more of this crust. The concertinas of barbed wire and concrete blocks were intended to prevent the landing of tanks, but Otto wasn't expecting anything so bulky to join him this evening. This ritual was designed to attract a very different kind of invader. It was one of the most demanding that Otto had ever attempted. He had found it in that same Assyrian grimoire, which described not only the precise details of what needed to be done, but also the grisly fate of all who had tried and failed to complete it in the past. It seemed the demons who granted such boons were quite demanding and particular about those to whom they would give such power. Otto was not fazed by such warnings, written by timid folk who lived in the light. Otto would ensure that the demons would fear him.

The body of the late Mrs Wallace – Nazi spy and budgerigar fancier – lay curled up on the shingle like a baby, her waxy skin dotted with crimson. She was surrounded by five stones. These had been the unexpectedly tricky part of the ritual for Otto. Finding the things, and getting them into the exact positions required by the ritual, had taken far longer than expected. And it hadn't helped that he had become aware of the approach of a pair of Air Raid Precautions volunteers in their tin hats. Thankfully, they hadn't spotted him – an oversight that had saved their lives – and he had been able to send them into a deep slumber. Death would have been preferable, but recently deceased bodies can draw the wrong kind of attention, and so they snored away for now and would wake in the morning, each blaming the other for falling asleep on the job.

Once they had been taken care of and the stones were in place, Otto had the messy business of Mrs Wallace's exsanguination to deal with. It was an unpleasant task, the sort of thing that he usually left to those hooded cretins in the Black Sun, but needs must when summoning the forces of darkness. Those demons demanded their blood, and the little old lady who had vowed to give her life for the Führer had done so with mindless compliance.

Otto used some of the blood to draw a pentangle across the stones, careful not to waste any. Eight pints sounded like a lot, but when it came to ritual sacrifice, every drop counted. The lapping foam mingled with the blood, turning pink in stark contrast to the black water.

According to the grimoire, he had until the stones were covered by the tide to complete the ritual. Over and over, Otto recited the ancient words of summoning. He offered blood in return for gifts from the sea.

Any ritual that summoned the dead should be a gruelling task, but this one put a fire in Otto's belly. The more he used this dark energy, the stronger he felt. His blood burned as it flowed through his body, and he glanced down to find the veins in his arms were a deep purple, bulging and throbbing. He knew there would be some reckoning for this power, but he would worry about that later.

The incoming tide was lapping around his shins when he saw the first one.

A hat came bobbing up from beneath the waves. A

sailor's cap with gothic lettering, an eagle emblem and a red, white and blue roundel, worn by a Kriegsmarine submariner. He walked from the seabed to the shore, answering Otto's call. His all-weather grey smock coat was stained with blood and his bearded face glowed china-white in the moonlight. He staggered through the beach defences and took his place by the first stone.

He was soon followed by a Luftwaffe pilot, his blue flying suit and face blackened by oil and flames. He, too, stood by the stones that surrounded Mrs Wallace's body, now all but submerged.

Finally came the gunner of a Luftwaffe bomber, his hulking body riddled with bullet-holes. He completed the circle, and Otto could feel the three undead minds and bodies come under his thrall as the ritual was completed. The tide covered the stones and washed Mrs Wallace's body away.

PLAYTIME

The Reverend Timothy Jacobs sat in his living room armchair by the fireplace in the vicarage cottage, his eyes wide open. On the occasional table, his dog collar curled at the base of an empty sherry glass. The Reverend wore his priestly blacks, though the top buttons of his shirt were loosened. A copy of Trollope's *The Warden* rested open on his thigh, as if placed there with the intention of picking it up again at any moment.

The wireless hissed from where it rested on the mantel. The BBC Home Service had retired for the evening after a lively concert from Billy Cotton and his band and a brief news broadcast, ending with the national anthem. Now there was only the white noise of the empty airwaves. The endless crackle of the universe captured by valves, tuning circuits and a loudspeaker. Reverend Jacobs listened to it intently, although his mind was not entirely his own.

'Good evening, Reverend.' Otto Kopp's Bavarian

voice came softly through the woven fabric of the speaker. 'I trust you have the information we discussed?'

Reverend Jacobs blinked and parted his lips. His voice was hoarse as he muttered a quiet, 'Yes.' He went on to list the locations of the telegraph and telephone poles around the village.

'Very good, Reverend.' Otto's words oozed with delight. 'Tell me, where will I find the Home Guard's machine-gun emplacements around Woodville?'

The Reverend Jacobs was footsore. At first light, before he had been discovered by Edith on the bench by the police station, he had wandered to the clifftop paths where the Home Guard had built machine-gun nests pointing out to the Thames Estuary. Then to the roads from Birchington, Canterbury and Herne Bay where roadblocks had been set up. To the winding Wode River where emplacements were hidden in the murky banks. The Reverend had found himself compelled to commit them to memory. Now he recited everything he had gathered to Otto.

'Very good, Reverend. *Wunderbar.* You have pleased me greatly. My gift to you is a dream of your former lover, Edith Palmer. Enjoy, Reverend. Rest well, and I look forward to speaking again tomorrow night.'

The Reverend's eyelids were unimaginably heavy. He surrendered to the darkness and let it consume him as thoughts of Edith and her gentle kisses warmed his soul. Little did he know that in embracing the void he had left that soul open and vulnerable, and something cold and unfeeling had crept in and begun to take root like a weed.

ॐ

Faye checked her wristwatch. It was nearly one in the morning. They'd been interrogating poor Petunia for hours to make sure that she really had encountered Otto Kopp. The poor lass had endured a lot in her short life – the death of her mother, chronic illness and an indifferent father – only to have it all topped off by being throttled by a Nazi occultist, and then questioned by witches in her ghostly limbo.

'Ladies, I think Petunia has suffered enough for one day,' Faye said. 'Shall we give it a rest?'

'Oh, don't mind me.' Petunia perked up, skipping around the standing stones. 'I haven't felt this alive in years. Doing something as simple as skipping, I'd be coughing up blood for hours.'

'Faye is right.' Mrs Teach clasped her handbag till it creaked, a sure sign that it was time to go. 'I think we have all we need. Thank you, Petunia, you've been most helpful.'

'My pleasure.' The ghostly girl stopped skipping as a thought occurred to her. 'I – that is, *we* – do quite like it here in the wood. You mentioned some sort of landlord. Will he let us stay?'

Faye cleared her throat as she glanced up into the canopy. 'I think you'll be all right for now. But if a big hairy man with a club gives you any trouble, just tell him that you know me, and that if he has any kind of gripe, then I'll deal with it. Actually . . .' Faye turned to face the trees and cupped a hand to her mouth. 'Hey, woodwose,' she cried. 'Leave them kids alone!'

'Well done, Faye,' Miss Charlotte said wryly, 'that ought to do it.'

'At least now he knows,' she replied with a shrug.

Ghostly giggles came from the wood.

'I think the others want to play hide-and-seek,' Petunia said, clapping her hands together. 'I haven't played that in years. May I?'

'Fill your boots.' Faye gestured to the woods. 'You don't need our permission.'

'Oh, goody. Playtime!' Petunia was a blur as she dashed into the trees to be greeted by the laughter of the other children.

℘

The witches marched back to the village. Faye could sense that the woodwose was following them but chose to ignore him. At least he was allowing the children to play.

'I shall call Vera and Bellamy,' Mrs Teach announced as they arrived at the Roman bridge. 'I think they'll want to know that the world's most notorious Nazi occultist is in town.'

'Good idea,' Faye said. 'We'll need all the help we can get.'

'I'll check the girl's story,' Miss Charlotte said. Then, after seeing Faye's disapproving expression, she added, 'It's not that I don't believe her – though little girls do have big imaginations – but if her story is true, then there's a chance that I can track Otto down and stop him before this all gets out of hand.'

'Don't try anything foolish.' Mrs Teach wagged a finger. 'Like taking him on alone.'

'Mrs Teach, when have I ever been so foolish?'

'Oh, I have a list, Miss Charlotte.'

'Nevertheless, I shall take Mr Gilbert's motorcycle and sidecar.'

'Are you sure he will allow it?' Mrs Teach asked. 'He was complaining about petrol rationing just the other day.'

'Leave him to me.' Miss Charlotte grimaced. 'I can't be waiting on buses and trains. Can you imagine?'

'I could fly you there,' Faye offered.

'Definitely not.' Mrs Teach drew herself upright. 'You have responsibilities, young lady. You have a wedding to plan.'

The wedding. A flush of guilt washed through Faye. She'd all but forgotten about the wedding. The guilt was followed by a wave of dread.

'Oh, blimey. Do you think that's why he's here?'

'Otto? To crash your wedding?' Miss Charlotte pursed her lips in thought. 'One wonders if he doesn't have better things to do with his time, though I wouldn't put it past the spiteful little wretch.'

'Let's not speculate on his motives.' Mrs Teach raised a palm. 'That man is as unpredictable as he is dangerous.'

As the pair exchanged theories about Otto's motives,

an unwelcome thought nudged into Faye's mind. She could call it off. No, not call it off. *Postpone* the wedding. Just for a while. Until they'd sorted Otto out. Or maybe till after the war? Just to be safe?

Faye shivered. What was she thinking? It was almost as if she didn't want to marry lovely Bertie. Of course she did. Didn't she?

She shook the thought from her head and returned to the real world, expecting to find Mrs Teach and Miss Charlotte still arguing. Instead, they were silent, looking over her shoulder. She turned, slowly. A ringing in her ears intensified as a dread feeling of inevitability crept up her spine.

The Corn Bride waited on the other side of the bridge.

She wore the same ivory dress as before, though her demure head looked less spiky now and her stems were more finger-like, clasped together around her belly. She hung mute in the air, gently rippling like gossamer. No one spoke. Faye's ears pulsed in time with her heart.

Now. Now was the time to ask.

'Mum?' she said in a small voice. 'Is that you?'

With a creaking like old floorboards, the Corn Bride raised her head. There were no features on her face, only intertwined sheaves of grain. She tilted her head to one side. With a rustling like leaves in the wind, she began to tremble all over. The Corn Bride unclasped her hands and held them up as if she was surrendering. Grain by grain, she broke apart, borne away on a sudden and strong breeze. The wind whipped around

Faye and she instinctively shut her eyes, the world tilting about her.

§

Faye stands in the Wode Road as flames consume Saint Irene's Church. Villagers flee, screaming as they run from their burning homes. Suddenly, daylight. Faye lies naked in a field. Someone wraps a blanket around her and helps her to her feet. They stand by a hawthorn tree. A black Spitfire waits, its engine purring, ready to take flight.

§

Faye's eyes snapped open and she staggered backwards into Miss Charlotte's arms. The Corn Bride's ivory dress fell, empty, but vanished before it landed. Soon she was only a memory, the wind fading with her.

Faye's heartbeat returned to something like normal, but her mind was still reeling. Frustration boiled inside her. Why did the supernatural never give a straight bloody answer to a question? Why all the riddles? She broke free of Miss Charlotte's grip, staring at the spot where the Corn Bride had just been.

Mrs Teach placed her fingers on Faye's clammy brow and peered into her eyes. 'Faye, darling, I don't wish to worry you, but you got a peculiar look on your face just now, as if you weren't quite all there.'

'Uhm, yes.' Faye chewed her lips as she pieced together her thoughts. 'You remember last summer when I had all those odd visions and premonitions about people dying and such?'

Miss Charlotte glanced from the bridge to Faye. 'You had another?'

Faye nodded.

Mrs Teach stepped back and held her by the arms. 'What did you see?'

'Oh, just the village on fire,' Faye said with a flick of her hand. She was trying to be flippant, but the wobble in her voice betrayed her fear. 'And then me naked in a field with someone.'

'Bertie?' Miss Charlotte arched a brow. 'Naked?'

'No, I was the one who was . . . I didn't see their face. Look, since I started my training, I've seen some peculiar things. Odd visions. And none of them have come true. I think it's just my noggin having a spring clean.'

'I'm not sure that's how the human mind works, Faye,' Miss Charlotte noted.

'It's how mine does,' Faye replied, before taking a breath. 'Anyway, let's not get distracted by stuff that's not real and concentrate on what is.'

'You would be unwise to dismiss what just happened, Faye,' Mrs Teach said softly.

'I'm not dismissing it. I simply don't understand what the blinkin' flip just happened.' Faye wriggled her toes. She had got into the habit of doing this when she needed to calm down. It wouldn't help for the others to see how rattled she was, and it wasn't as though they didn't already have enough on their plates. She took a deep breath. 'Now, we can stand around in the middle of the woods and waffle on about it all night if you want, but I would rather concentrate on what's really important. Namely, tracking down a homicidal Bavarian maniac and planning my wedding. Is that all tickety-boo with you pair?'

The older witches shared a look before Mrs Teach gave a smile. 'Of course, dear.'

'Splendid. If I have any more visions, then I'll let you know. We can keep a scrapbook or something. Right.' Faye clapped her hands together. 'I don't know about you, but I could murder a cuppa.'

OUT OF ORDER

Faye woke from a fitful sleep peppered with ghostly children and ominous corn dollies but, thankfully, no more apocalyptic visions. Frustrated at her inability to make any sense of the images whirling through her mind, she staggered downstairs in the hope of tea and toast, but instead found her father and Doris Finch taking chairs off the tables in the saloon.

Faye blinked at her wristwatch. 'How long was I a-kip?'

Terrence chuckled. 'We're not opening yet, Faye. Least, not for punters. Not today.'

'What's going on?'

'It's young Bertie's stag do today,' Doris said, sounding surprised that Faye had forgotten. 'The men are meeting here for a bit of Dutch courage before the main event.'

Faye's belly had begun to flutter every time anyone mentioned anything to do with the wedding. She really wished it would stop doing that.

'Actually, I need to have a word with Bertie when he gets here. I—'

'You can't do that!' Terrence gripped the chair he was holding like a child with a favourite toy.

'Why not?'

'It's bad luck. Well-known fact that, girl.'

'It's a silly superstition, Dad, and I'm no longer a girl.'

'Doesn't matter what you think, Faye. It's his big day today. You get yours tomorrow.'

'Last I heard, both me and Bertie are getting married. It's not just *my* day.'

'Faye, if I might?' Doris spoke softly, and Faye gave her a nod of assent. 'I remember all this silliness when I married my Kenny,' Doris continued. Her Kenny had been the milkman for years and also, without doubt, the most miserable sod in the village. The poor woman had endured his grumpiness for decades until he had died a couple of years ago. Doris had always been kindness itself, and Faye had often wondered how such different people could pair off for life like that. 'Let the boys have their fun for a day. After that, Bertie's all yours.'

'It's his last day as a free man,' Terrence added. 'You have to respect that.'

'Do I, Dad? Is that a fact?' Faye felt her overnight exasperation beginning to simmer. 'What do you take me for? Some sort of manhunter who's going to keep Bertie in a cage for the rest of his days? Blimmin' 'eck, Father.'

Terrence's body contorted in a shrug. 'It's only a bit of fun.'

'You make sure of that. Bring him home in one piece and ready to be wed. If anything happens to him—' Faye was interrupted by a knock from outside '—I'm holding you responsible,' she finished, glaring at her father as she unlocked the saloon door.

Mrs Teach stood imperiously on the doorstep in her green WVS coat and hat.

'Morning,' Faye greeted her, and the woman marched in without being asked. 'What's the word from on high?'

'I couldn't get through.' Mrs Teach gestured back the way she came. 'The telephone box by the church has been out of order all night. But that can wait. First, we must get you fitted for your dress, Faye.'

'What?' Terrence's head shook and little motes of dust dispersed around him in fright. 'Haven't you done that yet? You're getting married tomorrow, Faye.'

'Like people don't keep bleedin' reminding me every five bloody minutes!' Faye snapped, with an anger that surprised her and had Terrence and Doris flinching. Not daring to glance at Mrs Teach, she instead raised her glasses and rubbed at her eyes with a knuckle. 'Mrs Teach, this fitting malarkey, how long will it take?'

Mrs Teach looked Faye up and down, making measurements and estimates in her head. 'If you don't fidget or complain too much, half an hour at most.'

'Righto, so we'll do that as soon as you've called

147

Vera, like you said you would. You can use the pub's phone.'

'Can she now?' Terrence's lip twitched. He never let punters use the telephone. It was strictly for incoming calls from the brewery and such. Business purposes only. He'd even made Faye use the box by the church in the past.

'Dad, it's urgent,' Faye advised.

He made a wordless grumbling noise at the back of his throat, but then invited Mrs Teach to the secret little niche adjacent to the hall where he kept the sacred Bakelite phone hidden from prying eyes.

Mrs Teach raised the receiver to her ear, grimaced, then tapped the little buttons in the cradle. 'This one isn't working, either,' she said, glowering at Terrence as if it was his fault.

He took the receiver from her and, with the confidence of all men when faced with malfunctioning technology, did exactly what a woman had done first, only more aggressively.

'She's right,' he confirmed, slamming down the receiver with a *ding*. 'Bloody thing.'

Faye caught Mrs Teach's eye, sharing an unspoken suspicion.

'Oh, the telephone lines go down all the time.' Doris waved casually. 'Only last March, Larry Dell drove his brand-new tractor into a telegraph pole and we didn't have any telephones or telegrams for a week. It was really nice.'

'I think there's a telephone at Hayward Lodge,' Terrence suggested. 'That might be working.'

'Shall we?' Faye peered at Mrs Teach over the top of her specs and nodded in the direction of Hayward Lodge. 'Or we should at least check the telegraph poles.'

'All in good time, Faye. A word, if I may?' With a smile sweeter than honey, Mrs Teach took her by the elbow and escorted her over to the nook by the dartboard.

Faye's eyes darted back to her father and Doris, but they knew better than to interfere. 'What's the matter?' she whispered.

'Faye, I appreciate that something peculiar is afoot, but this is Woodville, my dear. Something peculiar is *always* afoot. You are clearly discombobulated by these visions, and I sympathise, but one must have the courage of one's convictions and not look for excuses to delay the inevitable.'

'What are you talking about? What inevitable?'

'One's wedding.'

Faye pinched her lips, before muttering, 'Don't be daft. But we've already got mysterious singing ghosts and a potential Otto Kopp sighting, and now all the phones are down. Aren't you worried?'

'The world is on fire, countless innocents are dying every day and the jackboot of tyranny is but a few miles over the water. Of course I'm worried, but one keeps one's chin up and perseveres, Faye. If we let every concern weigh upon us, we'd never get out of bed. Plus, Miss Charlotte and I can handle any trouble. If I didn't know better, I would think that you were trying to avoid getting married. Are you?'

'Definitely not.'

'Good.' Mrs Teach glided across the bar with Faye in tow, her voice returning to its regular tone of command.

'Fine, we'll do the fitting thing, *then* we'll check the telegraph poles,' Faye said, swinging the saloon doors open as she marched out into the morning air. She swore this wedding was going to be the end of her.

ø

The roadblock was high on the cliffs on an exposed country road facing the sea, over which the sun was rising and turning the placid water strawberry-milk pink.

Otto and his undead companions watched in silence, hunkered down in the long grass of a nearby field. Otto's blood no longer burned so intensely, but the bulging purple veins on his arms appeared to be a permanent change. He had briefly considered getting a tattoo to cover the unsightly streaks once this was all over, but in the end had decided to keep and display them as a mark of his power.

Raising the dead submariner's waterlogged binoculars, he observed the scene.

Two Home Guard volunteers were using a concrete pillbox as a shelter and manning an amateur assembly of sandbags, jerry cans and a bent flagpole that functioned as the roadblock itself. They waved through a rider in tan leathers and a black helmet, astride a black motorcycle-and-sidecar combination. Otto didn't know who they were, but that fortunate soul would be the last to escape Woodville before he sealed it off from the rest of the world. Already, he and his men had spent the evening cutting all the telegraph and telephone lines surrounding the village.

This pathetic excuse for a defence would be easy enough for Otto to circumnavigate, but that was not his goal this morning.

Voices echoed from the cliff path. Two more Home Guard volunteers. The day shift come to relieve the night shift. Old men. Simple minds. Perfect.

Their words were carried away by the breeze, but Otto caught chatter about the shame of missing out on 'Bertie's stag do' today. His black heart warmed on hearing the name of Faye Bright's intended and he wondered if this 'stag do' might present an opportunity to test his men. Perhaps, but first he had to attend to these new Home Guard volunteers at the roadblock. He must ensure that no one else came in or out of the village. And to do that he would need to control the minds of these poor wretches.

As the night shift pair ambled back to the village, the new duo began pouring tea from flasks and exchanging opinions on the niceness of the sunrise. This would be easier than he had thought. Otto closed his eyes and searched for their feeble minds in the aether.

Beltane Boy

The Green Man opened its doors a little after nine that last morning in April, quite against all licensing laws. And while a few villagers might have questioned the morality of such early morning boozing, none would begrudge young Bertie this rite of passage.

The lad watched, feeling somewhat out of sorts being the centre of attention, as the pub filled with locals. Terrence and Doris dealt with the first flurry of orders, beginning with Bertie himself who ordered half a cider. He knew it was going to be a long day and he wanted to pace himself. He also pocketed one of Mrs Teach's famous oatcakes. She made them every year for the May Day celebrations and they always went fast, so Bertie decided to get in early, tuck it away safely and treat himself later.

Mr Paine was next, along with the Roberts twins, who ordered matching pints of Guinness to go with their oatcakes.

Then came the village Morris Men, no doubt drawn

by the promise of free food. Captain Marshall and Mr Baxter – captain and squire of the Woodville Morris Men respectively – were absent, but their regulars were present and correct. Mr Loaf the funeral director carried his fiddle in a black case, Finlay Motspur's tambourine rattled with his every step, Henry Mogg cradled his concertina-like melodeon like a baby and Cecil Sutton peered into a mirror as he blackened his face with make-up. Bobby Newton – who had recently got his call-up papers for the Navy – took the role of the hoodening horse, its head tucked under one arm as he drained a pint with the other.

The Morris Men were dressed differently today. Gone were the breeches and hankies. They stood in long tailcoats and top hats and bowlers, all in black with colourful tatters of rags sewn into the cloth. Long and straight sticks of hazel and hawthorn protruded from their pockets, decorated with nailed-on bottle tops and a rainbow of strings and ribbons.

The bell-ringers of the village had been banned from ringing at the start of the war – Churchill would rather the bells be used to alert people of an invasion – but the Morris Men had been allowed to continue their ridiculous cavorting, and so the rivalry between ringers and Morris Men had only intensified as the war had progressed. But Bertie had always liked Bobby Newton at school, and he was the only person here younger than him, so he sidled up and said hello.

'Good luck with the wedding, Bertie!' Bobby said, slapping him on the shoulder.

'Thanks, Bobby.' Bertie took in the lad's costume. It was little more than a piece of sackcloth with a stuffed sock for a tail. 'You the hobby horse this year, then?'

'I am indeed the *hoodening* horse this May Day,' Bobby corrected Bertie, beaming proudly. 'I was the rear end of the horse in the panto a couple of Christmases ago, but now I get to be the whole thing.' He raised the horse's head. It was on a stick and its unblinking eyes stared straight at Bertie. 'Of course, I'm hidden under the cloth and bent over most of the time, so it plays merry hell with my back.'

'Make that yourself, did you?' Bertie asked.

'Oh no, Mr Hodgson borrowed it from one of the Morris Men over in Saint Nicholas-at-Wade. He says I have to be extra careful with it, or I'll—'

'Hold up, hold up.' Bertie raised a palm. 'What's Mr Hodgson doing consorting with Morris Men from other villages?' Bertie spun to find Mr Hodgson chatting at the far end of the saloon bar with a few pilots from Mansfield Airbase who were lodging in the village.

Mr Hodgson was wearing a summer frock with a spring floral pattern. One of Mrs Hodgson's, if Bertie wasn't mistaken. And the fetching ensemble was topped off with a black bowler hat adorned with colourful ribbons.

Bertie, confused and curious, threaded through the crowd to tap him on the shoulder. 'Mr Hodgson.'

The tower captain of Saint Irene's bell-ringers grinned and slapped Bertie on the shoulder, the same spot that Bobby had hit only moments ago. It was starting to get sore.

'Felicitations on your nuptials, Bertie!'

'Never mind my nuptials. What are you doing conspiring with Morris Men and their hobby horse?'

'*Hoodening* horse, Bertie.' Mr Hodgson repeated Bobby's correction. They were clearly touchy about the distinction. 'They're two completely different horses.'

Bertie leaned closer and whispered, 'You once told me that a man could be a Morris dancer or a bellringer, but not both. What's changed?'

'Nothing's changed, Bertie.' Mr Hodgson gestured to Bobby and his horse's head. 'I'm his mollie, that's all.'

'His what?'

'Whomever has the honour of being the hoodening horse cannot see from under that sackcloth. Therefore, he must be led by a mollie. That is, a man dressed in women's clothing, dancing before him while tugging him along on a leash. It's an ancient Kentish tradition.'

Bertie closed one eye as he pictured this in his head. 'Fair enough,' he said, satisfied.

'Normally, the hoodening horse only comes out for the Hoodening play at Christmas, but we thought we'd make an exception for you, Bertie. You should be honoured.'

Bertie smiled politely. 'I think I might be.'

A few more soldiers joined the crowd. Bertie had invited his father, but he had elected to work on the farm. It hadn't sounded like an excuse – there was never a moment to waste these days – but Bertie's heart had sunk a little. He might have enjoyed this.

They were joined by Private North and Lance Corporal Stedman, who were lodging in Mrs Yorke's spare room above the bakery, and they introduced an RAF sergeant called Black. They all offered Bertie cheery congratulations and there was yet more back-slapping, after which they ordered a round and the volume in the pub swelled significantly.

Last to arrive were Mr Brewer and Mr Gilbert, still wearing their Home Guard uniforms.

'Sorry we're late, Bertie,' Mr Gilbert said, tipping his hat back and raising his impressive nose. 'Just ended the night shift when Miss Charlotte arrived at the roadblock on *my* motorcycle and sidecar, wearing my leathers, too, if you please. Then she had the temerity to ask if she could borrow the bike she was sitting astride. The barefaced cheek.'

Mr Brewer peered out from behind his partner through his thick spectacle lenses. 'He still let her take it.'

'What was I supposed to do? The woman is incorri-gible. When she returns, I shall be serving her notice.'

'Oh, here we go again.' Mr Brewer rolled his eyes. 'Two sherries please, Terrence.'

'I mean it this time,' Mr Gilbert said, pouting. 'She's gone too far. And she had better pay me for the petroleum!'

'Simmer down, please.' Mr Hodgson stood glorious in his summer dress and bowler hat at the end of the saloon bar and all heads turned in his direction. 'Good morning and thank you all for coming to celebrate the impending nuptials of young Bertie Butterworth!' Mr Hodgson raised his bowler hat and got a raucous cheer in return.

Bertie found himself sprayed with foam from the pints of those surrounding him. He was beginning to have second thoughts about this. He knew that the stag do was a tradition, but he had never been much of a drinker. He always preferred to be on the other side of the bar, sober and busy. He wasn't sure he'd survive a whole day trying to keep up with this lot. He was equally puzzled as to why they had to start so early.

Mr Hodgson cleared his throat. 'What makes Bertie's marriage to young Faye . . .'

Bertie was delighted to hear her name get an approving cheer.

'. . . so special is that they are to be wed on the first of May. Known to us as May Day. A time for celebration as the first day of summer, and I'm very happy to report that we will have blue skies and a warm breeze.'

This would usually be the moment when those in the know would inspect Mr Hodgson's knees, which, as local lore would have it, could predict the weather with unerring accuracy. This morning they were covered by the skirt of his dress. But the gossip from Terrence – who had seen Mr Hodgson's knees when he'd crossed his legs at the bar earlier – was that they were the colour of unripe strawberries. Fair during the day, with the strong possibility of rain overnight.

'Get on with it!' Private North yelled, and Mr Hodgson waved the ensuing hubbub into a low murmur.

'In olden times, May Day was called Beltane, and on Beltane Eve the young men of the village would go into the woods wearing stag horns and deerskins to fight with the rutting stags.'

This got another cheer, and the hairs on Bertie's neck prickled. He didn't like the sound of where this was going.

'Whomever stood up to the stags the longest was declared the bravest, and that's where we get the tradition of the stag night from.' Mr Hodgson raised his pint, getting another cheer.

This lot were cheering at anything now, and Bertie knew that there was no way he was going to be able to keep up with them. He wondered if it was rude to slink away from your own stag do.

Mr Hodgson wiped the back of his hand across his mouth before continuing. 'Nowadays, you might find a few roe and fallow deer in the wood if you're lucky, and it's true that at this time of year they can get a little amorous—' Another cheer! '—but I think it best that we leave the creatures in peace.'

Bertie tingled with relief that he wouldn't be forced to fight a randy stag.

'However,' Mr Hodgson continued, leaning forwards and adopting a grave tone, 'it is true that if a man is to take a wife – our landlord's daughter, no less – then he must prove himself worthy!'

Bertie was nearly felled by the salvo of slaps on his shoulder.

'Bring forth the Beltane Crown!' Mr Hodgson hollered over the boiling cheers.

Bertie clenched with dread. He'd had his fill of crowns with the Holly King over Christmas.

Doris emerged from behind the bar carrying a pair of festive antlers made from card and attached to a headband. Bertie wasn't too keen on antlers, either, after his run-ins with the aforementioned demigod, but these ones looked harmless enough.

Doris placed them carefully on his head and kissed him on the cheek. Her lips were warm, and she wore bright red lipstick that – if the heightened whoops and pointing were anything to go by – had left a mark for all to see. At least Bertie would have witnesses to back up his story if he had to explain it to Faye later.

'Quiet, please.' Mr Hodgson raised his voice, but no one was listening. It took Terrence thumping his knobkerry on the surface of the counter to shut them up.

'Thank you, Terrence,' Mr Hodgson said, carefully unfolding a sheet of paper he had taken from a pocket. 'I have here a note from Captain Marshall of the Home Guard.'

'Ooh!' the crowd mocked.

'Indeed. He sends his apologies, Bertie. I believe he and Mr Baxter are on patrol?'

'Roadblock,' corrected Mr Brewer, then added in a saucy tone, 'They relieved us this morning.'

This got a filthy laugh that made Bertie's eyes boggle.

'Private Herbert Hercules Butterworth!' Mr Hodgson snapped, and Bertie instinctively stood rigid, wishing he was in his uniform instead of his Sunday best of a tank top and crisply ironed white shirt.

'Your captain has set you a challenge. You are to capture a dozen flags hidden around the village and its environs—'

'Ah, excuse me,' a voice chirped up.

Mr Hodgson continued undeterred. 'To find them, you must follow the cunning clues left by Captain Marshall.'

'Mr Hodgson? If you please?' the voice interrupted again.

Mr Hodgson lowered his sheet of paper to find Mr Brewer wiggling his fingers to draw his attention. 'Yes?'

'Apologies for butting in,' Mr Brewer said, ceasing the wiggling to push his glasses up his nose, 'but Captain Marshall did ask Mr Gilbert and myself to inform you of a late change of plan. Apparently, there aren't any actual flags, and he only managed to come up with four clues.'

Mr Hodgson curled his lip. 'Four? Four paltry clues? And no flags? I thought we'd agreed on a dozen clues, and that he had some flags in a trunk in his loft?'

Mr Gilbert, standing beside Mr Brewer, bobbed his shoulders. 'He said something about there being a war on and that he was somewhat busy. He hopes that Bertie isn't too disappointed.'

'Ooh, no,' Bertie said brightly. This meant he would

be out and about in the fresh air and wouldn't have to get blind drunk. 'Sounds like fun whatever the number.'

Mr Hodgson flexed his sheet of paper. 'Quite. Well, Bertie, are you ready for the challenge, albeit one not quite as challenging as originally conceived?'

Bertie vibrated with anticipation. 'Yes, sir. Very much so, sir.'

Mr Hodgson smiled. 'Splendid.'

Terrence chuckled. 'You loon, Bertie. Old Grand Marshall Marshall has got you doing capture-the-flag exercises on your stag do.'

Bertie was about to tell him that he really didn't mind, and that there weren't any actual flags, when Mr Hodgson swept a hand across the room.

'Bertie, to aid you in your quest, you may choose one squire to offer wise counsel and—'

'Mr Bright! I choose Mr Bright,' Bertie blurted.

Terrence glowered at him. 'I can't go gallivanting off on some silly treasure hunt. Who's going to look after the pub?'

'I'll do it, dear,' Doris said with a chuckle, planting a fresh kiss on his cheek and leaving a mark as ripe as a Red Devil apple.

'And Captain Marshall said you're behind with your hours this month, Mr Bright,' Bertie reminded him. 'You have to do a minimum of forty-eight hours' training or guard duty per month, or it's a ten-pound fine or a month in prison.'

This got an 'ooh' from Lance Corporal Stedman.

Terrence sneered. 'This won't count towards that, and anyway, I've been busy.'

'It might.' Bertie shrugged. 'If you ask him nicely.'

Before Terrence could protest further, Doris popped a smaller pair of antlers on his head.

'Go,' she said. 'It'll be fun. Enjoy yourself for once.'

'Fine.' Terrence wagged a finger at those assembled. 'Just don't burn the pub down while I'm gone!'

Another raucous cheer from the already well-refreshed crowd.

'Are the groom and squire ready?' Mr Hodgson asked.

Bertie said 'yes' and Terrence said 'no' at the exact same moment.

'Pray silence for the first clue!' Mr Hodgson cried, and was rewarded with fifteen seconds of intense shushing.

As his bell-ringing tower captain read the clue, Bertie took note of the odd emphasis that Mr Hodgson put on certain words.

'"You will *observe* the first flag around a *warty* tree lining the drive of the home of a *Brum* football team."'

Bertie and Terrence frowned at each other, cogs whirring in their heads.

'Brum football team?' Bertie pondered.

'Birmingham?' Terrence suggested. 'Aston Villa?'

Bertie snapped his fingers. 'Lord and Lady Aston lived at Hayward Lodge!'

'Which has an observatory: "observe".'

'And the drive is lined with silver birch, which are also known as warty birches.'

Bertie beamed at Mr Hodgson who gestured to the door. 'There's only one way to find out if you're right, Bertie.'

'Yes, come on, Mr Bright!' Bertie limped as fast as his uneven legs would carry him out of the door.

Terrence made a grumbling noise, but Doris assured him that all would be well in his absence and he trundled after Bertie. The lad felt the sun on his face and was almost skipping. Today's adventure had just begun.

A Poor Fit

Faye had been planted in the centre of Mrs Teach's living room like some kind of lace-draped hatstand. She had been crammed into an ivory wedding dress that was tight in all the wrong places, and far too baggy in many of the others. The dress – once Mrs Teach's – was beautiful. The skirt had a hanky hem that rippled whenever Faye turned, and the wreath was a crown that had yet to be filled with summer flowers, but Mrs Teach assured her it would be stunning.

'Something is pinching me armpits, Mrs Teach,' Faye noted, not wanting to complain too much as the older witch was proving to be a tetchy seamstress. 'And the less said about what it's doing to my bosom the better, but if I don't get this off soon, I think I might pass out.'

Mrs Teach stood back, assessing Faye and the dress with pursed lips and a disapprovingly scrunched nose. 'This is going to require more work than I thought,' she said. 'You used to be such a skinny little thing, Faye, but while you've been away, you've developed some very strange and unladylike bumps on your arms and legs.'

Faye, puzzled, glanced down at her limbs. 'Oh, those are called muscles, Mrs Teach. Climbing up and down ropes and going for long runs every day will do that to a girl.'

Mrs Teach drew herself up. 'I think it's unseemly.'

'If you want unseemly, those runs made me throw up every time, and I got callouses on my hands from the ropes, but I like the muscles a lot. It's nice to feel strong.' She raised her right arm, bending it at the elbow and flexing a bicep.

The short, sharp rip of a seam coming apart made Mrs Teach jolt.

Faye gave an apologetic smile. 'Oopsie.'

'For goodness' sake, girl, let me get you out of that dress before you destroy it completely.'

Mrs Teach spun Faye around to face the window as she unbuttoned the dress. Faye spotted Bertie and her father marching swiftly up the Wode Road. Both were wearing what looked like antlers.

'Now where do you suppose Laurel and Hardy are off to?' Faye muttered to herself. 'We should've asked them to check the telegraph poles.'

Mrs Teach wasn't listening. 'I should draft in Mrs Pritchett. What that woman can do with a needle and thread is its own kind of magic.'

'A shame that Corn Bride can't lend me her dress,' Faye mused. 'It looked about the right size.'

'Ask her next time you see her,' Mrs Teach suggested. 'Any more visions since we last spoke?'

'No, though I keep thinking about what they might mean. What is Mum trying to tell me?'

'You're sure it's connected to her?'

Faye shrugged. 'I can't talk with her like she's on the telephone, so I'm not certain. Speaking of which, don't forget we need to call Vera.'

'Yes, yes, we will,' Mrs Teach replied with a weary sigh.

'But I get this feeling,' Faye said wistfully. 'Almost as if Mum is standing next to me.'

'And those children are trying to tell you something, too.'

'Of course, I just wish they'd come out with it instead of prancing about.'

'Patience, Faye, dear.' Mrs Teach rested a hand on her shoulder. 'These things can take time to become apparent. A feeling might be all you need.'

Another figure dashed past Mrs Teach's living room window, so fast it was little more than a blur. Whoever it was rapped the triskelion knocker.

Mrs Teach tutted and bustled off to answer the door, leaving Faye half-unbuttoned and chasing after her.

As Mrs Teach opened the door, Edith Palmer all but fell into her arms, a mess of tears.

'It's Timothy,' Edith said between sobs. 'Something's happened to him. Please ... please help!'

✄

Faye wriggled out of the wedding dress, tearing more seams in the process, much to Mrs Teach's dismay. Once she was back in her comfy dungarees, the two witches took poor Edith in hand, leading her back to the vicarage cottage. The thatch on the roof was shedding, dotted with moss, and dipped in places. Even the garden's normally tidy herbaceous borders were a mess.

Faye had received letters from Bertie all through her training at Beaulieu. He had mentioned a few times that Reverend Jacobs' sermons had shortened recently, which you might think was a cause for celebration, but they had also been delivered in half-hearted mumbles that had Mrs Pritchett yelling, 'Speak up!' from the pews most Sundays. Certainly, what Faye had observed of the Reverend yesterday had her worried. This was more than just a case of the morbs. It sounded like Timothy Jacobs was having what Bellamy referred to as an existential crisis. Bellamy had explained the concept to Faye one night at Beaulieu after misplacing his favourite china teacup.

Edith produced a door key from a pocket of her Royal Mail uniform and let herself into the cottage. The first thing to hit Faye as she crossed the threshold was a warm fug of stale vomit.

Edith grimaced. 'I'm so sorry about that. He's been ill all night.'

These last two words solicited a suggestive glance from Mrs Teach. How scandalous that a single woman should stay with an unmarried man – and a vicar at that – all night. It was astonishing how much Mrs Teach could cram into a single brief expression.

Faye threw back one of her own – *Pack it in!* – as she followed Edith into the Reverend's bedroom.

It was a simple space. Oak beams propped up the walls and ceiling. A small lead-framed window looked out to where the bell tower used to be. The Reverend was a ringer himself, and Faye had enjoyed it when he occasionally popped up on practice nights. He made the rest of them look good. He had been full of beans back then. This morning, he was a shell of a man, lying flat on his back, his skin jaundiced and waxy as he stared at the small wooden cross fixed to the wall above his bed. Edith had placed a chamber pot on the floor nearby as a receptacle for vomit. There were fresh flecks around the inside of the rim.

'Oh, let me change that,' Edith fretted, taking the pot and scurrying from the room.

As she left, Faye felt the bare skin on the back of her neck prickle. A drinking glass half-full of water on the bedside cabinet was beaded with condensation. Faye's own specs misted at the edges.

'Bit nippy, isn't it?'

'Timothy?' Mrs Teach leaned closer to the Reverend.

He blinked his eyes open and they rolled about as he tried to focus.

'Reverend Jacobs, it's Mrs Teach.' She spoke to him as if he was stuck at the bottom of a well. 'What seems to be the problem, dear?'

The Reverend opened and closed his mouth silently a few times.

'That's about all he can manage.' Edith returned with a fresh chamber pot, placing it by the bed. 'Apart from the odd moan. And sometimes he talks funny.'

'In what way?' Mrs Teach asked.

'Begonne foule wommen!' the Reverend rasped, slicing a hand through the air before it fell limp by his side. 'Kisse mine olde breech!'

Faye looked at Mrs Teach, who could only shrug.

'Has he spoken like this before?' Faye asked.

'Not as such.' Edith shook her head. 'That's to say, he's quoted bits of the Bible in Ancient Greek, and he's always saying things in Latin that he expects me to understand – you know what he's like – but all night he's either been silent, sick or spouting nonsense, and I don't know what to do. Doctor Hamm popped over earlier, and all he could suggest was a hot bath and plenty of fluids.'

'I wol have esement!' the Reverend declared with a filthy cackle. 'Esement with you thre wenches!'

'That's not the Bible,' Mrs Teach noted.

'Sounds like Chaucer,' Faye said, getting a surprised look from her fellow witch. 'You don't go to school this close to Canterbury without being bashed over the head with *The Canterbury Tales* every year. I tried to like it, but it's mostly a load of old drunks groping and farting.' She glanced at Edith and added, 'I prefer detective stories.'

'My mouth has itched all day!' Reverend Jacobs licked his lips and lunged at Edith.

'Now, now, Reverend.' Faye moved fast, placing a firm hand on his sternum and thrusting him back onto the bed. 'We'll have none of that.'

'Don't hurt him!' Edith cried, a hand darting to her mouth.

For a moment, Faye caught a glimpse of humanity in the Reverend's eyes, but as Mrs Teach guided Edith to a safe distance from the bed, it faded to a blank, inhuman gaze and he began to thrash about.

Faye gripped his arms. 'Belts and braces, Mrs Teach!' she hollered over the creaking of the bedsprings and the Reverend's wordless ravings. 'We need to tie him down!'

'What is happening to him?' Edith wailed as Mrs Teach yanked open the dresser drawers, tossing aside socks and underpants until she found a couple of leather belts. She tossed one to Faye and they made quick work of tying the Reverend's wrists to the bedposts.

The Reverend snarled at Faye. 'A colt's tooth! Set me free and I'll catch thee by the queynte!'

'See,' Faye said, locking the belt buckle into place. 'Absolute filth. And to think they teach this in schools.'

The Reverend's head whipped from side to side, saliva foaming on his lips.

'Timothy, please stop this madness!' Edith cried, and once again Faye caught a pause in the Reverend's raving.

Mrs Teach steered Edith towards the door. 'This way, dear.'

'No, I can't leave him.'

'It's just for a moment. I must speak with Faye. We won't be long, I promise. Put the kettle on, will you, and make a nice brew, there's a good girl.' Mrs Teach all but shoved Edith out of the room and closed the door behind her. Leaning against the door and catching her breath, she looked from the Reverend to Faye. 'Are you thinking what I'm thinking?'

'Swyving!' The Reverend cackled, gyrating his hips lewdly. 'Taken me by the hand and hard me twiste!'

'Oh, be quiet, you dirty old man!' Faye snapped, then looked back at Mrs Teach. 'Demonic possession?' she guessed.

Mrs Teach nodded. 'Demonic possession.'

Faye puffed out her cheeks. 'And there I was, worried that today might be normal for once.'

MISS CHARLOTTE INVESTIGATES

A few folk on the roads around Stour might have recalled seeing a black motorcycle-and-sidecar combination pootling down winding country lanes. Fewer still might have noted the striking female rider clad in tan leathers, her long white hair tucked into her helmet, a few wisps brushing against her goggles. None, however, would have seen the ghostly child sitting in the sidecar, buzzing with the thrill of being a passenger on a proper motorcycle.

Miss Charlotte had gone to the wood at first light to simply obtain the address of Petunia's home, but the girl had insisted on coming along.

'I can see auras,' she had claimed. Miss Charlotte had no reason not to believe her. She just wished she would shut up for one minute.

'This is jolly exciting,' Petunia declared for the twenty-fifth time as they whizzed through another tiny Kentish hamlet. 'Father never let me ride along in the Rolls. Oh no, there was that one time for Aunt

Gloria's funeral, but he wouldn't let me come out for the service. Said I looked so ghastly pale that I might upset the other mourners. *Left here!*'

Miss Charlotte slowed to turn the motorcycle and sidecar into a long driveway. She pulled up and stopped by the drive's wrought-iron gate.

'What are you doing?' Petunia asked. 'The drive is a mile long. I know because Father was constantly bragging about it. He added extra bends to make it longer.'

Miss Charlotte dropped her goggles around her neck and wriggled out of the helmet, shaking her long white hair free. 'I have it on good authority that a young girl was murdered in this house, and I wouldn't be surprised if the place was teeming with the police. Therefore ...' Miss Charlotte wheeled the motorcycle out of sight behind a shrub ' ... we continue on foot. Or float, in your case.'

Petunia bunched up her lips and asked, 'Do you want to be sneaky?'

Miss Charlotte glanced about before answering, 'Always.'

Petunia's eyebrows bounced. 'I know a secret way in.'

Miss Charlotte smiled approvingly. 'Show me.'

They walked around the walls of the grounds until they came to a path lined with stinging nettles. Petunia led them to an ivy-covered gate that took some convincing to open, but which proved to be no match for Miss Charlotte's barging. They found themselves at the bottom of the gardens, the mansion rising in the distance. A lone gardener was weeding on his knees with his back to them, a black armband around his right arm.

'Ooh, what happened?' Petunia asked, stepping back from Miss Charlotte.

'What do you mean?'

'Your aura just changed. From light to, well, it's almost gone.'

'You noticed that?' Miss Charlotte made a little humming noise to show she was impressed. Petunia had no way of knowing this, but fewer than eight people had been the recipients of such a noise in Charlotte's long lifetime. 'I've cast a glamour. Most people won't see me unless they're looking for me. Now keep quiet. I need to concentrate.'

They passed the raised beds of vegetables and crept into the impressive red-brick house, stepping through a large doorway into a mirrored hall garlanded with chandeliers. Miss Charlotte's riding boots barely made a noise on the tiles as they headed for a pair of tall black doors.

'Take me to where it happened,' she whispered to Petunia as they entered a dusty hall.

They had barely taken two steps when a maid bustled past them. She, too, was wearing a black armband.

'Miss!' A man's voice called from the far end of the hall. Miss Charlotte turned to find a detective in a grey mac and trilby hat marching towards the maid, a notebook in his hand.

Miss Charlotte backed into the shadows, not wanting to risk being seen by the keen eyes of the detective.

The maid bit her lip as he approached.

'That's Betty,' Petunia whispered, even though she knew that only Miss Charlotte could hear her ghostly voice. 'She found me, poor dear. Screamed her head off.'

The detective flipped through the pages of his notebook. 'You are Miss Elizabeth Young, is that correct?'

Betty nodded, her eyes glistening.

'I believe you found Miss Petunia?' the detective asked softly.

Betty nodded again, her lips trembling.

'I'm sorry to bother you, Elizabeth—'

'Betty.'

'Betty, of course. I just have a few more questions. It won't take long. Shall we step into the library?'

'Have ... have they found the master's Rolls-Royce yet?' Betty asked with a sniff as the detective led her away. 'He's devastated about it. Inconsolable.'

Betty and the detective moved into the library, shutting the door behind them.

'Typical,' Petunia snapped. 'His only daughter is murdered, and the old goat is more worried about his rotten motor car.'

'Otto will have stolen it. He has a taste for the extravagant.' Miss Charlotte glanced down at Petunia, whose expression was one of fury. 'Want to see your father?'

'What's the point?' Petunia scowled. 'I could appear to him and give him a heart attack, but knowing my luck he'd become a ghost too and I'd have to spend all eternity with the old windbag. No, let the swine mope about his stinking Rolls, and if we find it, I want you to smash its windows.'

'Gladly,' Miss Charlotte replied, her red lips breaking into a beaming smile.

They sneaked up the carpeted stairs and slipped into Petunia's father's bedroom. They were alone, but the space was littered with numbered cards where the police had noted important evidence for their investigation. The wardrobe doors were still open.

'He stole some of your father's clothes?' Miss Charlotte asked.

'I caught him in the act and ...' Petunia froze. 'I can see it.'

'See what?'

The girl was staring at an empty spot in the air before them.

'Otto's aura. They linger sometimes, and this one ... It's like smog in the air. Smoke from a steamer. Oh gosh, now I know what to look for, it's so clear. Follow me!'

Petunia dashed out into the hall and raced down the stairs. Miss Charlotte had to move with more caution, slipping past the butler and a redundant chauffeur in the reception hall. It took her some time to rendezvous with Petunia by the iron gate at the end of the drive.

'He went that way!' Petunia pointed up the road. 'I can still see his aura snaking away. If we're fast, I think we might catch him.'

'Fast?' Miss Charlotte slipped her helmet on with a wink. 'That's my speciality.'

⚶

Not so fast were Bertie and Terrence. They had been correct with their first clue and found the second dangling from the branch of a birch tree at Hayward Lodge. Now they wandered back towards the village, antlers at a jaunty angle, as Terrence read aloud, trying to make sense of it.

'"Begorra! Where might I find the child of a model to a T?"' Terrence lowered the card bearing Captain Marshall's neat handwriting. 'That's not even proper English, Bertie. How am I supposed to make heads or tails of that?'

Bertie, for his part, was in no hurry to complete the challenge prepared by their Home Guard captain. The pub was a lovely place to work but couldn't compare with the breezy freedom of a stroll on the cusp of summer. Bluebells lined the road, and somewhere a chiffchaff cheeped repeatedly in competition with a willow warbler.

'"Begorra!"' Terrence repeated, putting the emphasis on different words this time in the hope that it might make more sense. '"Where *might* I find the *child* of a *model* to a T?"'

It did not make more sense.

'Were you nervous before your wedding day, Mr Bright?' Bertie asked.

Terrence blinked as he looked up from the card with the clue. 'Me? Not really. I s'pose I was nervous about little stuff, like making a speech, or my trousers falling down. Or my trousers falling down while making a speech. But I was never worried about the actual marriage part of it all. Kathryn and I were no spring chickens and we wanted to get on with it with as little fuss as possible.' Terrence smiled at the lad. 'Why do you ask? Case of the collywobbles?'

Bertie thought for a moment, stuffing his hands into his pockets. 'Whenever someone mentions the wedding, my belly does little flips, but I think that's because I'm excited.'

'You sure, lad? Don't take this the wrong way, but the pair of you have not long turned eighteen. There's no harm in waiting a couple of years. Just to be sure.'

'I've known Faye all my life, Mr Bright. What would waiting a couple of years do? No, I've never been more sure of anything than of marrying Faye.'

'Good for you, Bertie,' Terrence said, and turned his attention back to the clue on the card. '"Begorra—"'

'Harry Newton's barn.' Bertie stopped in his tracks. Terrence bumped into him. 'Eh?'

'The clue.' Bertie squinted as he concentrated. '"Child of a model to a T." A Model T is a Ford motor car, and the son of a Ford could be a Fordson.'

Terrence shook his head, making his candyfloss hair wobble. 'What's a Fordson?'

'Harry Newton has a Fordson tractor, an Irish N model. And "begorra" is something that Irish people say.'

Terrence, who had a few Irish relatives in his convoluted family tree, bobbed his head from side to side. 'It really isn't.'

Bertie corrected himself. 'It's something that Captain Marshall might think that Irish people say.'

'I thought Harry's tractor was an Allis-Chalmers? A manky old wreck from before the Great War.'

Bertie raised a finger. 'Last summer, Harry got a new Fordson with a special war grant from the government. It has blue paint on the body and red wheels.'

'You're certain?'

Bertie smiled. 'As certain as I am of marrying Faye.'

Terrence held up the clue. 'You know what this means, don't you?'

'We're going the wrong way,' they both said in unison.

The pair turned, adjusted the antlers on their heads, and took the path that led past the church and the pond towards Harry's farm.

Your Local Village
Exorcists

Faye and Mrs Teach huddled with a trembling Edith Palmer in the hallway outside Reverend Jacobs' bedroom. From within came a torrent of Middle English curses as the demon inside the vicar tried to break free of his bonds.

'Demonic possession?' Edith's voice rose in pitch with each syllable until she was only audible by dogs.

Faye and Mrs Teach had decided to be straight with her. No point in pussyfooting around when time is of the essence.

Edith's face creased in confusion. 'But demons aren't real, surely?'

'I'm afraid they are, dear.' Mrs Teach rested a gentle hand on Edith's forearm. 'And Timothy has succumbed to this one over the past few days. It accounts for all his odd behaviour.'

'I thought he was just a bit down in the dumps.'

Edith dabbed at her tears with a hankie. 'Not possessed by the bloody Devil.'

'A demon, dear,' Mrs Teach corrected her. 'Quite different.'

'How did it happen?'

Faye and Mrs Teach shared a look. They each had their theories, but they didn't want to overwhelm poor Edith with more than she needed to know.

'One of the risks of the job,' Faye said, bobbing her shoulders. 'Demons come after vicars and priests and nuns all the time.' This wasn't true at all, not these days, but the alternative didn't bear thinking about. Not yet.

More curses came from the other side of the door, and poor Edith recoiled in shock. 'Whatever can we do?'

'That's the good news.' Mrs Teach took Edith's hand. 'Demons are actually quite weak. They don't belong here and need a vessel to thrive.'

'A vessel?' Edith whimpered. 'Timothy's a vessel?'

Mrs Teach winced at her poor choice of words, but continued, 'The way they work is they wear one down with curses of self-loathing.'

Edith blinked in confusion.

'They're persistent buggers,' Faye added, 'who torment people by whispering a drip-drip-drip of doubts into your ear'ole.'

'This goes on until the possessed start to believe it themselves and eventually surrender.'

Edith's nostrils flared. 'What happens then?'

Faye didn't dare look at Mrs Teach. After all that kerfuffle with the crow folk, Mrs Teach and Miss Charlotte had schooled Faye on the dangers of possession. She knew that if the demon succeeded in wearing its victim down to the point where it had complete control, then the only thing to do would be to destroy the host. Miss Charlotte insisted that it be done with fire.

'We're not going to let it come to that,' Mrs Teach said in her most comforting tone.

'But we need your help,' Faye added.

'M-me? I'm not a ...' Edith's eyes widened as she gestured at Faye and Mrs Teach. It was generally accepted in the village that there were women that might be regarded as witchy, but no one ever said it out loud. Not twice, anyway.

Faye put Edith out of her misery. 'No, you're not a witch, but you are close to the Reverend. I noticed that whenever you spoke, Edith, I caught glimpses of the real Timothy coming through.' Faye leaned in. 'It's like Timothy is underwater, but your voice can bring him to the surface.'

'Do you care for Timothy?' Mrs Teach asked.

Edith nodded. 'Very much.'

'Good,' Faye said. 'Tell him how much he means to you. What you'll do together when all this is over, all the good things. Don't worry so much about what you say. It's more ...' Faye glanced at Mrs Teach. 'It's more the feeling that's important.'

'And ignore the demon,' Mrs Teach insisted, rolling up the sleeves of her blouse. 'You leave him to us.'

'Are you ready?' Faye asked, then shook her head. 'Silly question. Sorry, Edith. No one can be ready for this, but just keep whispering sweet nothings till we say otherwise. Understand?'

Edith nodded and raised her chin. 'Understood.'

'Righto.' Faye took hold of the bedroom's doorknob. 'Shall we?'

Mrs Teach smiled. 'We shall.'

✆

'Left! No, not this one, the next one!'

Young Petunia was unused to high-speed travel, particularly when following the ethereal trail of a Nazi occultist, and so her directions were tending to come maddeningly late as Miss Charlotte drove the motorcycle-and-sidecar combination up and down the country lanes.

'A right here!'

It didn't help that Miss Charlotte was also minus one eye, so her judgement of corners wasn't quite what it used to be and could make some of the bends rather hair-raising.

'Left!'

Of course, all road signs had been removed, too, in case of invasion, and Otto Kopp probably hadn't been in this neck of the woods for decades or more – if ever – so, wherever he was headed, he appeared to have taken a rambling route through Wingham, Bramling and Littlebourne, before turning north through Sturry. As they rattled past Herne Common, Miss Charlotte arrived at a fair idea of their destination, and it wasn't long before Petunia waved them to a stop by Herne Bay pier.

Miss Charlotte parked the motorcycle and sidecar by a row of tall houses facing the sea. She glanced around. The good people of Herne Bay and a fair few tourists were going about their day as normal, despite a beach littered with invasion defences, barrage balloons tethered every few hundred yards and a newly arrived witch and ghost.

Of course, none of them could see the ghost, which is why Miss Charlotte took off her helmet and used it to cover her mouth as she asked Petunia, 'Where now?'

'It's gone,' was Petunia's reply.

'What's gone?'

'Otto's trail. It was becoming fainter and thinner for the last few miles and then it tapered here and now it's completely vanished. I'm so sorry, Miss Charlotte. I don't know where he went from here.'

'Not to worry.' Miss Charlotte got off the bike, tucking the helmet under her arm. 'If there's a Nazi occultist in Herne Bay he'll stick out like a sore thumb. We'll find him sooner or ... later ...' She trailed off, her one eye narrowing.

'What is it?' Petunia asked.

Miss Charlotte's attention had been caught by the frantic behaviour of a blue-and-green budgerigar hopping about in a cage positioned in the bay window of one of the houses overlooking the sea, right where Otto's trail ran cold.

'Does anything strike you as peculiar about that bird?' Miss Charlotte asked.

Petunia jutted her head forward for a closer look. 'Its aura is like a kaleidoscope and . . . it's almost as if it's waving at us with its wing.'

'Indeed.' Miss Charlotte pursed her red lips as she ruminated.

'But what does a peculiar budgie have to do with this Otto chap?'

'When you've lived as long as I have, you learn to pay attention to the strange behaviour of birds. We should investigate.'

Miss Charlotte skipped up the steps and rapped on the door. She knocked three times, but there was no answer. The budgie's muffled chirping became increasingly distressed.

'Can't you simply—' Petunia waggled her fingers like a conjuror '—magic the door open?'

'Locks are impervious to magic, and besides, you're a ghost, so can't you just—' Now Miss Charlotte waggled her fingers like a conjuror '—drift through the door?'

'Oh.' Petunia's eyes boggled as if the thought hadn't occurred to her. 'I suppose I could. Forgive me, I'm new to all this, you see, so . . .' She faltered, sensing Miss Charlotte's impatience. 'Bear with me.'

Petunia closed her eyes and stepped through the door.

'I say,' came her voice from inside, 'that was rather odd. A bit like breaking into a million little pieces and then coming back together again. I'd rather not repeat that too—'

'Yes, yes, all very thrilling. Is anyone there?' Miss Charlotte crouched, propping open the letterbox and peering through. She watched as Petunia drifted from room to room.

'I don't think so,' the ghostly girl replied. 'It's difficult to concentrate. I can hear a voice and I think it's coming from the budgie.'

'What's it saying?'

Petunia cocked an ear as she floated at the threshold of the living room door. 'It's two voices. A woman and a man. He's demanding some cucumber he was promised, and she . . .'

'What?'

'It's rather an odd request.'

'Try me.'

'She says she wants her body back and— Oh, lots of rude words that I shan't repeat. She's really rather cross. "I want my body back" over and over.'

Miss Charlotte turned and looked up and down Herne Bay's Central Parade. There were too many people about for her to break in through the living room window unnoticed, but she had a sturdy motorcycle helmet and she reckoned that a well-placed barge should make short work of the door's lock.

'Wait there, Petunia,' she said. 'I'll be with you momentarily.'

Taking a step back, she raised the helmet like a shield, aimed it between the lock and the handle, and lunged forwards.

Advice on Marrying a Witch

Bertie and Terrence hadn't realised that Harry Newton owned so many barns. There were two for the cows, one for the tractors and his truck, one for grain and feed, a big coop for the chickens and, of course, one for the hay. That had burned down last summer and had quickly been rebuilt.

The pair surveyed the farm from a path that ran alongside Harry's field of carrots.

'We should pop into the farmhouse first,' Terrence said. 'It's not right to go snooping around a man's farm without his say-so.'

'Harry still got that blunderbuss?' Bertie asked.

'Aye, and it goes off at the slightest provocation.'

'Farmhouse it is, then.'

There they found a clutch of Women's Land Army volunteers busily repairing Harry's old Allis-Chalmers tractor.

'Morning, Ruby,' Bertie said, recognising one of the girls who worked on Harry's farm.

'Morning, chaps.' Ruby wiped her hands on an oily rag, looking smart in her Land Girls' uniform of a green V-neck pullover, brown corduroy breeches and rubber boots. She tipped her hat back as the tractor chugged into life. The other girls cheered at their success. 'Aren't carburettors simply fascinating?'

Bertie and Terrence shared a look. What they knew about carburettors could be written on the back of a beer mat, but, being men of the world, they would rather die than admit to ignorance and replied with a series of knowledgeable and approving murmurs.

'Fascinating,' Terrence began.

'Definitely,' Bertie agreed.

'Little ... carburettor ...'

'Very clever. What it does.'

'Marvellous.'

'How can I help you young stags?' Ruby asked.

Bertie crinkled his nose. 'Stags? How do you ...?'

'We've still got these on, Bertie.' Terrence tapped at the fake antlers attached to his head.

Bertie brushed a self-conscious hand against his antlers.

'Don't take them off, they suit you,' Ruby said, chuckling. 'If you're after chickens or eggs, I'm afraid Harry has told us he'll shoot first and ask questions later.'

'We thought that might be the case,' Terrence said. 'Though it's not chickens we're after. It's a clue for a little sort-of treasure hunt that me and Bertie are doing on account of him getting married on the morrow.'

'Ah, that explains the antlers,' Ruby said.

'Er, yes, so we reckon it's in or on or about one of Harry's barns,' Bertie chipped in, 'and we wanted to have a little nose about to find it, if that's all right?'

'I say, what larks.' Ruby rested her hands on her hips and grinned. 'I have no objection, but it's not my farm. If I see Harry, I'll let him know, but of course if he sees you snooping about then he might just—'

'Shoot first and ask questions later?' Bertie finished for her.

'Indeed. Fret not, we have plenty of first aid to hand,' Ruby told them. 'We've all had a little bit of Harry's buckshot in our behinds at some point, haven't we, girls?'

A chorus of pained sounds of agreement came from those gathered around the tractor.

'That's almost reassuring,' Terrence said, jabbing a thumb in the direction of the barns. 'We'll make a start, and if you do see Harry, we'd appreciate it if you'd let him know that we're not chicken rustlers.'

'Or stags,' Bertie added quickly.

'Most certainly. And congratulations, Bertie, on snagging a young beauty like Faye. She's a brick!'

⁊

Bertie suggested they use some of the guerrilla warfare tactics they'd learned in the Home Guard in order to move from barn to barn.

Terrence was less enthusiastic. 'Thing is, Bertie, that's skulking about. And if you saw someone skulking about, then you'd assume they were up to no good and shoot them.'

'But if Harry's going to shoot first anyway, then shouldn't we lessen the chances of being shot by keeping a low profile?'

'If I'm going to get shot, Bertie, I'll do it standing upright like a man,' Terrence said with a sudden defiance. 'Not to mention, my back's giving me aggro and I can't be crouching about like a chimpanzee. I'd never get up again.'

They checked the barns together, deciding to present a united front should Harry confront them. Having no luck, they walked across to the rebuilt hay barn last of all, and Bertie couldn't help but think of the events of the previous summer when the crow folk had burned it down. The two of them walked the ploughed field side by side, Terrence ambling with his hands in his pockets, keeping pace with Bertie, whose limp slowed him down on rough terrain.

'That was a day and a half, wasn't it?' Bertie didn't have to say any more. The barn was reminder enough.

'Certainly was, Bertie. Certainly was.'

Somewhere, a crow cawed. The pair stopped and turned about, the heels of their shoes kicking up little swirls of dust.

Bertie caught Terrence's eye and the pair of them chuckled.

'That was the day I knew there'd be no stopping Faye as a witch,' Terrence said as they resumed walking. 'I hadn't deliberately kept the truth from her, not as such,

I just . . . didn't mention it. She was always a smart girl. I knew she'd figure it out sooner or later. All I wanted was for Faye to have a happy childhood. No magic.'

'Did Mrs Teach and Miss Charlotte know what Faye could do?'

Terrence's shoulder bobbed. 'They knew her mother, of course, and I s'pose they reckoned it was only a matter of time before she figured it out . . . But, fair play to them, they respected my wishes and kept their distance.' Terrence stopped and stared into the wood that bordered the field. 'But once those straw hands got hold of me and dragged me into the wood . . .' He kicked at a rock. 'It was when I heard Faye coming after me. That determination in her voice. The same determination I'd heard from Kathryn so many times. That's when I knew things would never be the same again.'

The summer wind rumbled around the pair for a long moment. A robin bobbed by and Bertie followed its flight, his eyes drawn back to the barn.

'There's an envelope.' He shielded his eyes from the sun. 'There. Barn door.'

'Well spotted, lad.' Terrence chivvied them on. 'Let's get it before Harry starts taking potshots.'

'You and Mrs Bright were happy, weren't you?' Bertie asked as they approached the barn.

'Very,' Terrence said, somehow saturating the single word with both grief and happiness.

'Any advice?' Bertie asked as casually as he could. 'For marrying a witch?'

Terrence plucked the envelope from where it had

193

been tucked between the lapped planks on the barn door. He thought for a moment.

'It'll be hard,' he said. 'There'll be times when she'll face danger – you'll know this already, of course – but sometimes the dangers will be the likes of which you and me can barely get our noggins around. Corn Brides? Ghostly children? You have any clue?'

Bertie had a few half-baked theories, but now didn't feel like the right time to share them.

Terrence held up a finger. 'Rule number one: do not interfere. Even if you mean well. *Especially* if you mean well. Whenever I stuck my oar in, it caused more trouble than it was worth.' He held up a second finger. 'Rule number two: be there at the end of every day with a cuppa and a sympathetic ear.'

Bertie waited for more. It was not forthcoming. 'And that's it?'

'It sounds simple enough, but it can be a right palaver. And the wear and tear on your ticker can lead to an early grave. Just look at poor old Ernie Teach. But yes, that's it.'

'Don't interfere, and be there with a cuppa and listen,' Bertie summarised. 'I reckon I can do that.'

'Good. Right, what nonsense do we have here?' Terrence tore open the envelope, unfolded the card inside and read aloud. '"Don't thank me, but a terrible wind went up in flames. No more gas for an L-shaped key."'

'Who's got terrible wind?' Bertie asked.

'I sat next to Mrs Brew in church last Sunday. That woman needs to see a doctor.'

'A Hurricane!' Bertie clapped his hands together. 'That's a kind of terrible wind. And an L-shaped key is an Allen key, and Dougie Allen used to own the garage on Unthank Road – "Don't thank me" – and it blew up last summer when a Hurricane crashed into it!'

'Good work, Bertie.' Terrence tucked the envelope into his trouser pocket. 'Though I'm beginning to wonder why Captain Marshall's clues seem to be obsessed with gas and flames. I dread to think—'

Part of the barn door shattered into splinters. The crack of blunderbuss fire echoed across the field.

Terrence and Bertie spun to find Harry Newton trundling towards them in his new Fordson tractor. He was already reloading his blunderbuss, pouring shot from a cartridge into the weapon's pan.

'Get off my land!' he cried.

'Better do as he says,' Bertie suggested, limping as fast as his uneven legs could carry him.

'Always do what a man with a blunderbuss says.' Terrence ducked down and winced. 'Ow!'

'What? Have you been shot?'

'No, my bloody back's playing up. Move, move!' Terrence said, and the pair dashed around the side of the barn and out of sight.

BANNED BOOKS

The exorcism of Reverend Timothy Jacobs was not going well. Faye had lost all track of time, but some hours had passed with the two witches drawing various protective pentagrams around the bed, or chanting incantations remembered from the Ebers Papyrus, all while Edith whispered into Timothy's ear in an attempt to draw him out. All it had done so far was produce more insults and effluent from the possessed vicar.

Mrs Teach called for a break. The trio staggered from the chill of the Reverend's bedroom and into his kitchen. Faye filled the kettle and popped it on the stove.

'Is every day like this for witches?' Edith asked, flopping into a chair, her eyes drifting like clouds.

'There's not usually this much vomit,' Faye said as she wrenched the lid off the tea caddy. 'Are you getting any kind of reaction from Timothy?'

Edith bit her lip and shook her head.

Mrs Teach leaned across the table and rested her

hand on Edith's. 'What have you been talking to him about?'

'Oh, we did enjoy our walks in the wood, and on the path overlooking the sea. It's the only time we held hands outside. We had a lovely time planting carrots in his raised bed, and there was that day when we white-washed the crypt ...'

Mrs Teach glanced at Faye and grimaced. This was hardly the sort of thing to bring a man back from the brink of demonic possession.

'Did any of that get a reaction?' Faye asked.

Edith thinned her lips and squirmed. There was more, but she didn't want to tell.

'Darling, you're among friends,' Mrs Teach assured her. 'What is it?'

'I think I see him, the real Timothy ...' Edith began to blush. 'When I mention our *intimate* moments.'

'That's good.' Mrs Teach took a firmer grip on Edith's hand. 'That's what men live for, let's be honest. When I think of my Ernie ...' She drifted off for a moment, sighing wistfully. 'It's been a little over a year since he passed and I still dream of his weight pressing down on me when we made—'

'Mrs Teach!' Faye intervened, for all their sakes.

'Hm? Oh, yes. Edith, darling, draw him out with your most secret moments. Be as explicit as you like, dear.'

'E-explicit?' Edith's eyes vibrated with fear.

Faye crouched next to her and rested a hand on her shoulder. 'You don't have to tell us. Just whisper sweet nothings into his ear and keep using his name. Give him every reason to come back to us. Remember, it's the feeling that's important. Do you understand?'

Edith nodded.

Faye, still crouching, turned to Mrs Teach. 'And we have to try something new. The usual stuff isn't working.'

'Indeed.' Mrs Teach pursed her lips in thought. 'Faye, I need you to pop back to my house and fetch a book.'

'Book?' Faye's eyes narrowed. 'What book?'

'I have a copy of *The Book of Abramelin* in my—'

'That's a grimoire.' Faye raised a finger and wagged it oh-so-slightly. 'A book of magic and forbidden by the Council of Witches.'

'It's the ravings of a mad old German who, every now and then, somehow managed to get a few details correct.'

The kettle began to whistle as Faye rose from her crouch. 'You and Miss Charlotte made me burn my mother's book.'

'Faye, *The Book of Abramelin* has been freely available since the fifteenth century. You could get a copy from Mr McKendrick's mobile library if you really wanted it. It's mostly gibberish, but there is one page in there that might save the life of Reverend Jacobs, so could you possibly put aside any ire you have for just one—'

'Yes, yes, fine.' Faye scowled, catching sight of Edith's glassy eyes pleading with her. She took the screaming kettle off the hob and filled the teapot.

'You'll find it on my landing, top of the stairs,' Mrs Teach said. 'There's a bookcase, and this volume is two shelves down, three books from the left. Got that?'

Faye nodded.

'Do not – and I cannot stress this enough – do *not* tamper with any of the other books. Do not touch them, try and avoid even looking at them. Some are so dangerous they'll turn your hair white.'

'Think that's what happened to Miss Charlotte?'

'Go. Now.'

ø

Faye found the bookcase at the top of Mrs Teach's stairs as promised, and two shelves down and three books from the left there was a leather-bound volume with a flaking spine. She opened it to the title page, but it was all in German with a heavy gothic typeface that felt like it was shouting the bibliographic information at her. She caught the name 'Abraham' and the word 'Magie', which was close enough. Faye snapped the book shut, sending little eddies of dust spiralling about her. Despite Mrs Teach's grave warning, she gave the other books a quick once-over. She had expected an unholy library of deathly grimoires, and while there were a handful of crumbling tomes that fitted the bill, they were sandwiched between the likes of *Mrs Beeton's Book of Household Management*, Eliza Acton's *Modern Cookery for Private Families*, Miss Burgess' *Guide to Chicken Husbandry for Young Farmers* and a handful of Agatha Christie mysteries, a couple of which Faye had yet to read and had half a mind to ask if she could borrow. On the bottom shelf were a few untitled books. They looked more like ledgers, and one had black smoke smudges on its spine like it had been rescued from a fire. Faye knew from experience that the less magical something looked, the more dangerous it probably was, so she left them well alone. As she turned to descend the stairs, she caught a glimpse of herself in a full-length mirror that hung on the wall.

Standing behind her was the Corn Bride.

Faye's spine tensed, her muscles froze and her heart raced as the straw woman threw back her head and a wretched scream of anguish filled Faye's ears.

℘

Clad in an ivory wedding dress, Faye burned alive. Flames engulfed her from head to toe as the flesh on her face blackened and shrivelled, her glasses cracked in the heat and her eyes melted in their sockets.

℘

Faye found herself in a shivering pile at the bottom of the stairs with no memory of how she had got there. She flexed her fingers and toes. Nothing broken. And nothing on fire. Her mouth was dry and her vision blurred. Her specs had tumbled onto the rug in the hallway. As her shuddering subsided, she fumbled for them with trembling fingers, put them on and looked around her.

The Corn Bride was gone.

Another vision. This one more petrifying than any other, though mercifully brief. That dress. She was certain it was the same as the Corn Bride's. The same as her mother's.

Already the image was fading in her mind's eye. Somewhere, a clock chimed the hour. Heart thumping in her ears, Faye got to her feet, retrieved Mrs Teach's grimoire and took a deep breath before heading back to the vicarage on wobblier legs than she had arrived with.

Ø

As soon as Faye stepped through the front door, Mrs Teach took the book from her and flipped through its delicate, yellowing pages. Moans reverberated from the bedroom above them.

'How's Edith doing?' Faye asked as nonchalantly as possible, deciding to keep her vision to herself for the moment.

'The girl is a champion sweet-talker and has thus far kept the demon at bay,' Mrs Teach said, slowing her page-turning, searching more intently. 'Aha!' She slapped a hand down on one page in particular and showed it to Faye, who tried to make sense of what she was seeing. Word squares covered the pages.

'They look like word puzzles. Sator Squares,' Faye said, then snapped her fingers. 'No, wait. Are these talismans?'

'Very good, Faye. And almost correct,' Mrs Teach said, reining in the full weight of her usual patronising tone. 'Most people associate talismans with some kind of object – a medallion or a ring – but it's always the words inscribed on them that convey the true power. In *The Book of Abramelin*, many of these squares are gibberish at first glance, but look closer and you will find the names of demons hiding in plain sight.'

'And once you know the name of a demon, you can cast him out,' Faye said.

'Quite. There is one teensy-weensy hurdle that we must overcome.'

'Most of them are in Hebrew,' Faye noted.

'Indeed.' Mrs Teach gave Faye a winning smile. 'I don't suppose Bellamy covered ancient Hebrew in your training, did he?'

'I can ask the way to the train station and buy a newspaper,' Faye said, returning the smile with some added cheek.

'Impudent girl,' Mrs Teach snapped, glancing down at the impenetrable word squares. 'We shall recite them in turn. This could take some time.'

How to
Interrogate a Budgie

Breaking into Mrs Wallace's home was easy. Making sense of what had happened was proving to be altogether more frustrating for Miss Charlotte. Petunia did her best, repeating the words of the two entities sharing the body of the chittering budgerigar like some bizarre Punch and Judy show, only minus the puppets.

'I have a right to be heard! *Don't listen to her, she's a spy.* A man came in here and took my body. *She's completely barmy, you can't trust her.* I demand my body back!'

'Silence!' Miss Charlotte's voice made the bay windows rattle so hard that it was only the criss-crossed anti-blast tape that saved them.

It had the desired effect. Petunia's mouth shrank into a quivering moue. Miss Charlotte took a moment to savour the peace.

'They're still blethering on in my head,' Petunia

informed her quietly. 'You could probably hear it yourself if you tried. It's quite simple, really. It's odd how straightforward this all becomes once one is dead. Their voices can be heard in between all the other noises in the world. Give it a try.'

Miss Charlotte was impressed at how well Petunia was adjusting to the afterlife. Most ghosts she had encountered took years to accept the cold embrace of death. For Petunia, it was all an awfully big adventure, full of new skills to discover. And it turned out she was right about the voices. Miss Charlotte closed her eyes, allowing the gentle ticking of the clock in the hall, the budgie's tweets, the trundle of traffic on the street and the hiss of waves on shingle to all wash over her. There, at a frequency somewhere between long-wave radio and the echo of creation, were two voices. One had the manner of a cantankerous older woman, the other that of an equally cantankerous lifelong prisoner. Or a caged budgie.

'I can hear them.' Miss Charlotte opened her eyes, the overlapping voices creating a chaotic din in her ears.

She moved to the mantel, where a few letters and postcards were stacked. All had the same addressee.

'Mrs Jessica Wallace,' she said, loud and clear.

'Speaking.' The woman's voice somehow came from the budgie in the cage.

'I will hear you first.'

'That's not fair,' the male voice objected. 'She's a spy!'

'Be quiet, Harold,' the woman snapped. 'You're a budgie and confused. Leave this to Mumsy.'

'Harold, I will hear you next. You have my word,'

206

Miss Charlotte vowed. She replaced the letters on the mantel, tapping with a long fingernail. 'Mrs Wallace. You are resident here?'

'Of course I am, you silly woman. And who the devil are you? What right have you to break into my home? You're like him, aren't you? Some sort of occult deviant. I don't know what you're playing at, but I demand to be set free. I demand the return of my body.'

'Tell me more about this deviant occultist. What did he look like?'

'Bald chap. No eyebrows. He spoke with a—' Mrs Wallace stopped herself.

'Did he have a foreign accent, Mrs Wallace? A distinct Bavarian accent?'

Mrs Wallace's silence spoke volumes.

'And why would a Bavarian occultist come knocking at your door, Mrs Wallace?'

''Cos she's a bloody spy!' Harold blurted.

'Be quiet, you little wretch, or no more treats!'

'Diced cucumber is not a treat, and she's a spy, I'm telling you. Agent Siskin, he called her.'

'You lying little—'

'I will listen to Harold now,' Miss Charlotte declared.

'He's a liar and you mustn't—'

'Mrs Wallace, if you ever want to see your body again, you would do well to obey my commands. I am the only person who can save you from a short life trapped in a cage, on a diet of millet.'

Miss Charlotte waited until she was certain that Mrs Wallace understood.

'Harold, you are remarkably well versed in espionage for a small house bird,' Miss Charlotte suggested.

The budgie hopped along his stand and jerked his beak at the wireless on a table by the window. 'I've not got much else to do other than listen when she has the news on. And if you go up to her bedroom, you'll find a two-way radio hidden at the back of her wardrobe.'

'Petunia, could you kindly check, please?' Miss Charlotte asked, and the ghostly girl rose upwards, vanishing into the ceiling.

'I could hear her sending Morse code messages at night,' Harold said. 'Tap-tap-bloody-tap. How was I supposed to get any kip with that racket?'

Petunia drifted down through the plaster ceiling rose light fitting. 'Oh, I say, there's a radio and code books and maps with swastikas, and all sorts of Nazi paraphernalia.'

Miss Charlotte's red lips thinned into a cruel smile. 'That all sounds quite damning, Mrs Wallace. Do you have anything to say in your defence?'

Mrs Wallace remained silent.

'You were in cahoots with this occultist?' Miss Charlotte asked.

'Certainly not.' Mrs Wallace found her voice again. 'I never even believed in any of this nonsense.'

'Few do, till it becomes their reality,' Miss Charlotte said.

'It's remarkable how quickly you get used to it,' Petunia noted cheerily. 'And at least I'm not poorly all the time. I quite prefer it, if I'm honest.'

'I do not,' Mrs Wallace declared. 'Therefore, I am ready to come to an arrangement.'

'And what arrangement might that be?' Miss Charlotte was genuinely curious. 'I hardly think you're in a position to negotiate.'

'I have all kinds of information about the Nazi spy network in Great Britain that your superiors might find very useful.'

'You imagine I have superiors?' Miss Charlotte gave a hollow chuckle at the very idea. 'How amusing. Nevertheless, we have a common goal: to find your body and, along with it, Otto Kopp.'

'Otto Kopp?'

'The occultist you encountered, Mrs Wallace. He is a very powerful and dangerous man. How long ago did he leave here?'

'Yesterday afternoon. In a Rolls-Royce, if you please.'

'Father's car!' Petunia said. 'But that means he could be anywhere by now.'

'Did he give you any clue as to where he was headed?' Miss Charlotte asked.

'No,' Harold said, hopping across his cage, 'but he went east up the Central Parade. Does that help?'

'Thank you, Harold, Mrs Wallace.' Miss Charlotte gestured for Petunia to follow her into the kitchen, out of earshot.

'How does one find a stolen car?' Petunia pondered. 'Ask a policeman? I'm sure that Daddy would have reported it stolen to the police.'

'Indeed, so Otto would be wise to keep it out of sight.'

'I have a question.'

'Go on.'

'Why would Otto want Mrs Wallace's body in the first place?'

'Oh, that's simple.' Miss Charlotte waved a hand casually. 'Some kind of sacrificial blood ritual.'

'That sounds horrid.'

'It is.' Miss Charlotte peered back towards the living room, where the budgie bounced back and forth in frustration. 'I have a suspicion that even if we do find Mrs Wallace's body, it will either be drained of blood, chopped into little pieces or burned to ashes.'

Petunia turned pale, even for a ghost, and Miss Charlotte was reminded that she was still dealing with a little girl.

'Sorry, but I have every reason to believe that's what he's up to. Though keep that to yourself. We need Mrs Wallace to cooperate until we find Otto.'

Petunia grimaced. 'I'm not sure I want to now.'

'Petunia, I wasn't joking when I said Otto was dangerous. He's here on the eve of my friend's wedding . . .' Miss Charlotte faltered, wondering if that was the first time she had referred to Faye as a friend. 'A friend who has thwarted his plans more than once. He's out for revenge, and he's got a Rolls-Royce and the body of a septuagenarian spy. Where would he go first?'

'The woods?' Petunia suggested. 'The woods around Woodville village are jolly strange.'

210

'They are, but there are things in the wood that scare even someone like Otto.'

'Monsters?'

'No, mostly birds and trees and . . . Of course, there's a woodwose who could tear him limb from limb, so I don't think he's there. Oh, bugger.'

'What?'

'If he's done what I think he's done to Mrs Wallace—'

'The draining of the blood and chopping-into-bits?'

'Keep your voice down. Yes, that. If he's done that, then he's likely performed some exceptionally powerful magic. I could go into a trance and search the aether for traces of the ritual.'

'Like the black trail that he left?'

'Yes – and this one would be very dark indeed. If I find it, then we would have his location.'

'That sounds splendid. Off you pop.'

'It's not that simple. It takes hours and it's bloody exhausting.'

'Well, it's not like we have anything better to do.'

Miss Charlotte tried to contain her grin. There was no denying that Petunia's moxie was intoxicating.

'Indeed,' she said. 'Let's begin. I'll need a blanket, a pillow, warm milk and a budgerigar.'

REVELATIONS

Free of buckshot in their behinds, Bertie and Terrence came to the remains of Dougie Allen's garage on the corner of Unthank Road by the railway bridge. Bertie checked his wristwatch. It was coming up to five o'clock. They had been wandering for hours! He gave thanks that he had spent this day in the sunshine and open air, not being coerced into boozing in the confines of the pub.

The site of Dougie's former garage brought back vivid memories for Bertie. That morning last July had been quite something. Bertie and Faye had been on the bus coming back from seeing a splendid George Formby flick in Canterbury, when a Hurricane had crashed into the garage and sent the whole thing up in flames. Bertie had never seen anything like it. The flames had stung his face, and if he closed his eyes, he could still sense the tingle of petrol, oil and smoke in his nostrils.

Now the garage was gone, leaving only a scorched

patch of concrete on which the Army could park their vehicles. This morning, Bertie was delighted to find a Bren Universal Carrier sitting facing the railway bridge. Complete with tank tracks, there was also a Bren gun mounted on the back, and a heavy chain hung across its front in a metallic smile.

'I know this is an old man's thing to say,' Terrence said as they approached the garage's former forecourt, 'but all this used to be fields, and Dougie Allen's garage started as a stable where folks could get their horses fed and watered and shod. Then old Mr Unthank sold up and Dougie turned it into a garage.'

Bertie noted the weeds growing through the cracks in the concrete and wondered how long it would be till the fields claimed the land back. The village was peppered with trees and roots in odd places after all that fuss at Christmas, and Bertie wouldn't be surprised if he woke up one morning to find the whole village gobbled up by the wood.

'Righto.' Terrence snapped back to the task at hand and surveyed the garage plot, hands on hips like an explorer. 'Where's this bloody clue, then?'

☙

'Oren, Uruk, Heka, Enok, Noaj, Baal, Sceve . . .' Faye and Mrs Teach continued to recite names from *The Book of Abramelin*. Edith did her bit with aplomb, whispering sweet nothings into the Reverend's ear. The poor man writhed about as the demon tormented him.

214

As far as Faye knew, Edith and Reverend Jacobs had only been stepping out since December. What did Edith have to talk about? Faye was uncertain that she'd be able to keep whispering into Bertie's ear for so long. One of the things she liked about being with Bertie was that they could happily sit in silence for ages without feeling the need to witter on about nothing.

'Hrek, Flen, Duck.'

'Duck?' Faye asked as they reached the final name on their list. 'There's a demon called Duck?'

'Apparently so, but he's not present in Reverend Jacobs' body and is therefore of no use to us.' Mrs Teach flipped a page in the dusty book, inspecting the inscrutable word squares. 'We could try longer variations, I suppose.'

'That could take for ever.' Faye's mind boggled at the array of letters on the pages.

'It certainly won't be quick,' Mrs Teach said, failing to hide the weariness in her voice, 'but we have to try for the sake of the Reverend. Resilience is everything in this game, Faye.'

'Yes, of course, you're right.' Faye glanced at Edith's red-rimmed eyes as she brushed Timothy's hair back. 'Okey-dokey, where do we start?' she asked with a sigh, just as the poor Reverend pitched forwards making a ghastly retching noise. All that came out was a clear spittle.

Edith looked at the witches with tears in her eyes. 'Can we please call the doctor? He left his telephone number somewhere.' She scrabbled to the bedside

215

cabinet, tossing aside books as she looked for the scrap of paper.

Faye had just opened her mouth to say something about the phone lines being down when a dread thought gripped her mind. 'Oh, blimmin' 'eck!' she blurted.

Mrs Teach glanced up from her grimoire. 'What is it?'

Faye pressed the heel of her hand to her forehead. 'How did I not see this before?' She whipped around, gesturing at Edith and Timothy. 'This morning we found the Reverend on a bench and he says he's been visiting all the telegraph poles, but then fobs us off with some hooey about woodpeckers.' She spun back to face Mrs Teach. 'Then all the phone lines went dead.'

Mrs Teach's mouth crinkled into a little 'o' of realisation. 'And poor Petunia had a run-in with Otto not so very far from here.'

'Otto's cut the phone lines.' Faye snapped her fingers. 'And he knew which ones to cut and where to find them because he somehow got inside our Reverend's noggin and had him do a recce. We don't need to know the name of the demon because there isn't one.' Faye spun dramatically and pointed at the ailing Reverend Jacobs' face. 'It's Otto Kopp himself!'

The Reverend froze, his back arched. Slowly, as in some terrible nightmare, he floated off the bed. His wrists were still tied to the bedposts, and his feet rose to touch the ceiling, putting Faye in mind of a half-inflated barrage balloon. The belts around his wrists tightened and his fingers twitched as they turned red. He wailed in agony. Edith screamed and tumbled back into the dresser, just as the lightbulb above the bed exploded.

'Otto!' Faye cried, untying the belts. *'Let him go!'*

℘

'Gotcha!' Terrence snapped a finger and dashed across the concrete. There were few remaining relics of Dougie Allen's garage – mostly scorched tin advertisement signs for Esso Methyl and Raleigh bicycles – but miraculously one of the pumps was still standing. It looked to Bertie like a green lighthouse topped with a white glass bulb. The words SHELL and MEX formed a cross with the E in its centre. The bulb was smeared with streaks of oil from the fire. The body of the pump had a couple of panels. Terrence opened the first one, revealing a dial for measuring the gallons of petrol being pumped, a pair of brass fittings and a white envelope.

As Terrence tore into the envelope, Bertie recalled that fateful day. He had somehow summoned the courage to ask Faye to come with him to the village Summer Fair, and he had thought himself so brave. Then he had watched as she dashed fearlessly into the flames to save Max, Magda and Rudolf, the Kindertransport children whose short stay in the village had been fraught with peril. Oh, and poor Klaus, their handsome guardian who came a cropper later on. There were moments when Bertie had been worried that Faye might have had a thing for Klaus, but it had never really bothered him. He had known, when he saw her emerge from the smoke with those children, that he would always love her, no matter what.

ℰ

Faye wiped the vomit from her spectacles. From the moment they had begun the ritual to oust Otto, he had taken out his spite on the poor Reverend by having him leak from every orifice while rotating him in the air like a pig on a spit.

'Edith, stay back,' Mrs Teach warned as Faye recited the words of a short ritual from *The Book of Abramelin* over and over. She didn't fully understand their meaning, and she knew she didn't have to. They carried their own power, and Faye's task was to channel their strange and ancient energy to drive Otto out.

Mrs Teach held Edith closer as the Reverend's body stopped rotating and instead convulsed, arms and legs twitching. This was it. With a final flourish, Faye declared, 'I cast you out!'

Her ears popped as the air in the room flexed then shrank, rattling the glass of water on the bedside table.

Reverend Jacobs dropped like a stone onto the bed, its sheets wrapping around him in a clumsy embrace.

'Timothy!' Edith broke free from Mrs Teach and took her place at his side, kneeling by the bed and mopping his brow with her hankie. He was snoring loudly. 'Is he . . . ?' Edith looked imploringly at Faye and Mrs Teach.

'He's free,' Faye assured her. 'Though he'll probably be a bit wobbly on his pins for a while.'

'I prescribe a hot bath and plenty of fluids,' Mrs Teach said, before turning to Faye. 'Well done, dear. Splendid work.'

Faye, unused to such unqualified praise from Mrs Teach, was wondering how to reply when the Reverend spoke.

'Faye Bright, how wonderful to see you in action again.' He sat up, eyes unblinking. His voice had a familiar, breathy, Bavarian quality to it.

'Otto.' Faye stiffened with shock. His voice turned the sweat on her forehead to ice. Her specs began to steam up at the edges of their lenses.

'At your service. Fear not. I've had my fun with the Reverend. You'll need him for your big day, of course. Rest assured, Faye Bright, I wouldn't miss it for the world.'

A chill wind blew through the room and Otto was gone. The Reverend's eyes darted about as if he'd just woken up from a nap. He looked in disgust at the various drying fluids on his person and the sheets, then glared at Mrs Teach and Faye, blurting in his own hoarse voice, 'I say, what the devil is going on?' He looked glassy-eyed at Edith. 'Have I ...? Have I disgraced myself?'

'Oh, Timothy,' Edith said, giving him a warm smile and brushing her fingers across his cheeks. 'Such guilelessness.'

ʕ

'Bertie?' Terrence's voice was a distant echo in Bertie's daydream. He savoured visions of long summer days with Faye in a happy little cottage on the edge of the wood, children frolicking in the garden, butterflies dancing in the air and the sweet scent of honeysuckle—

'Bertie, you dozy ding-dong, snap out of it!'

A few rapid blinks returned Bertie to the dusty reality of Dougie Allen's former garage. Terrence was flapping a slip of paper at him. The latest clue.

'What do you think it means?' Terrence asked impatiently.

'Oh, er, read it again?'

Terrence gave Bertie a concerned look before flexing his wrist, straightening the paper and reading aloud. '"Forget Ruby, Gladys and Gustav, go straight to the hoarder's mouth."'

Bertie silently mouthed the clue again before declaring, 'Ivy!'

'Eh?'

'Ruby, Gladys and Gustav are the names of Larry Dell's barns, but they've left out Ivy Barn, and that's where he hoarded all his scrap, before all that business with the ... y'know ...' Bertie didn't want to say the words 'ghost' or 'poltergeist' out loud for fear of bringing back discombobulating memories, but from the way Terrence brightened he knew he had got the gist.

'Good work, Bertie. Onwards and upwards!' He started to march off, but Bertie didn't follow. He remained staring at the black stains on the old garage forecourt.

'Bertie?' Terrence shuffled back to the lad. 'You all ship-shape, sailor?'

Bertie smiled and nodded. 'Did you ever feel so happy, so certain that you're doing the right thing, and so sure that everything's going to be tickety-boo that you don't have a single care in the world?'

Terrence thought for a moment. 'I think I did, Bertie. I think it was the night before I got married, funnily enough.' He scruffed Bertie's hair. 'C'mon, sunshine. By my reckoning, this will be the last one.'

They walked off together, Bertie full of happiness and hope.

ᛈ

Faye and Mrs Teach stepped into the fresh air outside the vicarage cottage. Faye dabbed the vomit from her dungarees. She was thinking less about Otto's warning and more about Edith's face as she had held Timothy. The Reverend had endured a terrifying ordeal. His face was gaunt, the skin around his eyes bruised and grey, and his hands had trembled as he embraced the woman who had stayed by his side throughout his torment. Edith had clasped his hand and whispered words of love and encouragement. She had been the very definition of steadfastness and resilience. But as she had returned Timothy's embrace and rested her chin on his shoulder, Faye had thought she could read a new question in Edith's exhausted expression. *Was it worth it?*

She tried to shake the uncharitable thought away, but

after that and her fiery vision on Mrs Teach's stairs, one thing was very clear to her now. She turned to Mrs Teach. 'There's no other option,' she said. 'We have to stop the wedding.'

GOLDEN SLUMBERS

It was Henry's turn with the binoculars tonight. As the sun dipped towards the western horizon, he pointed the lenses east, searching for any signs of an imminent Luftwaffe attack. Not that any raid would begin until much later, when it was dark, but Henry desperately needed something to distract him from Young Bill's wittering.

'Found curled up, I heard,' Young Bill blethered. 'The pair of them. Right where we're sitting. Can you believe it?'

Henry had been pensioned off from the bank in the summer of 1939, hoping for a quiet retirement. Then Hitler had his way, and Henry had been urged by his good lady wife Vera to volunteer for this, that and the other, and any dreams he'd had of spending his twilight years with his feet up in the garden, listening to the cricket on the wireless, had faded away to nothing. At least with the Air Raid Precautions duties he had hoped for some semblance of quiet order in the long nights, but he hadn't counted on being paired up on a regular basis with Young Bill.

'Didn't think they were the sort to snooze on the job.' Young Bill was just a lad, and prone to gossip. 'Been kipping all night, apparently. Sleeping like babies.'

Henry lowered his binoculars. 'Odd phrase, that,' he said thoughtfully.

'What is?'

'Sleeping like a baby. Vera and I had three children, all grown up now, of course, and if you're suggesting that last night's shift woke up three times, making an awful racket and wetting themselves, then I'm inclined to believe you.'

Young Bill, a stranger to irony, flared his nostrils and gaped. 'What are you on about?'

Henry sighed. 'Never mind.' He wondered about this war and how much longer it might go on for, and how many more nights he might have to listen to Young Bill's inane waffling, then considered it a small price to pay for freedom. Lost in his thoughts, he was aware that Young Bill had asked a question and was expecting an answer.

'Sorry, miles away. What did you say?'

'Do you think they'll get a proper rollicking?' Young Bill asked again. 'For sleeping on the job?'

Henry had heard about last night's ARP shift sleeping through till morning but had yet to formulate an opinion.

'It's most unlike Samuel and Richard,' he began. 'Both are stalwart chaps. Yes, I would imagine they will be disciplined, but we need all the volunteers we can get, so one would hope they'll get a stern talking to and that will be the end of it.'

Young Bill straightened his back. 'But what if we'd been invaded? What if last night the beach had been stormed by Nazi commandos, eh? Where would we be then? What if—'

'What's that?' Henry waved Young Bill into silence and cocked an ear.

'What's what?' Young Bill hurried to his side.

Henry had heard something odd – a sound he was familiar with, but didn't want to share quite yet; at least not until he had heard it a second time. He could have sworn he'd caught the comforting trill of a budgerigar on the breeze.

Then something caught his eye. He raised his binoculars again, but this time he wasn't pointing them at the sky. There was something peculiar on the beach.

'What is it?' Young Bill hopped to his feet, reaching for the binoculars that Henry had no intention of giving him.

'Something . . . strange,' was all Henry could manage. He wasn't quite sure how to put it into words. It was as if a small patch of light was drifting across the beach, like someone was carrying a mirror and hiding behind it, and again he was certain he could hear the song of a budgie. Then, for one hallucinogenic moment, he was positive he saw a birdcage floating across the sand. He lowered the binoculars, squeezed his eyes shut, then tried again.

'What do you see?' Young Bill was all but perched on his shoulder like an eager parrot.

Whatever it was, it had gone. Henry felt a little less judgemental about Samuel and Richard now. Perhaps after a year and a half of long nights watching the skies, they all needed to sleep like babies every so often. He lowered the binoculars again and stifled a yawn.

'Nothing. It's nothing,' he said. 'Fetch the flask, will you? Time for a cuppa.'

Henry turned to find Young Bill curled up asleep in the long grass. Just at that moment, a woman's voice inveigled its way into his thoughts, and it suggested in the most soothing tone that a little sleep was precisely what he needed. Henry was overcome by a sudden weight on his eyelids. 'Just what I thought,' he muttered as he lowered himself next to Young Bill and finally got the peace he was longing for.

☙

Miss Charlotte's glamour skills had been honed over centuries of sneaking into castles, palaces and boudoirs, and she considered herself to be one of the best in the business. But even she could not remain hidden if something like, say, a budgerigar's insistent trilling drew attention to her. And such attention would mean all kinds of awkward questions, not least, 'Why are you out so late with a budgie in a cage?'

The answer was that Miss Charlotte's trance had brought her here. While unconscious, she had crossed over into the aether – that place between worlds – and found what she was looking for. The echo of a powerful ritual. Opening her mind to the magical reverberations, she had seen visions of the sea. A beach with sand the colour of milky tea, peppered with rocks and draped in seaweed, and framed by giant chalk stacks with mossy bottoms. She had known exactly where to go, and they had reached Botany Bay, only a short ride from Herne Bay, without incident. That said, the exact spot of the ritual eluded her, so she and Petunia and the budgie needed to explore in peace, hence the decision to send the ARP volunteers on the clifftop into a deep slumber with a simple bit of suggestive thinking. It was a method frowned upon by other witches – Mrs Teach considered it unsporting – but needs must in an emergency, and in war it was always an emergency.

Now the ARP men had been dealt with, she just needed the budgie to shut up.

'Harold, if you can't keep this noise under control, I swear I will wring your neck and end both of you,' she said, without a hint of malice, which made it all the more terrifying.

'It's not me,' Harold insisted. 'It's Mrs Wallace. She's learned how to make bird noises and she won't shut up.'

'Mrs Wallace, if you can hear me, you should know that we are close to our destination and to finding your body, and if you don't put a sock in it now, I shall toss you into the sea.'

The chirping ceased and Miss Charlotte continued in silence.

'You certainly have a way with people,' Petunia said. 'Might it be too much to ask for a please?'

'You can put a sock in it, too,' Miss Charlotte said, then added, 'please.'

'That's more like it.'

They passed beyond the chalk stacks as the tide crept ever closer. It wasn't long before Charlotte found what she had seen at the end of her vision. In a nook that even the locals might overlook was a circle of five stones. Two of them had toppled over. The sand surrounding them was stained red, and there were boot prints all around. Heavy and deep, as if whoever it was had been dragging their feet. Miss Charlotte held her breath. She had hoped the vision had been wrong, but here it was.

'Why have you brought me to this place?' Mrs Wallace's voice complained. 'Where's my body? There's nothing here.'

'Is this the place you saw in the vision?' Petunia asked.

Miss Charlotte nodded as she lowered the birdcage to the sand. 'This very spot.' She gestured to the stones. 'These were part of the ritual.'

Petunia leaned closer to whisper, 'And the red stain on the sand?'

Miss Charlotte glanced at the birdcage before nodding.

'Oh dear,' Petunia said.

'Er ... what's that?' Harold spotted it first. Budgerigars are blessed with superior vision to humans, with wide-set eyes for spotting predators and prey.

'Oh dear again,' Petunia said, and Miss Charlotte wondered if ghosts had better vision, too.

The cliffs and the beach were blending into the grey shadows of dusk. She followed Petunia's gaze out a hundred yards or so to where something was being rocked about by the waves.

'Wait here,' Charlotte ordered, wading into the sea.

'What are you doing?' Mrs Wallace's voice called after her. 'This is no time for a paddle.'

The water was cold and soaked through Miss Charlotte's riding leathers, weighing them down. She was up to her waist by the time she reached the body floating face down in the sea. It was naked, the skin marble-white and ice-cold to the touch. Miss Charlotte was not the squeamish type, but even she had to recoil when she rolled the corpse over to discover dozens of tiny little crabs feasting on Mrs Wallace's face. There were deep cuts on her neck, arms and legs where Otto had drained her of her blood. Miss Charlotte knew this ritual. An ancient and evil black magic that had been attempted and failed by many fools; but if anyone could succeed at this blasphemy, it was Otto. And if he had been successful in his attempt to resurrect the dead, then he was no longer alone. Whatever his plans were, he needed a number of undead allies, and to control them he was drawing on dark and powerful forces that would make him unstoppable.

Miss Charlotte released Mrs Wallace's body to sink

beneath the grey blanket of the sea and turned to face the shore, where the ghost of a young girl stood pensively by a budgie cage.

They had to get back to Woodville, and fast.

PARTY CRASHERS

Sitting in the driver's seat of the Rolls-Royce, Otto contemplated his next move. It was difficult to focus as his blood simmered; an uncomfortable sensation, but it also bestowed upon him a kind of ecstasy. The more of this dark magic he used, the stronger he felt. Controlling someone like Reverend Jacobs, and also these men – if indeed they could be called men – was no small thing. And Otto had not stopped since fleeing the clutches of the Black Sun. His heart raced, thumping in his ears, and all his nerve endings tingled as he ran through the plan in his head, over and over.

It was a shame to lose contact with the good Reverend, but he had served his purpose in keeping Faye Bright distracted while Otto's men went about fulfilling his orders. All the telephone lines had been cut and the roads blocked. Woodville was isolated from the outside world. It wouldn't last for ever, but Otto only needed this one night.

He gripped the steering wheel of the Rolls, not to

drive anywhere, but simply to ground himself in something tangible in the real world. The skin on his hands was pink as a lobster's shell, as though he'd been in the sun for too long. He looked at himself in the rearview mirror to find his face was a similar hue. Strangely, it suited him.

The Kriegsmarine stood guard in front of the car, silent and still. The gunner and pilot flanked the vehicle, protecting Otto from any unwanted attention while he was in his meditative state. Not that he expected anyone to find them down this secluded path on the outskirts of Woodville. There were no tyre tracks or footprints, and it was dark and forbidding. They had remained undisturbed.

Otto wound down the window.

'Get in,' he told his sentinels, and they obeyed, rocking the car as they squeezed into the back.

He started the engine, leaving the headlights off, and drove down winding country lanes for a few minutes until they brought him out by the main road at Saint Irene's Church. From here, he could look down on the whole village.

Applying the handbrake but leaving the engine running, Otto stepped out. The trio instinctively followed, extricating themselves in a series of awkward lurches before standing almost upright, forming a line and staring blankly ahead. Their training served them well, even after death.

Otto inspected them, wondering which he should choose for the next crucial task.

The gunner felt like the obvious choice. Otto glanced at the bullet-holes in the man's flight suit, briefly fanta-sising about what those final moments must have been like as the poor wretch met his fate in the front bubble of a Heinkel. Such men were not meant for greatness. They were doomed to be used by the likes of Otto to bring about greatness. It was the way of things. Yes, he would be perfect.

'You,' Otto addressed him directly.

The gunner's body flinched. His head turned and milky-white eyes gazed back at Otto.

'Heed my words,' Otto said softly. 'I have a very important task for you.'

Moments later, the gunner was hunched over in the driver's seat of the Rolls-Royce, fingers wrapped around the steering wheel.

Otto calmly took a spare petrol can from the boot. He unscrewed the cap and liberally splashed gasoline over the rear seats, then pulled a book of matches from the pocket of his tweed suit, struck one, savouring its tangy phosphorous aroma, and tossed it into the car.

Flames silently spread across the leather upholstery and filled the interior with smoke.

Otto leaned in through the passenger door and re-leased the handbrake.

'*Tschüss!*' he told the gunner, before slamming the door shut. He gave a signal to the Kriegsmarine and the pilot, who began to push the Rolls from the rear. With the rumble of rubber tyres on cobbles, the flaming car began to roll downhill.

'Halt!' Otto commanded the pair. They did as ordered, and he stood by their side as the Rolls-Royce picked up speed.

'And so we begin this evening's entertainment,' Otto said with a smile. 'Come, come. No time to waste,' he told his undead companions. 'We have a village to burn.'

⌀

Faye decided that going in through the front entrance of the Green Man's saloon bar would be a big mistake. She had no time for all the attention she would get from the revellers at Bertie's stag do. Instead, she and Mrs Teach slipped through the backyard and into the kitchen, startling poor Doris, who was drying a tray of pint glasses.

'Oh, thank the Lord,' she said, wiping the back of one hand against her brow. 'I've been run ragged all day with that lot.' She jerked her head towards the bar, where the ambience was at a deafening level of raucous jeering normally reserved for significant birthdays, Christmases and weddings. 'Faye, can you serve? And Mrs Teach, would you help me with—'

'Wait, wait, wait.' Faye raised a hand. 'You're on your tod? Where's Dad and Bertie?'

Doris shrugged. 'Still on their treasure hunt, I suppose.'

Mrs Teach curled her lip in disapproval. 'Treasure hunt?'

'Yes, they had to follow clues around the village.'

Doris presented a faltering smile. 'It's all a bit of a lark, you know.'

'But they're still not back?' Faye asked.

Doris shook her head.

'It's nearly closing time.' Faye's voice hardened. 'Where did they go looking for this treasure? Timbuk-bloody-tu?'

Mrs Teach positioned herself between poor Doris and Faye's rage. 'Faye, calm yourself. Doris, dear, who arranged this treasure hunt? Who might know their whereabouts?'

'Captain Marshall,' Doris said. 'He's in the bar. Shall I fetch him?'

'Please do.'

Doris dried her hands on a tea towel before scurrying away, glad to be out of range of Faye's glare.

'It's not her fault, Faye. Let the poor woman be.'

'I know, I know.' Faye bunched her hands into fists. 'But it's too dangerous with Otto about. We should send them all home.'

'Before closing time?' Mrs Teach shook her head. 'That will only arouse suspicion and might lead to confusion and panic, none of which we need more of at this moment. Let them have their fun till last orders. I shall ensure they all get home safely while you search for Terrence and Bertie.'

'B-Bertie? I say, is he back?' Captain Marshall staggered into the kitchen, the remains of a pint of bitter sloshing about in his glass. He looked around the room, his eyes drifting in their sockets. 'You big fibber. He's not here. Where have you put him?' He opened the larder door, then peeked under the cloth covering the kitchen table. 'Here, Bertie-Bertie-Bertie!'

'Oh, perfect.' Faye gestured at the normally upright captain crawling under the table. 'He's half-cut.'

'How dare you, madam!' The captain made to stand but bashed his head against the table. 'Bugger me.'

Faye and Mrs Teach took an arm each, extricated him from the tablecloth, and stood him almost upright.

'You drink I'm thunk, don't you?'

'Where's my dad and Bertie, Captain?' Faye asked, gripping his shoulders. 'Where did you send them?'

'Bertie?' Captain Marshall recoiled in shock. 'No, no, no, you can't see him. Not before the wedding. S'bad luck!'

'Captain, if I don't find him soon, we'll have more than bad luck. Where is he?' Faye grabbed him by the lapels and drew him closer.

He burped gently, the warm waft of stale bitter rolling against Faye's nostrils.

'Can't tell,' he said. 'That would be cheating. But . . .'

Faye waited for the rest of the sentence, but it was not immediately forthcoming. 'But what?'

'What?' He blinked and smiled.

'Where can I find Bertie and Dad, Captain Marshall? Please, just tell me.'

'S'easy,' he said, scratching his ear. 'You will *observe* the flag around a *warty* tree lining the drive of a *Brum* football team.' He smiled broadly, as if that explained everything.

Faye released her grip on his lapels and looked at Mrs Teach, who was equally baffled.

'He's lost his bloody marbles,' Faye said. She was about to ask the captain to explain himself, but at that moment the lights flickered and died. There was a brief pause, followed by a confused-sounding cheer from the saloon.

'Power cut?' Doris pondered.

Faye's spine tingled. No, there was something about this that felt different. She didn't want to say it out loud, but the lights going out felt ... intentional.

'Wait here,' she told the others as she dashed down the hall and into the crowded bar. With the blackout boards in place, the room was a gathering of confused, murmuring shadows. Faye was certain that one of them looked like a man dressed as a horse.

One voice rose above the hubbub as Mr Hodgson asked, 'Does anyone have a match?'

Faye was about to reply when a flaming Rolls-Royce came crashing through the wall of the pub.

OTTO'S INFERNO

It was like a bomb going off. For a few moments, Faye thought a stray Luftwaffe Junkers had shed its load on the pub. But as the dust began to clear, she could make out shapes. A familiar shining grille, an emblem with overlapping 'R's, round headlights smashed to pieces and the figurine of a winged woman – the Spirit of Ecstasy – knocked askew after the crash.

There was a Rolls-Royce where the saloon's wall and doors used to be.

Flames pulsed from inside the car, smoke poured from the shattered windscreen and Faye could make out the form of somebody flailing in the driver's seat.

Mr Hodgson was the first to get to his feet, blinking at the carnage and wondering what the hell had just happened. Others joined him, similarly baffled and shocked. Most were so inebriated that even after being flung aside by the flaming Rolls, they were able to dust themselves off in stunned silence.

'Everybody out!' Faye cried, pointing to the hole

the car had made. The heavily soused villagers didn't need telling twice as the gravity of the situation rapidly became clear, clambering over broken bricks and shards of glass into the Wode Road.

Faye was about to follow them when the door of the Rolls juddered open. She gasped as the burning figure of a man in a Luftwaffe flight suit hauled himself out. Blazing from head to toe, his boots thudded as he grasped at the air, flamelets dripping from his swinging arms. Bottles and glasses smashed in the intense heat. Faye shielded her face as the alcohol-soaked floorboards and walls caught on fire with alarming speed.

As great slices of plaster came crashing down from the ceiling, she scrabbled backwards, peering through the smoke only to find that her exit to the Wode Road had been cut off. Batting away her panic, she got to her feet and ran blindly down the hall to the kitchen, where she bumped into an unusually startled Mrs Teach coming the other way.

'Back, back!' Faye stuck to commands of one syllable. 'Fire! Out. Back yard. Now!'

Mrs Teach turned on her heels and moved with surprising agility as she whisked through the kitchen, somehow taking both Doris and Captain Marshall by the scruffs of their necks and steering them out into the yard.

The back of Faye's own neck suddenly flushed with heat as a wave of cinders enveloped her, accompanied by a terrible crash. She kept moving, ignoring the cold dread in her belly, not daring to look behind her. Something told her the pub's ceiling had just caved in.

As she stumbled into the back yard, waving smoke from her face, Mrs Teach was already guiding Doris and Captain Marshall out through the gate, into the alley, then onto the Wode Road. Faye stumbled after them, feeling the familiar cobbles under her feet, until she was out of the worst of it. Catching her breath, she raised her head.

The village was ablaze.

Faye needed a few thumping heartbeats to take it all in.

The church roof leaked smoke from its eaves and gutters, and its slate tiles popped and spun through the air. The newsagent's, baker's, butcher's and several homes in the Wode Road were also belching smoke from doors and windows, their residents tumbling out into the street in a blind panic.

Faye's vision of a burning village, the nightmare gifted to her by the Corn Bride, had come true. She began to feel lightheaded, her breathing coming fast and short.

The former revellers of the Green Man could only stand and stare in utter shock. Most of them were Morris Men still in their hats and tails, along with Bobby Newton, still dressed as what she now realised was a hoodening horse.

'Call the fire brigade!' Bobby cried.

'The phone lines are dead,' Doris replied in a numb voice.

'Buckets!' Faye clapped her hands together. Partly to snap everyone out of their stunned stupor, but mainly to shove aside any further thoughts she might have of visions and instead focus on doing something useful. She'd put out fires before, and this would be no different. 'Everyone grab a bucket and fill it up. Form a line and—'

'There's no water!' Mrs Pritchett came running towards her, cradling her two Yorkshire terriers. 'I tried filling a kettle just before all this started, but the taps ran dry.'

'She's right.' Mr Hodgson was hunched over the standpipe outside the butcher's, turning it in vain. 'There's nothing.' He glanced up, and his face began to tremble as he caught sight of something in the distance. Other villagers wailed in fear.

Faye followed Mr Hodgson's terrified gaze to find two men silhouetted against the smouldering church. They carried flaming torches and moved with a kind of inhuman lurch.

'Otto,' she muttered to Mrs Teach. 'This has to be Otto's doing.'

Mrs Teach stood at Faye's side and narrowed her eyes at the lurching men. 'I think you might be right, dear. And, if I recall, you had a vision of such a disaster when you last encountered the Corn Bride.'

'Don't remind me.'

'I don't suppose you recall anything from those visions that might help us?' Mrs Teach prompted.

Faye considered telling Mrs Teach about the brief vision she'd had on her landing. Of Faye burning alive and the Corn Bride screaming. But she reckoned it wouldn't be useful right at this very moment. 'Help us? No.'

'Then might I suggest what is known in military circles as a tactical withdrawal?'

Faye's heart tightened. 'You're saying we should give up and run?'

'I'm saying that one has been caught with one's pants down, so to speak, and we should not go haring into a situation about which we know very little,' Mrs Teach replied, her voice steady and calm. 'We need to regroup and plan our counterattack.'

Faye gestured wildly at the flames. 'The village is on fire, Mrs Teach!'

'Leave that to me,' the older witch said, looking up at the overcast sky. 'In the meantime, get everyone to the safety of the wood.'

'But—'

'Now!' Mrs Teach snapped. Turning her back, she pootled off down the Wode Road, away from Otto's men, as if she was about to do a spot of shopping.

Faye watched her go for precisely one heartbeat, then cupped her hands to her mouth. 'Everyone leave the village now!' she cried. 'Head for the woods, to safety. Everyone, please.'

The villagers continued to twist taps, or dash back into flaming buildings to collect precious belongings. Milly Baxter was holding Betty Marshall back from rushing into her burning home as she cried despairingly, 'My nylons!'

Faye set her jaw. If she'd learned anything while training with Bellamy and his military chums, it was that the chain of command was everything.

She marched over to where Captain Marshall was gawping with the other pub revellers. She spun him like a top and gripped him by his shoulders.

'Cap', I need you to sober up pronto,' she snapped, giving him a shake.

'I am, I am,' he said as his eyes blinked back into focus. 'What on earth is happening?'

'I'll explain later, but you need to order a withdrawal to the woods now or people will die. Do you understand?'

For a moment, it looked like Captain Marshall was going to object. How dare this imp of a girl give him orders? But just then a gut-wrenching crash came from the bakery, sending white-hot embers spiralling into the night.

Captain Marshall straightened his cap, snapped his heels together and yelled, 'Withdraw to the woods! Everyone withdraw to the woods in an orderly fashion. That's an order!'

For a moment, the villagers remained frozen, but as the captain repeated his commands over and over, they were soon bustling down the Wode Road towards the wood, guided by Constable Muldoon, Private North, Lance Corporal Stedman and Sergeant Black.

Faye and the captain were the last to leave, checking for stragglers. Faye glanced up the road. In the distance the lurching men were still closing in, now applying their flaming torches to Mr Brewer and Mr Gilbert's antiques shop. Faye's heart boiled with rage to see the village, her home, gutted like this, and she had half a mind to go for these mindless thugs. But there was something odd about the way they moved. Like puppets on strings. And she recalled Mrs Teach's advice about not rushing into unknowable situations.

'Come, Faye,' Captain Marshall said. 'We must hurry.'

Faye took one last look at Woodville. There, standing by the lychgate of Saint Irene's, was the unmistakable silhouette of Otto Kopp. She couldn't hear him over the crackle of the fire, but he threw his head back in laughter.

'Yes, Captain,' she said bleakly, and the pair of them began to run, past the war memorial, down the bridle-way and out of reach of the flames.

It wasn't long before they arrived at the Roman bridge, where they paused to catch their breath. Faye took a moment to compose herself, trying to shake off the devastating scenes she had just witnessed.

She and the captain noticed them at the same time. A family of frogs hopping away from the river and down the path, as if they had been startled by an invader.

The captain marched to the edge of the bridge and leaned over. Faye joined him. Both were surprised to find Mrs Teach lying on her back in the water like Millais' Ophelia, her eyes half-closed and her palms raised.

'Mrs Teach,' Captain Marshall blustered. 'What do you think you're doing, woman?'

Faye silenced him with a gentle touch on his forearm.

The water around Mrs Teach was rippling. Thunder rumbled in the clouds above and the sky darkened. Faye felt the first cold spots of rain on the back of her neck. In moments, it was tipping it down, and by the time Mrs Teach rose from the water, helped by Captain Marshall, the downpour had intensified into something torrential.

They stood on the old Roman bridge, watching the glow of the flames in the village subside. Woodville had been saved from destruction for the moment, but there was no doubting that Otto Kopp was back. And now Woodville belonged to him.

THE HORSE'S HEAD

Otto savoured the thrill of the smoking ruins and the distant cries of fear. Yes, the torrential rain had doused the flames, but the damage to the village was done and Faye Bright had fled into the woods. Exactly where he wanted her.

He wiped rainwater from his bald head and took a moment, allowing his mind to drift on the aether. He could sense the terrified villagers darting aimlessly between the dense trees and thickets of the woodland. Beyond them, he saw Faye's father and her fiancé lost in the gathering gloom. Further still, his old rival Charlotte Southill was coming at speed down twisting roads. Both of these were gifts to be unwrapped. Still, Otto could not afford to be complacent.

He opened his eyes to find the smouldering form of the gunner shuffling towards him, a mess of charred-black and red-raw skin after his crash in the Rolls. His uniform was in tatters, the patchy remains of his hair steaming. Otto was impressed by the tenacity of his undead minions. The ritual to raise them had been more than worth the effort.

'You.' He pointed at the pilot. 'Follow the villagers into the wood. Make them fear you. Kill one of them, preferably the older witch. If you can't find her, then kill a child or a woman. Return here when you're done.'

The pilot immediately turned and ran down the road towards the wood.

'You.' Otto pointed at the hulking Kriegsmarine. 'Find the witch on the motorcycle. I will do what I can to slow her down, but you must kill the woman and her companions.'

The Kriegsmarine nodded and ran off, his boots slapping on the wet cobbles.

'And you, my indestructible friend,' Otto said, smiling at the gunner. 'I have a very special task for you. Find the girl's father and her fiancé. Capture one. Kill the other. I don't care which.'

⌀

Bobby Newton knew it had been a mistake to run while still in the hoodening horse sackcloth, but what with a bloody Rolls-Royce crashing through the wall, half the village on fire and everyone fleeing in a panic, there hadn't been time to think properly. He'd just followed the others into the wood. Until he'd lost them, that is.

Bobby had never really liked the wood, even when he was a boy. He'd always been an outdoorsy type and had loved climbing trees, but his parents had often warned him to keep away from Woodville's shadowy arboreal labyrinth. That was how his mother had referred to it, fancying herself a bit of a poet. And, being a good boy, Bobby had done as he was told. Now he was deep in the trees, he began to realise just why his mother and father had warned him off. There was something about the wood that ... *Hate* was too strong a word. The wood simply didn't care about you. Bobby couldn't be sure how he knew this, but he had an inkling deep inside him that the wood was indifferent to his presence; that he didn't matter. He sometimes got a similar feeling when he was at sea in his uncle's fishing boat. The ocean didn't care if you lived or died; you had to respect its wishes when it became angry and head straight for shore.

Bobby had always felt most at home during those excursions on his uncle's fishing boat. It was one of the reasons he'd volunteered for the Royal Navy. Even in the worst storms at sea, you could rely on a compass to find your way, but not in this wood. That said, the canopy was protecting him from the torrential downpour. At least he wasn't soaking wet. Just completely adrift.

'Hello?' he cried out, but his words were lost between the shifting trunks of oak and ash. He turned in every direction, but somehow the wood had hidden every villager who had fled for their lives.

And what had they been fleeing from, anyway? The fires were bad, but it was raining. And even if the rain didn't douse the flames, why not form a line of buckets from the river? Why keep running? What were Faye and

Mrs Teach so afraid of? Even Captain Marshall had ordered a retreat, which seemed unthinkable to Bobby.

He would go back. Yes, he would return to the village and put the remaining fires out. Anything was better than loafing about in the woods dressed as a hoodening horse. The only problem was, he'd got so turned around he didn't have the first bloody clue which direction was home. He looked up for the stars, but the darkening sky was still overcast.

His ears were tickled by the faraway *pat-pat-pat* of feet running over foliage. The sound flitted between the trees. Bobby's head jerked about as he tried to locate the runner.

'Hello?' he called. 'It's Bobby ... Who's that?'

The pace of the feet picked up. There were few in Woodville who could run that fast. The soldiers and airmen who lodged in the village trained regularly. Perhaps it was one of them?

'Hello? I'm from the village. Who's there?'

In the distance, a silhouette darted onto a path that Bobby could have sworn hadn't been there a moment ago. Whoever it was, he was running like the clappers, and it looked like he was wearing a uniform.

'Ahoy!' Bobby waved his hands high. 'I'm joining the Navy soon and I'm a bit at sea without a compass,' he called, hoping that making light of his situation would temper the humiliation of being lost.

The runner did not waver from his path, his arms blurring like Spitfire propellers as he closed in on Bobby. An alarm began to ring at the back of the young man's mind. Through the gloom, he could just about make out that the figure was wearing a blue flight suit with fur lining around the neck. Somehow, a pilot was running straight at him. And something about this pilot's demeanour suggested that he might not be the friendliest of chaps.

Bobby would worry about things like direction and destination later. Now was the time to run. Only it wasn't easy with the weight of a sackcloth hoodening horse on his shoulders. It was even less easy while carrying a hoodening horse head on a stick. Bobby tried to think of it as a baton as he ran. But it wasn't a baton. It was a handmade hoodening horse head from a chap in nearby Saint Nicholas-at-Wade, and it weighed a tonne, and Mr Hodgson had warned Bobby to be careful with it and not lose it, otherwise he couldn't be the hoodening horse on May Day. So why did the bloody thing keep catching on branches and snagging on—

Bobby tumbled over, tipping into a patch of damp bluebells. The stick with the horse's head spiralled away. He jolted upright and was halfway to his feet when the pilot barged him aside, sending him crashing into the trunk of an oak. Bobby saw flashes of white as the pilot pounded his head. The lad's terror was compounded by confusion as he caught sight of an eagle emblem through the hail of blows. His attacker was a Luftwaffe pilot! And one wearing a flight suit riddled with bullet-holes. Bobby's skin crawled and his heart seized as he looked up into the German's eyes, only to find them pale as egg whites.

Bobby could only flail helplessly as the undead pilot battered him, his own blows weak, barely slapping against his attacker's face. Bile rose in his throat as cold, bony fingers closed around his neck. Their grip tightened suddenly and his lungs ached for air. His vision darkened at the edges. He knew he was falling into a hole from which he would never return. Bobby didn't want to die. Not yet. Not like this. At sea, perhaps. For his country, and his king, and his fellow sailors; not lost in a wood, confused and afraid.

The darkness had all but consumed him when suddenly the grip of those cold fingers released and he could breathe again. Gasping to fill his lungs, he could just about make out shadows clashing, the ground shaking as huge feet thundered close by. He was dimly aware of the pilot being dragged away, bones crunching, something heavy slapping against flesh.

Bobby found himself on all fours, his mouth dry, his arms like wet rope. Colour returned to the world; there were leaves on the trees, and a nightingale sang somewhere nearby. He looked up and, through blurry eyes, saw the pilot staggering about aimlessly, as lost as Bobby had been just a few moments ago. The big difference here was that the pilot was missing his head.

Bobby struggled to breathe once more as shock gripped his body. The headless pilot took a few steps, stumbled over something, then crouched on his hands and knees. After some frantic brushing aside of the undergrowth, he retrieved whatever it was he had tripped over – pale, dotted with mud and leaves, an expression of wide-eyed terror frozen on its face. His head. Bobby slapped a hand over his mouth to stifle a scream as the pilot tucked his bonce under his arm like a rugby ball and ran back the way he had come.

As the rain battered the leaves around him, Bobby sank into the wet mulch of the forest floor, too overcome to move. He tried to make sense of what he had just seen, but his thoughts failed to gel. He allowed his mind to go soft. He rubbed his forehead and wondered when the cold weight in his belly would fade.

Then his jaw clenched and his pulse began to race. He could sense a presence behind him, as if the indifference of the wood had taken a physical form. It was breathing like a wolf after a hunt. It reeked of musky sweat and blood. Bobby didn't want to turn to face whatever it was, fearing what seeing it might do to his already fragile mind.

The head of the hoodening horse swung into his vision, startling him and making him yelp. He could only stare at it at first, then it jerked a few times. It was being offered to him, and something told Bobby that he should take it with sincere gratitude.

'Th-thank you,' he croaked, his voice hoarse from his near-death experience. He drew the horse's head closer to him, stroking its hair like a doll's.

At the edge of his vision, he caught sight of a long, hairy finger pointing down a path that most definitely had not been there a few minutes ago. Bobby discovered he was no longer inclined to question such things and gratefully got on his merry way, staggering to his feet on quivering knees and following the path. To his left, a long shadow swooped across the woodland floor. It was as tall as a bear and it appeared to be carrying a club. Just as Bobby screwed up his courage to turn and look, the shadowy figure vaulted into the canopy and melted into the darkness.

THE LIVING DEAD
OF IVY BARN

Terrence and Bertie's first error was to take a shortcut through the wood. It was a path they had walked down together dozens of times before when they were working on the Griffin – Faye's flying bicycle – but Bertie realised he should have known that there was no such thing as a shortcut in this wood. Somehow, it knew if you were in a hurry and would do its best to turn you around at every opportunity.

'Bertie, far be it from me to dampen your enjoyment, lad,' Terrence said as the pair ambled side by side, still wearing their cardboard antlers, 'but it's dark, tipping down with rain, and we've been on this path for what feels like bloody hours. I'm starting to worry what that rabble have been doing to my pub.'

'Doris will have things under control, won't she?'

'I don't doubt that for a moment, but it's hardly fair on her now, is it?'

Bertie could see the longing in Terrence's hangdog expression. They *had* been in the wood for an unusually long time.

'Righto, Mr Bright, we'll head back soon, I promise, but we're so close to finishing that we might as well do it.'

'Bertie, it's a silly little treasure hunt. We'll probably find a jug of cider at the end of it as our reward. I've got cider back at the pub. Good cider. Not the homemade poison that Hodgson serves up, 'cos that's what it'll be, Bertie. Your guts'll never forgive you.'

'I know, Mr Bright, but I want everything to be right and proper for the wedding, and that includes the stag night. I don't want to look back at the day and wonder if anything could have been done better or if I could've worked a little harder. I want it to be perfect.'

'Bertie, perfect doesn't exist.' Terrence patted him on the shoulder. 'Just enjoy the day and whatever it throws at you, come rain or shine. All that matters— Ooh, look, the barn!'

He went haring down a winding path between brambles to where the trees finally tapered into long grass.

Bertie limped after him, hoping that the wood wasn't about to change its mind and trap him in here for ever.

He emerged from the trees and hurried to where Terrence waited for him on the muddy path. Rain was coming in sheets and the sky was a blanket of clouds – lilac, charcoal and gold. Swifts darted about, hunting for insect treats, and the echo of Larry's dogs barking came to them across the fields.

There, at the end of the path, was the familiar shape of Ivy Barn.

Bertie was not attuned to magic, like Faye. She would often sense things that he never could – a knack that had saved their bacon more than once – but every now and then he got a taste of what it must be like to have that added perception of the uncanny. This was one of those moments.

The swifts swooping away across the field was the first sign, followed by a bustling in the hedgerow. As they crossed the threshold into the barn, Bertie felt a strange tingling at the back of his neck. The rain drummed on the tin roof, and he was put in mind of Roman soldiers banging their swords on their shields before a battle.

'Has old Larry had a spring clean?' Terrence asked.

The barn was unusually tidy. Last summer, it had been full of aircraft scrap that the farmer had salvaged from his fields. What Bertie and Terrence found this evening was a recently swept floor and a clear work-bench with nails, screws and bolts neatly arranged in old baked bean tins. Saws, spanners, chisels and hammers all hung in size order on the wall. The Griffin leaned against the workbench, tyres pumped, chain greased and frame gleaming as if recently cleaned. Larry's experience with a poltergeist last summer had certainly set him straight.

There was one anomalous object, however.

'Told yer, didn't I?' Terrence gestured at a big, corked glass jar standing in front of the rows of tins.

It contained a dense, cloudy amber liquid. Bertie wasn't a betting man, but he would put good money on the concoction's ability to remove rust from girders.

Terrence took off his cardboard antlers, tossing them onto the workbench. Bertie did the same, brushing his hair back. His belly rumbled, and he remembered he still had one of Mrs Teach's oatcakes in his pocket. Now felt like the right time for a quick nibble. He took it out, delighted to discover that it was still in one piece. Of course it was. Mrs Teach's oatcakes could have been used as discuses in the Olympic Games.

Terrence leaned forwards to peer at the amber liquid in the jar. 'That's either Mr Hodgson's homemade cider or someone is literally taking the—'

'Er, who's that?' Bertie interrupted, his oatcake brushing his lips but remaining uneaten.

Terrence looked up from the cider.

A man stood outside, just yards from the barn. He was a good six feet tall, with glistening, charred skin the texture of pork crackling, and he was steaming in the rain like a freshly served spotted dick and custard. To top it all off, Bertie recognised the brown flight suit as that of a Luftwaffe Unteroffizier, most likely a navigator or a gunner on a bomber.

Bertie recalled a Hurricane pilot once telling him how quick decisions saved lives. The lad did not hesitate. He tucked the oatcake away and rushed as fast as his uneven legs would move to the barn's doors to heave them shut.

Terrence didn't question Bertie's instinct, following hot on his heels.

They had barely moved the heavy wood an inch when the gunner began staggering in their direction, arms outstretched, fingers grasping.

Thankfully, he staggered rather than ran, giving the pair enough time to slam the doors shut just as the gunner smashed into them with enough force to shake the whole building.

'That's something you don't see every day,' Bertie muttered.

'Nah, round here you only get this sort of thing once a month,' Terrence quipped as the undead gunner barged into the doors again.

'That won't hold him for long.' Bertie winced at another crash. His heart raced as his eyes darted about, hoping to find inspiration from Larry's tools. The idea of using something like a handsaw blade to defend himself made him queasy. He found himself wondering what Faye would do. 'Any ideas?'

'How about this?' Terrence dashed over to grab a club hammer from the tool display. He hurried back, leaning against the doors as he weighed the hammer in his hand.

'Y'know, he might just want to talk?' Bertie suggested as the gunner careened into the woodwork again, cracking the grain.

'Bertie, you're a nice lad, and I know you like to see the best in people, but there are times like this, when a Nazi is kicking down your door, that you need to—'

The ear-splitting crash of the barn doors collapsing interrupted Terrence's speech. Both men tumbled back as the gunner lurched over the splintered planks. Terrence scrambled to grab the club hammer, which had fallen to the floor and been kicked into the corner in the commotion. The gunner planted a boot on his back, pinning him down.

'Bertie!' Terrence cried, wheezing as his lungs were squeezed under the dead weight.

Bertie, acting on instinct, rushed to the workbench, grabbed Mr Hodgson's jar of homemade cider and, in one swift movement, uncorked it and splashed its contents into the raw, puffy face of the gunner.

The undead Luftwaffe officer gave an inhuman wail of agony as his tender flesh sizzled.

He lunged at Bertie, who ducked under his arms and rolled across the floor, kicking out at the officer's boots and sending him tumbling.

The gunner floundered into the workbench, managing to stay upright by slapping his big meaty hands down onto its surface.

Terrence had got his breath back and sprang into action. Snatching up a pair of six-inch nails from one of Larry's baked bean tins, he raised his club hammer and pounded them into their assailant's hands, pinning him to the workbench.

The gunner threw his head back and roared like a wounded bear.

'On your feet, Bertie,' Terrence said, grabbing the Griffin's handlebars and swinging his leg over the crossbar. 'We're done. We're going home to warn the others.'

'Good idea!' Bertie scrabbled onto the saddle behind him, daring to glance back. The gunner howled as he stood pinioned to the workbench, his skin smoking gently from the remnants of the home brew. Bertie and Terrence cycled through the shattered doors and down the path to the village, out into the rain and the deepening night.

MRS WALLACE
MAKES A SACRIFICE

Mrs Wallace – finding herself an unwilling passenger in both the body of her own pet budgie, and on the motorcycle-and-sidecar combination presently hurtling down a series of dark country lanes – reflected on all she had lost. Her home, her career as a spy, any affection she had for her budgie and, last but not least, her body. Seeing her pathetic naked form floating in the sea had brought home to her just how pointless her life had been. All that strife, and for what? You wind up as nothing more than cold, mutilated fish food. All her work to change the world, all she had risked to serve a greater cause – it all meant nothing.

'You've gone quiet.' Harold's voice swirled around the recesses of what remained of her mind.

She tried to ignore him as she wallowed in her pity.

'Mrs Wallace?' A new voice came to her. She ignored that, too.

This was her fate. One worse than death. Budgerigars might live perhaps ten, maybe even fifteen years if they were lucky? Harold was only five, and she instinctively knew the little twerp was destined for a long and annoying life.

'Mrs Wallace?'

Another ten years of this? Unthinkable. There had to be another way out.

'*Mrs Wallace!*' The voice was not Harold's but was still chillingly familiar. Old and breathy and Bavarian. She felt her feathers ruffle as it gave a cruel chuckle. 'Oh, Mrs Wallace, are you sad? Have you discovered what I did with your body? Take some solace from the fact that your fate was sealed from the moment we met. There was nothing you could have done to stop me.'

'Fate? What kind of cruel trick is this, Otto Kopp? Yes, I know your name now! What perverted pleasure can you possibly take from my imprisonment in the tiny mind of a dumb animal?'

'Oi, I object to that,' Harold broke in, then immediately started badgering the girl and the witch. 'Petunia, Miss Charlotte – that Otto fella, he's back!'

Mrs Wallace let him wail. The witch was too busy concentrating on the road to hear him.

She reserved all her venom for Otto. 'You are a monster, Otto Kopp. A degenerate, cold-blooded murderer who has no place in the Führer's glorious Third Reich. It's people like you who give the Nazis a bad name!'

Otto chuckled. 'Mrs Wallace, I bring good news.

There is a way out of this. One last service you can provide for the cause. Do this, and you will be free.'

A way out. Despite herself, Mrs Wallace trilled at the thought. She didn't trust Otto, of course she didn't . . . but what other way was there? Her heart warmed to think of simple comforts, like sitting in her armchair, sipping tea and enjoying a sea view.

'What service?' she asked, her thoughts laced with suspicion. 'What must I do?'

℘

Miss Charlotte wiped the rain from her goggles before leaning forwards over the handlebars of the motorcycle. She slowed to take a tight bend in the road, the wheels slicing through a black puddle. This thing wasn't as fast as she would have liked, and the sidecar carrying Petunia and the birdcage made it all the more awkward to steer, but she estimated that she would be back in Woodville within minutes. The first order of business would be to find Faye and Mrs Teach. If her assessment of Otto's ritual was correct, then he had summoned the dead to do his bidding. This was ancient, powerful and downright reckless magic to be playing with. She had always known the man was dangerous, but this was the kind of necromancy that hadn't been attempted since the Middle Ages, and for good reason. The dead did not take kindly to being woken from their slumber. Miss Charlotte was grouchy if someone was fool enough to wake her from a nap. Take that ire, multiply it to the scale of the promise of eternal rest and suffer the consequences. The undead were very angry, and not at all shy when it came to expressing their rage in violent ways.

'Miss Charlotte! Miss Charlotte!'

She was aware that Petunia and Harold had been trying to get her attention for some time, but this road had more kinks than a willow branch. Not to mention it was dark, raining hard and the headlights of the motorbike – hooded to meet with blackout regulations – were worse than useless. She had to apply all her concentration simply to see where she was—

'*Whoooaaah!*'

The ghost of Mrs Wallace appeared directly before Miss Charlotte's eyes. Miss Charlotte didn't think ghosts made such hokey noises as 'Whoooaaah!', but Mrs Wallace looked just as surprised to manifest herself as Miss Charlotte was to see her, so perhaps the expression was justified this once.

'Bastard!' Mrs Wallace scowled. 'He lied to me again!' Pathetic last words from the Nazi spy before her ghostly form congealed into ectoplasm, but effective enough to distract Miss Charlotte, who didn't have time to ponder their meaning as the former Mrs Wallace's ectoplasmic residue spattered onto her goggles, blinding her instantly. Charlotte applied the brakes, but she hadn't seen the next turn and the motorcycle-and-sidecar combination were sent skidding into a ditch at high speed. She and the budgie cage were thrown clear of the bike, and the world was a brief spinning rush as she tumbled through the undergrowth, coming to a sudden stop at the foot of an oak tree. A sharp crack in her ribs sent a flare of pain through her body, but otherwise Miss Charlotte was unharmed.

For a moment, all she could hear was the steady rhythm of the rain gently dabbing the leaves around her in time with her heart thudding in her ears. She removed her gooey goggles and surveyed the damage.

The sidecar was detached from the motorcycle, which lay on its side, wheels buckled, the engine billowing white smoke. The budgie cage was several feet away, its bars bent and its little door wide open. Miss Charlotte glanced down to find more ectoplasmic residue on her riding leathers. Mr Gilbert would not be happy about this. Not one little bit.

'She's gone!' Harold the budgie, newly released from his incarceration, fluttered before her. 'The old bat is gone. My mind is my own again,' he chirruped, swooping about in the air. 'I'm free! Free as a ... well, as a bird!'

'I'm glad someone's happy,' Miss Charlotte said, hissing in pain as she got to her feet. 'But our current mode of transport is, for want of a better word, knackered. We'll have to continue on foot.'

'I think that might not be our biggest problem.' Petunia drifted to Miss Charlotte's side. The girl was staring off into the distance.

Miss Charlotte turned, one hand on her cracked ribs, to follow her gaze.

A hulking man stood in the middle of the road. He

wore a distinctive sailor's cap with gothic lettering. Noticing his pale skin and white eyes, Miss Charlotte realised she had to be looking at one of Otto's recently resuscitated minions. A Kriegsmarine, back from the dead.

He raised his fists like mallets and ran directly at her.

'I'll fetch help,' Petunia said, vanishing into thin air.

'I'll, er, not get in the way,' Harold added, flitting away and hiding in a cluster of honeysuckle by the side of the road.

Miss Charlotte had but a few heartbeats to decide on a strategy. As she shifted on her feet to steady her balance, she was rewarded with a stabbing pain in her ribs. A straight fight wouldn't be the best option.

The Kriegsmarine was bearing down on her fast, stretching out his arms, and she waited until the last possible moment before ducking under his grasp and sticking out a foot to send him tumbling. Rolling across the wet road, she winced at the white flashes of pain before scrambling to her feet. Running was her best chance for survival, and so she hopped off the road and over a nearby fence into the field beyond. She was sure it was one of Larry Dell's. Planted with barley last summer, it had been left fallow this year. A hundred or so yards away, she could make out the edge of the wood, where she knew she stood a better chance of losing the Kriegsmarine. Doing her best to ignore the paralysing jolts from her ribs, Miss Charlotte kept her one good eye on the finishing line of trees.

The *thud-splash* of the Kriegsmarine's boots drew closer behind her. Before she was even halfway across, she felt a sharp tug on her long white hair. Her head jerked back and she tumbled into the sodden dirt.

He was on her in seconds, pushing her face into the soft soil as she tried to rise. Miss Charlotte couldn't breathe, but she refused to panic. This goon wasn't the first thug to try to kill her. With a sharp kick, her heel found his knee, popping it out of place. For any normal human, this would be agonising. For the undead, it was a minor inconvenience. Still, he tumbled to one side, giving Miss Charlotte the moment she needed to heave herself out of the mud and scrabble away.

'Tally-ho!' came a voice in her head, and Harold the budgie darted around the prone sailor, flapping in his face and pecking at his pale eyes as Miss Charlotte ran.

'Come on, then, big fella!' Harold cried, puffing his chest as he flitted about. 'Let's have you, sunshine! Is that the best you've—'

The Kriegsmarine's meaty fist swatted the poor budgie out of the air, sending him spiralling into a puddle where he lay on his back, legs stuck straight out above him.

The Kriegsmarine hauled himself free of the mud and came after Charlotte again. He was bulky, but fast. She was limping and clutching her ribs. It took mere seconds for him to close the gap between them. He reached for her with his outsized hands, shoving her into the mud. Miss Charlotte rolled three times as the huge silhouette loomed over her.

'We're here!' came a jolly voice, and out of nowhere Petunia swept between the witch and the undead man. She was joined by the gaggle of ghostly schoolchildren, who immediately began dancing in circles around the baffled Kriegsmarine.

> *'Oats, peas, beans and barley grow,*
> *Oats, peas, beans and barley grow,*
> *Can you or I or anyone know*
> *How oats, peas, beans and barley grow?'*

Charlotte knew she should probably run again, but her ribs burned, and the rain was so heavy now that it was easier simply to lie here rather than risk running, falling and breaking something else. Besides, she couldn't look away as the children continued their dance.

> *'First the farmer sows his seed,*
> *Stands erect and takes his ease,*
> *He stamps his foot and claps his hands,*
> *And turns around to view his lands.'*

The Kriegsmarine swiped his fists at the children, but his punches passed straight through them.

'No, you silly fool,' said a familiar voice. Miss Charlotte looked around, but there was no one else there. 'They're just ghosts,' the voice insisted. 'Ignore them!'

> *'Next the farmer waters the seed,*
> *Stands erect and takes his ease,*

He stamps his foot and claps his hands,
And turns around to view his lands.'

Miss Charlotte felt something tremble beneath the field. The water in the puddles rippled. Taking advantage of the Kriegsmarine's distraction, she crawled over to where Harold lay nearby and cradled him in the palm of her hand.

He sneezed and weakly turned his head towards her. 'I think I've broken my beak,' he said.

'Next the farmer hoes the weeds,
Stands erect and takes his ease,
He stamps his foot and claps his hands,
And turns around to view his lands.'

The Kriegsmarine was raging now, and Miss Charlotte was reminded of that splendid film about the big gorilla climbing up the Empire State Building. She'd only seen the end, and had felt sorry for the poor thing.

'Leave the children and kill the witch!' That voice again. It sounded an awful lot like—

'Mrs Wallace?' Petunia asked. 'Is that you in there?'

'Last the farmer harvests his seed,
Stands erect and takes his ease,
He stamps his foot and claps his hands,
And turns around to view his lands.'

The children clapped their own hands and the rumbling in the earth intensified. Shafts of barley sprouted from the mud like spears, wrapping around the Kriegsmarine's legs, the spikes holding him still.

'Miss Charlotte!' Petunia cried. 'I do believe Mrs Wallace's spirit is now inside this sailor chap!'

'Indeed,' Miss Charlotte replied. 'Do keep up, Petunia.'

Before the Kriegsmarine could break free, the barley stems shot back down into the earth, rooting him in place. They jerked and tugged, and his body shook from side to side as they began to pull him down with them, further and further until only his head and shoulders were visible. He wriggled in vain, moaning wordlessly as Mrs Wallace's voice wailed, 'Let me free, you idiots!'

Miss Charlotte crawled towards the submerged sailor, a thin smile on her face. 'This isn't me, Mrs Wallace.' She glanced at the children dancing around the Kriegsmarine's head. 'And I don't think it's them, either. There's something bigger guiding their hands.'

'Stop talking in riddles and help me. I'm sinking.'

It was true. With each passing moment, the Kriegsmarine was sucked a little deeper into the moist soil.

'I've seen this before,' Miss Charlotte said. 'The earth reclaiming body and soul to nourish the soil. Whatever grows in this field next year will be a bumper crop, I guarantee it.'

'I don't want to nourish a crop. Make it stop. Set me free!'

'I can't honestly say that one is inclined to dash to the aid of a Nazi spy.' Miss Charlotte remained lying on her front in the mud. It was cold and wet, but at least her ribs weren't on fire. She propped her chin on a balled fist.

'I hear his thoughts, you know,' Mrs Wallace said. 'This Otto Kopp fellow, I know his plans. I know everything, and I can spill the beans.'

'Can you indeed?'

'Yes, but you won't like it.' Mrs Wallace's voice turned priggish. 'He's already won, you see.'

Miss Charlotte lowered her balled fist and edged forwards. She was almost nose to nose with the sinking Kriegsmarine now. 'Won how?'

'Look to the sky, where the village is,' Mrs Wallace replied, and Charlotte did as she said, noting an unusual orange glow on a horizon that should have been in blackout. 'Woodville has burned to the ground. Its occupants have scattered into the wood like frightened mice.'

Miss Charlotte recalled Faye's vision of the burning village and felt a chill at the back of her neck.

'The feeble groom and his useless father-in-law-to-be are most likely dead already,' Mrs Wallace continued in her sneering voice, 'and the blushing bride will be next.'

The Kriegsmarine moaned as he raised his chin, but it wasn't enough to stop him sliding further into the mud.

Mrs Wallace's voice still had that superior tone. 'I know what Otto's endgame is. I'll tell you. It's not too late to save the girl. You just need to pull me free and find me a more suitable body than this oaf.'

Miss Charlotte wrinkled her brow. 'Let me get this straight, Mrs Wallace, because I'm a little confused. You want me to pull you free, then find a new body for your disembodied spirit, and in return you'll tell me every detail of Otto's plan?'

'Yes, what's so confusing about that? Now hurry before—'

'No.' Miss Charlotte allowed herself the first hint of a smile.

'No? What do you mean, no?'

The Kriegsmarine's upturned face was all that remained above the surface of the mud, which continued to creep slowly over his cheeks as his panicked white eyes darted about. His nose looked like the sail of a scuttled ship.

'I mean no.' Miss Charlotte stood with a series of grunts and gasps, the pain in her side making even the simplest action an exercise in agony. 'If there's one thing I've learned from this damned war,' she said, 'it's to never trust a Nazi.'

With that, Miss Charlotte placed the sole of her right boot on the Kriegsmarine's face and leaned all her weight onto it, hastening his descent beneath the soil.

'No, no!' Mrs Wallace's voice rose in pitch as she panicked. 'I've got more. Names of contacts, spies, traitors. Don't throw it all away.'

'Goodbye, Mrs Wallace,' Miss Charlotte said, removing her boot from the new indentation in the soil and allowing the water from an adjacent puddle to flow in and wash over the Kriegsmarine's eyes. As Mrs Wallace continued to wail and curse, Miss Charlotte used the side of her boot to scrape mud over to fill the hole. It wasn't long before Mrs Wallace fell silent.

Miss Charlotte looked up to find Petunia gawping at her in horror. The ghostly schoolchildren had gone.

Harold was the first to speak. 'Remind me to never get on the wrong side of you, Miss Charlotte.'

The witch smiled at the budgie snug in her hand. 'And don't you forget it,' she said, then turned to Petunia. 'Faye and Mrs Teach. Where are they?'

PLAN OF ATTACK

The villagers were gathered in the clearing by the hollow oak. Faye had never seen so many people here at once. As the rain continued to fall in sheets, they sat around the clearing in little huddles and cliques. The Morris Men mingled with the Home Guard, the shopkeepers and their families sat with the church volunteers, and a couple of soldiers and an RAF pilot were trying to start a fire.

'This isn't everyone,' Faye noted as she attempted a headcount. 'Some might still be lost in the wood. And I think a few folks headed off to stay with friends and family in places like Herne Bay and Margate.'

'Maybe they'll bring help?' Doris Finch suggested hopefully.

Faye scruffed her hair and shrugged. 'What help would they bring? As far as most people are concerned, there was a fire and now that's been put out by the rain. No, we need magical help and Mrs Teach will ... Oh, here she comes.'

Faye had caught sight of Mrs Teach over Doris' shoulder. The older witch was returning from a quiet spot away from the clearing. She carried a compact make-up mirror in her hand.

The look of dismay on her face told Faye all she needed to know, but still she asked, 'Any luck?'

'No, dear. It was always unlikely. For scrying to work I need a proper chalk circle, wax and gold tablets, and this—' She handed the compact mirror to Doris '—should be made of obsidian. Thank you for the loan, though, Doris dear. Much appreciated.'

'My pleasure.' Doris inspected her little mirror, quite unsure as to what Mrs Teach had been doing with it.

'And of course, to speak directly with Vera or Bellamy I would need a vial of their blood. No, Faye, it was worth trying, but I never held out much hope for scrying. That said, we should prepare emergency scrying packs once all this nonsense is over. Mustn't get caught short again.'

'Duly noted,' Faye said. 'Who else could we call on for help? Sid?'

'The woodwose is guardian of the wood, Faye. He doesn't take sides.'

'But he's letting us remain here. That tells us something.'

'Perhaps.' Mrs Teach held up her palms. 'I don't suppose Laura Long Arms would be of help?'

'I've used up my one favour with her,' Faye said, smiling at Doris, who had been helped by the wood's wish-giving naiad Laura last summer.

'As have I,' Mrs Teach mused.

'I'm sorry.' Doris pressed her fingers to her fore-head. 'I'm struggling to keep up. What does all this mean?'

Faye thought for a moment. 'It means we're on our own. No help is coming. Not anytime soon. What I suggest is we wait for Miss Charlotte to get back—'

'*If* she gets back,' Mrs Teach interjected. 'We've no idea where she went, and I couldn't make contact with her, either. For all we know, Otto may have done for her, too.'

'She'll be back,' Faye insisted, for the alternative was unthinkable. 'And when she is, we can work together to ... What on earth are that lot up to?'

Faye brushed past Doris to where Captain Marshall was leading Mr Brewer, Mr Gilbert, Constable Muldoon, Private North, Lance Corporal Stedman and an RAF pilot she didn't know down the winding path back to the village, like deadly ducklings all in a row.

Faye rushed past them to intercept the captain. 'Captain, may I ask where you're going?'

Captain Marshall raised a hand, bringing his troop to a halt. 'That, young lady, is top-secret information, given only on a need-to-know basis.'

'Yes, but I really need to know.'

'Do you indeed? Faye, I'm aware that you and Mrs Teach like to think you rule the roost, but I am a cap-tain of the Home Guard, and these men are trained to fight. And you – and I mean no disrespect when I say this – are a landlord's daughter. Kindly stand aside and let us do our job.'

'Do your job?' Faye inspected his troops. 'You're all unarmed. What are you going to do? Tickle them to death? If I let you go, you'll all be marching to your doom and I can't allow that to happen.' She made sure to say this loud enough for all the captain's men to hear. Mr Gilbert and Mr Brewer exchanged looks of concern.

Captain Marshall remained unimpressed. 'Thank you for your consideration, but we've trained thoroughly for scenarios such as this. And I think we can handle one pyromaniac.'

'That's what you think you're dealing with?' Faye scoffed, then leaned closer so that only the captain could hear. 'Captain, that man is a Bavarian Druid – a member of the Thule Society, the SS and the Black Sun, and one of the most powerful and dangerous practitioners of magic there has ever been. You haven't trained for him, believe me.'

It was the captain's turn to scoff, though he was rather less certain with his scoffing than Faye had been. 'And how would you know all this?'

'It's on a need-to-know basis.' Faye couldn't resist giving him a cheeky wink before turning serious again. 'And you do really need to know this. Otto is impetuous. He can't help himself. Eventually, he'll do something provocative, or stupid, or both. We just need to be patient. He can't hold the village for ever.'

A polite cough came from over Captain Marshall's shoulder. Mr Gilbert raised his impressive nose.

'Permission to speak, Captain?'

'If you must.'

'Begging your pardon, sir, but in my experience, I've always found Faye's advice on such matters to be invaluable.'

'Thank you, Private, I'll take that under advisement. We will proceed to engage the enemy as planned. And as for you, Faye Bright—'

Just then a voice called from the depths of the wood. 'Faye!'

She spun on her heels to find Bobby Newton staggering up the path, still draped in sackcloth and gripping his hoodening horse head like a wizard's staff.

'I've found you,' he cried. 'Oh, thank God.'

Faye ran to meet the lad. His legs gave way and he collapsed in her arms.

'He ... he saved me,' Bobby said, his eyes drifting about in their sockets. 'The big hairy man saved me.'

Faye knew immediately who he meant. 'Did you see anyone else, Bobby? Any other villagers? Reverend Jacobs and Edith, perhaps? Bertie? Or my dad?'

Bobby shook his head, then passed out, snoring loudly as Faye cradled him.

Captain Marshall and his men hurried to carry Bobby back to the clearing. Soon the lad was resting by a fire, briefly half-awake as he recounted his adventure, Doris mopping his brow with a hankie all the while, before falling back to sleep.

Faye and Mrs Teach huddled together by the hollow oak.

'Good grief, that boy can snore,' Mrs Teach noted.

'At least we know the woodwose is on our side now,' Faye said.

'We know no such thing,' Mrs Teach replied. 'I told you. He doesn't take sides.'

'No? Then why did he rip the head off a Nazi and leave Bobby be? Not only that, he showed Bobby where to find us. I think we can count the woodwose as an ally.'

'Oh God, his head!' Bobby jolted awake from his slumber, startling poor Doris. 'He ripped his head right off!'

Mrs Teach bustled over to help calm the boy. Faye was about to follow when something niggled at her. Something was missing. She narrowed her eyes and it took a few seconds for her to realise. 'Buggeration,' she snapped. 'Where the bloody hell are Captain Marshall and his men?'

⌀

'He wasn't quite dead, was he?' Bertie clung to Terrence's waist as the Griffin rattled down the bumpy path towards the village.

'No, Bertie, I don't reckon he was,' Terrence replied matter-of-factly. 'Which might account for his short temper and violent disposition.'

The pair of them had not said a word since fleeing Ivy Barn, but Bertie had decided it was time to expel all the fearful thoughts in his brain at once.

'Where do you think he came from? Are there more

like him? Is this an invasion? I need to spend a penny. Stop the bike!'

Terrence gently applied the brakes, bringing the Griffin to a halt near the bottom of Gibbet Lane.

Bertie hopped off the back and dashed into the trees by the side of the path. Though not too far, because who knew what else lurked in the shadows? The truth was, he didn't need a wee. Instead, he vomited the contents of his stomach onto a cluster of unsuspecting stinging nettles.

'Sorry,' Bertie apologised to the spattered plants.

'You all right, Bertie?' Terrence offered a hand to the boy as he emerged from the trees.

Bertie nodded, though without much conviction. 'Sorry, Mr Bright, but for some reason our encounter with that undead chap has given me a bad case of the heebie-jeebies.'

'For some reason?' Terrence echoed with a chuckle. He patted Bertie on the shoulder and steered him back to the Griffin. 'I think after any encounter with the undead you're entitled to a case of the ... What did you call it?'

'The heebie-jeebies. I read it in a comic book. It's like the collywobbles, only American.' Bertie rested a hand on his aching belly. 'So, why aren't you all shaky and sick?'

Terrence idly scratched the back of his neck. 'Me? I'm terrified, lad, but I've been around long enough to know that in situations where all seems lost, you have to keep buggering on, as Mr Churchill would say.'

Bertie frowned. 'I've never heard him say that on the wireless.'

'No, you wouldn't've. An RAF officer in the pub once told me Churchill ends his telephone calls with that little phrase. No idea if it's true or not, but I quite like it as a motto in these dark times. Besides which, there's always a new challenge. That, for instance.'

Terrence nodded to the orange glow on the horizon. It wasn't the setting sun – it was in the wrong place, for a start, and it pulsed like a bonfire. The night air was laced with the aroma of burning wood.

'That's ... that's Woodville,' Bertie said, not wanting to believe it.

'Come on,' Terrence said grimly, swinging his leg back over the Griffin's crossbar. 'Let's go home.'

THE ARMOURY

Captain Morris Marshall tensed as he and his men approached the back of the Woodville Village police station. The incessant hiss of rain had covered the sound of their footsteps as they'd sneaked up Gibbet Lane, but this was the most dangerous part of the mission. They were exposed and unarmed as they waited for Constable Muldoon to unlock the heavy iron back door. The constable had warned them in advance that going through the front entrance would mean they'd be spotted, but sneaking in through the back meant opening the heavy iron door, and there was a knack to doing it quietly that only he knew. Get it wrong, and the screech of scraping metal would bring the enemy down upon them in moments. Without weapons, they would be goners. Captain Marshall had his trusty Smith and Wesson revolver, but he suspected that wouldn't be enough to save them.

It didn't help that the captain's mind was drifting somewhere between the grog of drunkenness and the impending doom of a colossal hangover. His head was thumping, his skin was clammy, his throat was dry and it was taking more effort than usual to remain upright. He dearly hoped this wouldn't take long.

Constable Muldoon's moustache bristled as he quietly slid in the key. Then he gripped the door's handle, keenly observed with bated breath by the captain's little platoon. Mr Brewer and Mr Gilbert were stalwarts of the Home Guard, though they'd had no rest since their last watch and were exhausted. Private North and Lance Corporal Stedman were more of an unknown quantity. The soldiers had the air of thugs in uniform; a pair of shifty chancers, they cheated at darts in the pub and, unbeknownst to them, were on the verge of being booted out of their lodgings above the bakery by their landlady, Mrs Yorke, on account of their loutish behaviour after a few too many pints. Captain Marshall could only hope they were ready to obey his orders. The RAF pilot, one Sergeant Black, put on a good show, though he had become twitchy as they'd skulked into the village, no doubt preferring the autonomy and distance of a fighter aircraft.

The lock clicked and Constable Muldoon oh-so-gently nudged the door open, just enough for them all to squeeze through. Captain Marshall waved the others in.

The constable led them down a dark staircase to the cells. A shadow shifted within number three, and the captain raised a hand to bring the party to a halt. He nudged past Muldoon and aimed his pistol at the cell door, slowly edging forwards. The soles of his boots squeaked on the tiles like a bum note on a busker's fiddle.

'I say, who's there?' came a woman's voice from inside the cell.

'This is Captain Marshall of the Home Guard. Advance and be—'

'Oh, Captain Marshall, how marvellous!' Edith Palmer's head popped out. 'Have you come to rescue us?'

The captain holstered his pistol. 'Not as such. What are you doing here, Edith?'

'I'm here with Timothy,' Edith said, swinging the cell door all the way open to reveal Reverend Jacobs asleep on the bunk. Private North and Lance Corporal Stedman made suggestive noises.

'Quiet, you two!' the captain snapped.

Reverend Jacobs was pale, and beads of sweat rested on his brow. His fingers trembled.

'He's rather under the weather,' Edith said by way of explanation, though Captain Marshall wondered if there was more to it than that. 'We saw the church was on fire, and the flames were so intense that I feared the vicarage could be next. So I bundled poor Timothy into a wheelbarrow and brought him to the police station. Constable Muldoon wasn't here, so I took it upon myself to hop over the desk—'

This got a disapproving grumble from Constable Muldoon.

'And take the keys—'

Another grumble with added intensity.

'To put Timothy in the most secure place in the village. A cell in the police station.'

'Wish I'd thought of that,' Mr Brewer muttered.

'You are to be commended for your quick thinking, Edith,' Captain Marshall said. 'There's no doubt that you have saved the good Reverend's life. However, I am sorry to report that we are not a rescue mission as such. We've come to eliminate the enemy, so I would suggest that you remain safely in here until our objective is achieved.'

'By enemy, do you mean that bald chap who set the village on fire?' Edith lowered her voice, glancing at Reverend Jacobs. 'You're here to, what, attack him?'

'We are indeed, though first we're commandeering weapons and ordnance from—'

'Is Faye Bright with you?' Edith asked hopefully. 'Or Mrs Teach? Or Miss Charlotte?'

'No. Why would they be?'

Edith's face drained of hope. 'Well, because they're used to dealing with ... this sort of thing.'

The captain bristled. 'My dear Edith, "this sort of thing" is what I and my men have been training for since war was declared. Please leave this to us. Remain safe in this cell, and we'll fetch you when it's all over.'

'But, Captain, he's taken over the church. It's like a fortress—'

'And he's alone?'

'Yes, but—'

'Thank you for the intelligence, Edith. We'll handle it from here.'

'He's using some sort of magic, I think.'

Captain Marshall couldn't help scoffing. 'Oh, good grief. Yes, right, thank you, Edith.'

'You really should get Faye and the others here. They called him Otto Kopp. He's a Druid and they've dealt with him before—'

'Yes, yes, thank you!' Captain Marshall pushed the cell door closed, leaving Edith and the Reverend behind bars. 'Lay on, Muldoon,' he said, before muttering, 'I don't know, honestly. What does the vicar put in his sherry to foster such delusions, hmm?'

The constable led them down another flight of stairs to the basement, where they came to a huge cage that dominated the room.

'I say, the rumours were true,' Mr Gilbert said in awe.

The cage was full of metal shelving units, which were stacked with enough weaponry to start another war.

'Don't get your hopes up, Private,' Constable Muldoon advised. 'Most of these have had their firing pins removed, and there's very little ammunition. However ...' He gestured to the last rack of shelves. 'These were stored here on Captain Marshall's orders in anticipation of an invasion. Help yourselves, gents.'

North and Stedman were the first to dash in, like children in a sweet shop.

As they bickered over who got the Sten gun, Mr Brewer sidled up to Captain Marshall. 'Begging your pardon, Captain sir, but Edith's point is well made. If there is something ... odd about this Otto chap, then perhaps we should work with Faye Bright and her—'

'Private Brewer, we are the Home Guard, the greatest citizen army that this country has ever seen. We are tasked with providing an effective countermeasure to enemy invasion. We will not flinch from that task under any circumstances, and certainly not on the basis of ridiculous rumour and hearsay. Do I make myself clear?'

'Sir, yes, sir.' Mr Brewer saluted.

'Now get yourself a weapon before they're all gone.'

A few moments later, the men mingled before Captain Marshall, comparing weaponry.

Private North and Lance Corporal Stedman had opted for Tommy guns in the end, which seemed fitting given their gangster-like countenances. Mr Brewer and Mr Gilbert had found a Sten gun each, Constable Muldoon had a hunting rifle, Sergeant Black had a Browning pistol and the captain had his revolver.

'Very good.' Captain Marshall nodded. 'I understand we have two grenades with Privates Brewer and Gilbert, and we have a rubber truncheon each.'

'Not forgetting the knuckledusters, Captain.' Constable Muldoon turned over said brass knuckledusters in his hand.

'Who the devil ... ?'

'Confiscated from Mrs Pritchett,' Constable Muldoon explained. 'Claimed they were a family heirloom.'

'Quite. Well, I'm sure they'll come in handy,' Captain Marshall said as the constable slipped them into a pocket. 'A shame we don't have the spigot mortar, but it's on loan to the Herne Bay Home Guard for a demonstration. Still, this should all be more than adequate. Attention, men.'

The soldiers and pilot stiffened their backs, arms by their sides. Chins up, chests out, stomachs in.

'Our plan is to use the guerrilla warfare techniques that we've spent so long practising,' the captain began. 'This will entail using tactics that some might consider underhand and downright ungentlemanly, but this isn't cricket or bridge. This is war.'

Stedman let out a snort.

'Something to add, Lance Corporal?'

The man straightened his face hastily. 'No, sir.'

'Very well. Our target is this Otto Kopp fellow, some kind of Nazi deviant and pyromaniac. As far as we can ascertain, he's alone and hunkered down in the remains of Saint Irene's Church. We are to advance with stealth up the Wode Road, using the shops as cover—'

'With respect, Captain, if it's just one man, why are we pussyfooting about like this?' Stedman said.

'Yeah, just one bloke. We should hit him fast,' Private North agreed.

'I hate to break rank like this, Captain,' Sergeant Black of the RAF said, 'but I'm in agreement with these chaps. Speed and surprise are of the essence.'

'And we've seen our share of action on the front line, Captain,' the lance corporal added. 'We know what needs to be done, so why not leave it to us, eh? We'll pop out, zip up Perry Lane and surprise him from the rear.'

'Perry Lane is too narrow,' Captain Marshall objected. 'If you were to meet an enemy—'

'Then we'll shoot his legs off,' Private North said with a chuckle, readying his Tommy gun. 'You lot wait here. We'll be back in a jiffy.'

'Private, stand down. All of you, I order you to stand down,' Captain Marshall bellowed, but the trio of Stedman, North and Black barged past him and up the stairs.

Watching them go, the captain's head throbbed and he thought longingly of a glass of water, two aspirin and a nap.

'We're still with you, sir,' Mr Brewer said, raising his chin.

'Good man, Private. Good man.' Captain Marshall puffed out his chest, pushing his hangover aside. He readied his revolver. 'Now, shall we?'

INGLORIOUS BAR STEWARDS

As Captain Marshall and his men quietly slipped out of the police station and back into the rain, he reflected on their objective. It sounded so simple. Wipe out the enemy, secure the church, find a radio and make contact with the outside world, then it's bacon and eggs for breakfast. A good fry-up would do wonders for his hangover. Captain Marshall had fought in the last year of the Great War at Megiddo in Ottoman Palestine. A victory, to be sure, but not without cost. He'd had a horse then. Good old Arthur. One of the greatest lessons he had learned from those days of blood and sweat in the desert was that it's all well and good having a plan, but rarely does that plan endure beyond the first maddening encounter with the enemy. What you needed most during the chaos of battle were nerves of steel. And a good horse, if possible. He'd loved that Arthur. Captain Marshall allowed himself a momentary wallow in the past and tried to conjure up the heat of the desert and the joy of victory once more.

He had seen T. E. Lawrence, you know. At least, he had thought it was him. He'd been quite far away, and it had been difficult to tell what with all the heat haze.

What the captain wouldn't give for a little heat now, as the rain hammered on his Mark I steel helmet. He gave the signal to his men to huddle by a low wall adjacent to the police station and wait. Hunkering down, he felt a twinge in his shoulder where he had been wounded by an arrow during some drunken revelling last Christmas. He couldn't quite recall exactly how it had happened now, though he had a hazy impression that it had been fired by Miss Gordon. Most of Christmas was a blur. Someone had cleaned and bandaged the wound, enough for it to heal well, but it always ached when it was damp. Still, no point dwelling on such nonsense now. They had a mission to accomplish.

He gave the nod. They dashed from the police station, past the butcher's, then hurried through the smashed door of the baker's, taking cover behind the toppled racks where Mrs Yorke usually kept the fresh loaves. Captain Marshall listened for any sign that they had been spotted, which was easier said than done while his heart was pounding in his ears and the rain drowned out any other sounds. It didn't help that his head was throbbing again.

It took him a moment to assess the devastation. Shards of glass littered the cobbles. Almost every house and shop on the Wode Road had smashed windows, and a few bore black smoke stains on their walls. The front of the Green Man pub had collapsed, and the rest of the building was a smouldering wreck. Beyond, the church billowed smoke like a factory and flames flickered from within.

The captain was estimating how fast they could hurry across to the pub and use what remained of the saloon bar for cover when screams echoed from Perry Lane. Someone who sounded a lot like Lance Corporal Stedman cried, 'Run!' This was followed by a short blast from a Tommy gun and more screaming.

Private Brewer shifted as if to check on the commotion, but the captain rested a hand on his shoulder, not wanting to give away their position. Brewer nodded and remained crouched beside him.

Captain Marshall couldn't be sure when the screams ceased, blending into the crackle of the rain, but it didn't take long. He would assume that Lance Corporal Stedman, Private North and Sergeant Black were dead and proceed accordingly. His head ached more intensely, his blood chilled in his veins.

'Good evening, gentlemen.' A voice drifted from the top of the Wode Road, startling him. It sounded German. Cautiously, the captain peered through the cracked glass and blast tape in the bakery window.

The silhouette of a man appeared in the near distance, backlit by the glowing amber of the burning church, and began to walk along the glistening cobbles. He extended his arms in greeting, though Captain Marshall was sure that he hadn't spotted them yet.

'I'm afraid your friends' attempt to attack us has failed. Such a senseless waste of life.'

Captain Marshall's heart sank at having his fears about the others confirmed. He gripped the handle of his revolver tight.

The bald German drew closer to the Green Man and the captain could see him more clearly. He wore a rather natty three-piece tweed suit, and the flames from the church reflected off his bald head. Captain Marshall couldn't be sure, but it looked like the German had red skin.

'I'm sure we've seen this Otto chap before,' Private Gilbert whispered.

Captain Marshall nodded, recognition dawning. 'Last summer when we sent those Kriegsmarines packing on the beach.'

'He was wearing an SS uniform then,' Private Brewer added. 'And he wasn't bright red. You tend to notice things like that.'

'Indeed,' Captain Marshall said, noticing that Constable Muldoon's fingers were trembling. The captain wondered how wise it had been to bring the constable with them. He wasn't trained for this, poor chap. Too late now. 'Ready your weapons.'

Otto strolled further down the road. 'I thought I'd save you the trouble, gentlemen. Here I am. Shoot me.'

'Who am I to argue with that?' Captain Marshall muttered. One quick breath to steady his nerves, then he hollered, 'Open fire!'

This was what they had trained for. All those drills, all those exercises, and it all came down to a moment like this. Captain Marshall exhaled as he rose and fired six rounds from his revolver. Around him came the flash and thunder of the Sten guns, the crack of Constable Muldoon's hunting rifle. On any other day, they were a pair of antiques dealers, a village constable and a retired bank manager and captain of the bowls team, but tonight they were a formidable fighting force, ready to see off this invader. Captain Marshall would have hoped for more men by his side in a situation like this, but most of the Home Guard were far too inebriated from today's celebrations to be allowed weapons, and the remainder – including Terrence Bright and Bertie Butterworth – were still missing. Of course, Captain Marshall wouldn't technically pass muster, either – not after all the pints he had downed today. But if there was one thing he had really learned from T. E. Lawrence that September in 1918, it was that duty must come above all else, and to lead from the front.

As he fired, he noticed something strange happening. The bullets appeared to be swerving around this Otto chap. Captain Marshall was no crack marksman, but he could hit a man at thirty yards. Yet every one of his shots went wide, as did the hail of bullets from the Sten guns and the hunting rifle.

Otto, not a scratch on him, stopped in his tracks. He turned towards them and smiled. 'There you are.'

Captain Marshall blanched. He had given away their position, and now there was nowhere to run. They could try to escape out the back, but if the cries from Stedman and his men had told him anything, there was a nasty surprise waiting in Perry Lane.

'Reload!' the captain ordered, and there was a scrabble as he and his men grabbed bullets and magazines with shaking hands.

They were interrupted by a crack of splintering wood from the rear of the bakery. Their heads turned as one to find a pair of shadowy figures kicking in the back door. A huge hand bearing a stigmata-like wound ripped the remnants from its hinges to reveal a hulking Luftwaffe officer, his uniform dotted with bullet-holes. He was accompanied by a walking nightmare of a pilot, clumsy stitches encircling his torn neck.

Constable Muldoon was the first to fire, shooting the bigger one in the head. The thing staggered backwards, flailing its hands bearing their bloody holes, then righted itself and kept coming.

'Fall back!' Captain Marshall ordered, his voice trembling as he realised with a cold dread that this was no ordinary enemy. 'Follow me.'

He ran out into the downpour, loosing more rounds in Otto's direction. The crazed man was enjoying himself, laughing amid the torrent of bullets and raindrops.

There was only one place where they could quickly take cover on the Wode Road, and the captain was struck by the grim irony of it being the stone memorial to the Great War.

'Here! Behind me,' he ordered as he half hid himself at the foot of the towering cross. Brewer, Gilbert and Muldoon crouched around its base, weapons ready. Out of the corner of his eye, Captain Marshall spotted a few familiar names etched in the stone. Young men who had marched off to war with their heads held high but had never come back. Edgar Reed. He had been in the village cricket first eleven back then. A slow left-hand bowler with a swerve. Nice chap with buck teeth and a pencil moustache, and now there was his name carved into the stone for posterity. Captain Marshall wondered if there would be another memorial for this war, and if his name would be on it.

'Captain!' Private Brewer yelled, and he snapped out of his daze to find the duo of bullet-riddled Nazis lurching towards them through the rain.

'Fire at will!' Captain Marshall ordered, and countless bullets punched into the bodies of their attackers. They stumbled and staggered, but they kept on coming, and Otto continued to cackle beyond them.

'Out of ammo, sir!' Private Gilbert declared.

Captain Marshall checked his revolver. He was, too. They all were.

The two Nazis began to run at them, boots slapping on the cobbles. They had only seconds left.

'What do we do, Morris?' Private Brewer asked quietly.

Captain Morris Marshall realised he had been a fool. He should have taken young Faye Bright's advice. Too late for that now, but these men didn't deserve to die like this. They could run, though at the rate their assailants were coming at them they would be caught before they reached the bottom of the road.

'Truncheons ready!' Captain Marshall stood firm and drew his weapon, as did his men. He noticed with a flash of gallows humour that Constable Muldoon was wearing Mrs Pritchett's knuckledusters. 'Forward!'

He took a deep breath and heaved himself off the memorial, ready to die on his feet, but death and glory were interrupted by an armoured vehicle – a Bren Universal Carrier – skidding to a halt before him. It slammed into the pair of Luftwaffe officers, crushing the big one under its tracks and sending the pilot's head flying clean off its torn stitches and crashing through the butcher's window.

'Hurry!' Edith Palmer peered over the hull of the vehicle, her arms outstretched.

As she spoke, a Bren light machine gun fired through a slit in the carrier's armour, lighting up the Wode Road like it was Bonfire Night, flashes pulsing on the fronts of the houses and shops. Otto Kopp remained where he stood; the bullets continued to swerve around him, but he had stopped laughing. This wasn't part of his plan.

'Come on!' Edith cried. 'Mind the bike,' she added, and as he and his men clambered over the hull Captain Marshall noted a bicycle that looked a lot like Faye Bright's Pashley Model A.

Jumping inside, they discovered Terrence Bright at the wheel and young Bertie Butterworth firing the Bren. Terrence stared grim-faced at what remained of his pub. Bertie gritted his teeth as he pulled on the light machine gun's trigger.

Edith wrapped her arms tightly around Reverend

Jacobs where he sat in a corner as the armoured vehicle moved off, its tracks rattling on the cobbles, taking them away from the village and to safety.

'Will this count towards my hours, Captain?' Terrence asked drily, with a sarcastic chuckle.

'I certainly think so, Terrence,' Captain Marshall replied over the chugging of the engine. 'I certainly think so.'

'Good. Back soon, darlin',' Terrence said, and it took Morris a few moments to realise that he was talking to the Green Man pub.

The captain's head throbbed with a vengeance, and it looked like the hangover to end all hangovers was inevitable, but as they rode away, he simply relished the fact that he would be alive to endure it. A small price to pay.

WOUND LICKING

Faye rises from the earth, soil tumbling from her skin. She takes a first breath, filling her lungs as her eyes fall on a hawthorn tree standing alone in a field. She is reborn. Naked and shivering. Blood rushes in her ears and every nerve tingles anew.

⚥

Faye jolted from her nap. She had nodded off while resting against the hollow oak. Another vision. Or was it just a dream? Whatever they were, she still had no idea what any of them meant. Shaking her head clear, she got to her feet just in time to see her father and Bertie emerge from the gloom of the wood. Her legs turned to jelly and tears welled in her eyes as she raced to greet them. She didn't know which one to hug first, so she wrapped her arms around both at once. She gave Bertie a clumsy kiss that was meant for his lips but ended up on his cheek. Then she gripped her father's hand.

'Dad ... the pub ... our home.'

Terrence nodded, and he took a couple of deep breaths before speaking. 'I know. I saw. Still ... could've been worse, eh?' He drew Faye into another embrace.

'Privates Bright and Butterworth!' Captain Marshall led Mr Gilbert, Mr Brewer and Constable Muldoon up the path. Their stooped posture told Faye all she needed to know about their mission. Otto had not only survived but had sent them packing.

Bertie and her dad snapped to attention and saluted.

'Oh, at ease,' Captain Marshall said, exhaustion weighing down every word. 'Report.'

Terrence glanced at Bertie, who nudged him to speak.

'Bertie, er, that is, Private Butterworth and I had completed the tasks you set out for us, Captain. However, we encountered and engaged an enemy at Ivy Barn. Big fella, uh, what did you reckon he was, Bertie?'

'Luftwaffe Unteroffizier,' Bertie said, adding an unnecessary salute. 'From his flight suit, I'd say he was either a navigator or a gunner on a bomber.'

'And, as previously mentioned, a big bruiser of a fella,' Terrence added. 'After briefly disabling the enemy by nailing his hands to a workbench, we decided to retreat and regroup at the police station where we reasoned there might be some weapons we could requisition.'

Bertie raised a hand. 'Oh, but before that I had to stop for the toilet.'

Terrence blinked. 'Not sure the captain needs to know that, Bertie.'

'At least, I thought I needed the toilet, but then I was a bit sick, and then I had to have a moment because I got a bad case of the shakes.'

'Bertie.'

'Because the enemy was one of those fellas you encountered, Captain. The one with the holes in his hands, and for some reason he isn't quite dead. And, as I'm sure I don't have to tell you, he was an unsettling character to encounter, and he gave me what some folk call the heebie-jeebies. And Mr Bright, that is *Private* Bright, gave me words of encouragement that got me back on my feet. "Keep buggering on!" Mr Churchill says it over the telephone, rumour has it. Anyway, that's why we were so late, and I've realised I'm wittering because I'm still a bit wobbly, so apologies for that and over to you, Private Bright.'

Terrence gently rocked on the balls of his feet for a moment, just to make sure Bertie was finished, before continuing, 'It was at the police station that we discovered the Reverend Jacobs and Miss Edith Palmer, who alerted us to your action on the enemy. With that in mind, we decided to commandeer the Bren Universal Carrier parked at the old garage on Unthank Road and see if you could use our assistance. The rest, well ... you was there, sir.'

'Indeed.' Captain Marshall shook both men's hands with a sharp yank. 'Your bravery back there was exemplary, gentlemen. And Bertie, I've seen other men get the ... What did you call it?'

'The heebie-jeebies, Captain,' Bertie said, saluting again for no reason other than that he was nervous. 'I read the phrase in a comic book.'

'Did you? Hmm. Yes, I have seen other men affected in such a way in the Great War, but for you to throw yourself back into the fray with such determination ... Well, it fills one's heart. I shall see to it that you both receive the appropriate commendations ... should we ever see another dawn.' The captain patted Terrence on the shoulder.

'What about the others?' Faye asked. 'The pilot? North and Stedman?'

Captain Marshall's lips tightened. He took a deep breath before shaking his head and sloping off to join the other villagers in the clearing.

Messrs Brewer, Gilbert and Muldoon also expressed their gratitude to Terrence and Bertie with shell-shocked pats, handshakes and – a first from Constable Muldoon – a bear hug.

'Oh, Bertie, my love, how are you?' Faye asked when they'd trundled off after the captain, her fingers tangling with his.

'I fired a Bren light machine gun, Faye,' Bertie said, eyes wide, his voice a whisper. 'In action. At Otto. I ... I didn't hit him. The bullets went around him. But ... it was bloody brilliant.'

Faye smiled and kissed him on the cheek.

'Come on, lad.' Terrence squeezed Bertie's shoulder. 'Let's sit by the fire and see if we can get dry, eh?'

Faye was about to join them when she caught sight of

another pair coming up the path from the village. Edith wore a stoic smile as she led Reverend Jacobs slowly by the elbow. His eyes drifted as he walked. But then he saw Faye and broke free from Edith. He scrabbled towards her and took both her hands in his.

'He's not leaving, Faye,' the Reverend said, his voice ragged. 'He won't go till he gets what he wants. Otto won't go till he gets you.'

⌀

'Our position on this is clear.' Captain Marshall stood in the centre of the clearing, summoning his best Churchillian bearing despite his lack of sleep. 'We do not hand over villagers to the enemy to be taken prisoner, or hostage, or worse. And you, Faye Bright, are under orders to remain here with us. Is that understood?'

'But Captain,' Faye protested, 'if I just turn myself in, you'll all be—'

'I'll keep a close eye on her, Captain,' Mrs Teach interrupted. 'The girl won't leave my sight.'

Faye wasn't sure what wound her up the most. That no one could see that the simplest solution was for Faye to confront Otto, or that Mrs Teach was still referring to her as a girl.

The hollow oak clearing was filled to the brim with villagers. The rain had stopped but the ground was sodden, so people either stood or found a slightly less damp patch to squeeze themselves onto. Mrs Teach somehow had her own tartan blanket. Terrence huddled with Doris among the hollow oak's gnarled roots, on the same spot where Faye had first opened her mother's book only last summer. So much had changed since then, not least Faye herself. And she knew that if she hadn't opened that book and embarked on learning magic and witchcraft – and, as a consequence, pissing off the most powerful Druid in the world – none of them would be here.

'We can't just give up,' she said firmly, drawing every eye.

Most people in the village had become used to the strangeness that went on around them, and few took much notice anymore, what with the war and everything. They had enough on their plates already, thank you very much. So what if some strange scarecrow people went gallivanting about, or that last Christmas was little more than a half-remembered Bacchanalian fever dream? There were rations to be sorted, essential duties to be attended to. All that other odd stuff could go hang.

But now they had lost their homes, and the man responsible for it wanted Faye. No one quite understood why, but for this short moment it felt easy to blame Faye Bright and her peculiar ways. And Faye could feel that resentment radiating at her as she spoke, as sure as she could feel the damp on her backside.

She stood up, patting the leaf litter from the bottom of her dungarees before pushing her specs up her nose and stuffing her hands into the pockets of her flight jacket. 'We can't give up,' she repeated. 'But you don't want me confronting Otto. And we'll lose in a fight—'

'There's nothing worth fighting for,' Mr Loaf the funeral director said in despair, jabbing his Morris stick at Faye and making its nailed-on bottle tops jingle and its ribbons flutter. 'Half the village is burned to the ground. Why risk our lives for a ruin?'

'With all due respect, Mr Loaf, don't be such a berk,' Faye snapped, getting a few gasps. The funeral director looked like he'd just been slapped. 'A village isn't just buildings and things. It's us. *We* are what we're fighting for, and that's what we have to ask ourselves now: are we worth the fight?' Faye looked around her, hoping for a few rousing cheers, but so many folks kept their eyes downcast that she couldn't help but falter. Only Bertie gave her an eager smile. 'There ain't nothing to stop us going our separate ways,' she continued. 'A few of us have done it already. And we've had a good run in Woodville. For centuries, we've shown the world who we are. Maybe our time is up?'

Bertie's smile faded. Like everyone else here, he was probably wondering where Faye was going with this little speech. Truth be told, she was, too.

Turning towards Captain Marshall, who was standing nearby, she caught sight of the dark shadows under his eyes – testament to the responsibility he felt for those who hadn't come back from the last fight. Something cracked open in her. Could she really let them die in vain?

Taking a deep breath, Faye turned back to the villagers. 'Or do we still have something to give?' She swept a hand across all those gathered. 'There's still a bigger war to be won. Crops to grow, food to share, people to love and cherish.' Her eyes fell on Bertie again, and his smile returned.

He sat up straight. 'So we fight?'

Faye shook her head. 'Otto can beat us in a fight. He's proved that over and over. Fighting and guns ain't the answer.'

'Then what is?' Captain Marshall asked.

Faye pressed a hand to her chest. Her voice was flat and determined. 'We give him what he wants.'

'No.' Terrence was on his feet, wagging a finger at Faye. 'I can rebuild a pub, but I can't rebuild you.'

'I agree,' Mrs Teach said, rising imperiously from her tartan rug. 'And we know Otto is not the sort to go meekly off into the setting sun. Once he's done with you, he'll take more and more.'

'Then what *is* the answer?' Bertie asked.

There was a pause, everyone shuffling their feet, at a loss. It was broken by Mr Loaf. 'I'm off to stay with my brother in Ramsgate,' he said, throwing his bowler hat with its ribbons and bells to the ground. It bounced and jingled, somewhat lessening the impact of his solemn declaration.

Other voices joined him, and in moments the clearing was heaving with villagers waving their hands and wailing in despair.

Faye's heart sank. There was a solution to this, she was sure, but she needed a little time and space to think. Quietly, she slipped away from the chaos and into the wood.

CONSIDERATION FOR BLUEBELLS

Faye found a quiet spot a short walk from the clearing, sitting down heavily on a fallen oak trunk with an exhausted puff of breath. She thought about drawing a glamour around herself to ensure her solitude, but the villagers back in the clearing were all so wrapped up in their arguments that no one had noticed her leaving. No one but Bertie.

'I can bugger off if you want me to?' He stood a little distance from Faye on the other side of a carpet of bluebells, hands stuffed into his pockets. 'If you need some time alone?'

'I've had so much time on my own while training, Bertie . . .' Faye patted a space next to her on the trunk. 'And I'd never turn you away.'

He limped around the bluebells, careful not to bend any. Faye's heart warmed to see that even now, in such a dark and hopeless moment, Bertie had consideration for bluebells.

They sat side by side in silence for some time. His hand slipped into hers, his skin rough and warm.

Faye wondered how she could summon the courage to tell him the decision she had made, knowing that it would surely break his heart. Facing Otto was a doddle in comparison. Bertie didn't deserve heartbreak. Not like this. One reason was his unerring ability to know what she was thinking, and to save her the pain of speaking first.

'I'm guessing the wedding's off?' He gave her hand a gentle squeeze. 'What with the church being on fire and all.'

Faye rested her head on his shoulder. 'I'm afraid so, Bertie, my love.'

'Here's the thing,' Bertie began, clearing his throat. Faye could feel his heart beating so hard and fast that it resonated throughout his body. 'Is it just postponed? Or . . .' He shuddered. Even brave Bertie couldn't bring himself to say it. Until he did. 'Or is it off completely? Because I know you've been having doubts. I could tell from the minute you came home. You'd changed . . . and not in a bad way. But it was like you'd opened a door, and whatever you'd seen on the other side meant you could never be the same.'

Faye raised her head. 'You got all that in the first minute I came back?'

Bertie shrugged and examined a cluster of mushrooms at the base of the log. 'Must be magic of a sort.'

Faye smiled, took the tip of his chin and turned his

face back towards her. 'You know I love you, don't you?' she said. 'I want that clear from the start.'

Bertie nodded, his eyes turning glassy.

Faye took a breath. 'If the world wasn't off its rocker, Bertie, then marrying you would make perfect sense.' She couldn't bear to watch his face crumble, so she looked at the bluebells. They grew back in this same patch every year, and every year there were more of them. 'But you're right – I have changed. The war's changed us all. If it wasn't for Hitler, I think I'd be more like my mum. Ready to settle down and start a family. But since I began training, I've realised I could make a difference. A real difference. I don't want to blow my own trumpet too much, but me and Bellamy and Vera – we might be able to end it sooner rather than later. But it means I'd be gallivanting all over the place, getting into all kinds of danger, and that wouldn't be fair on you.' Faye decided to dare to look back at Bertie and it was worse than she'd imagined. His freckles were wet with tears, his mouth fixed in a sympathetic smile, but there was no doubting the crushing heartache in his eyes. 'Oh, Bertie.' She wrapped her arms around him tightly, fighting back tears of her own.

His lips rested by her ear and he spoke softly, 'Can I ask a question?'

'Of course you can. Is it, "Why is Faye a complete cow?"'

His body hitched with a chuckle. 'No. But how is you going off to stop the war any different from all those men who've left their wives and girlfriends behind?'

313

'It's not, I suppose. It's just not fair. None of it is. But if I can avoid hurting you, if I can stop you worrying about me, then I will.'

Bertie gently drew back. He sniffed and dried his cheeks with the heel of his palm. 'You think if we don't get married that I'll stop loving you?' He shook his head. 'You just said a village isn't the buildings or things. Well, a marriage isn't about putting on fancy clothes and going to some church. It's about promising to love and care for someone. I'm doing that right now. Have been for some time. And I will continue to do so for the rest of my days.' He was about to say more, but Faye saw him stop himself, and she knew why. He was going to ask if she could love and care for him for the rest of her life, too. A few days ago, he would have been certain of her answer. And now he didn't know for sure, and that for Bertie was like a wall coming down on top of him, tumbling and crushing his hopes. As all this ran through Faye's mind, she realised she hadn't answered immediately, which only added more bricks to that wall. She knew she should say yes. She wanted to say yes. But in doing so, she'd be condemning Bertie to an even worse heartbreak if anything else happened to her.

Bertie blinked, still waiting for Faye to say something, but she was worried that she had lost the ability to speak.

'Thirty-seven,' Bertie said eventually.

'Eh?'

'I've heard your dad say how he and your mum

weren't married till they were thirty-seven years old. You and me, we're eighteen, so if you go and help Bellamy and Vera stop Hitler and do it before we're both thirty-seven, then I can wait if you can.' He brightened at his solution, the smile reaching his eyes.

Faye chuckled. 'You want to get married in ...' She half closed one eye as she did the sums. 'Nineteen sixty?'

'I like a nice round number.'

Faye's heart quickened, and she was reminded of just how much she loved being with this young man. She wanted him in her life.

'You're right,' she said, cupping his cheek. 'We don't need a dress or some vicar to prove we love each other. There's a better way.' She kissed him on the lips, gently at first, then deeper and more hungrily.

'Oh, yes, I like that way,' Bertie gasped.

'It doesn't stop there, Bertie.' Faye took off her specs and rested them on the oak log. She took Bertie by the hand and they lay among the bluebells. She began to unbutton her dungarees.

'Found them!' a voice cried. The effect it had on the couple was not dissimilar to a direct hit from a bolt of lightning, and they jolted upright in a blink. Faye reached for her specs and found the ghost of Petunia Parker looking down at them with the same mixture of disgust and confusion that a child exhibits when encountering frogspawn for the first time.

Miss Charlotte was right behind her, clad in muddy biking leathers. On her shoulder sat a budgerigar, which, combined with the scarlet-and-gold eyepatch, made her resemble a leather-clad Anne Bonny.

She sighed wearily. 'Honestly, you two, we're under attack from the most dangerous Druid who ever lived, and all you can think about is getting your end away.'

Faye and Bertie tried to protest, but all that came out were half-formed vowels.

Miss Charlotte waved them into silence. 'Save it. We have to defeat Otto,' she said, an enigmatic smile on her face, 'and I reckon I know how to do it.'

Faye felt a flicker of hope at Miss Charlotte's declaration, though she was distracted by Bertie, who glumly took an oatcake from a pocket and contemplated it as a poor consolation prize compared to a life of wedded bliss. As he opened his mouth to take a bite, Miss Charlotte snatched it from his hand.

'Perfect,' she said. 'We'll need one of these. Good thinking, Bertie.'

The lad's eyes widened as she tucked the oatcake into one of her own pockets.

'Get back to the others, Bertie,' Miss Charlotte commanded him. 'Don't let anyone leave. And reassure them that we'll have a plan very soon.'

'Will we?' Faye asked.

Miss Charlotte gave her a wink. 'We will. I think I've found a way to turn the tide in our favour, Faye.'

THE REACH OF THE WOOD

Miss Charlotte, Mrs Teach and Faye found a quiet nook and conjured a glamour around themselves in order to confer in peace. Petunia was exploring the woods, and the budgie, whom Faye had learned was called Harold, was stretching his wings. Faye felt a familiar warmth rising within her. Just the three of them in the wood reminded her of a simpler time when all they had to deal with were marauding scarecrows.

'I have news,' Miss Charlotte declared.

'You've defeated Otto and we can all go home?' Faye suggested. 'That sort of news?'

'No.'

'Worth a try.'

'If you're that desperate for a sliver of positivity, I did manage to vanquish one of Otto's undead minions,' Miss Charlotte reported, with the merest hint of a proud smile. 'A Kriegsmarine twice my size.'

'Well done, dear,' Mrs Teach said with sincere admiration. 'Now what's the *news* news?'

Miss Charlotte shifted on her feet and folded her arms. Faye instinctively knew that this was going to be bad.

'Otto Kopp is drawing on some of the most powerful magic I have ever seen,' Miss Charlotte began ominously. 'Necromancy, blood magic, demonology.'

'I didn't think any of that was allowed,' Faye said.

'He's a Nazi occultist, dear,' Mrs Teach said, fluttering her lashes. 'They're not exactly renowned for sticking to the rules.'

Faye bobbed her shoulder. 'Righto, but that's good news, surely?'

'What do you mean?'

'Doesn't power like that corrupt the user?'

'That's right.' Miss Charlotte nodded. 'Otto's body will decay as the magic takes its toll. If we wait long enough, then he'll destroy himself.'

'But that could take years, couldn't it?'

Mrs Teach pursed her lips. 'There's no telling without seeing him. It could be hours, months or, indeed, years.'

'We haven't got years. We've barely got hours.' Faye gestured back the way they had come. 'What we have got is a lot of very confused and frightened people who want to go home. We can't camp out here in the woods, twiddling our thumbs while he burns down our village. We have to take the fight to him.'

Mrs Teach brushed a sympathetic hand over her arm. 'Faye, darling, if Otto is using the kind of magic that I think he's using, then even our combined power could not stop him. I doubt even Vera could help us.'

Faye felt a tightness in her chest. She clenched her fists. 'I'm not waiting, I'm not hiding, and I refuse to run.' She glanced at the spots of blood on Miss Charlotte's biking leathers. 'That Kriegsmarine you came across – twice your size, you said?'

Miss Charlotte tilted her head. 'He was.'

'How did you stop him?'

Mrs Teach exhaled loudly. 'Facing Otto won't be the same as—'

'I know that,' Faye snapped, 'but I'm thinking out loud. If Miss Charlotte could take him on her own, then maybe—'

'Truth be told, I had some help,' Miss Charlotte interrupted. 'I was crossing one of Larry Dell's fields – the one where he grew barley last summer. The thing attacking me was dragged under by the barley and consumed by the earth.'

'Dragged under?' Faye narrowed her eyes.

'You doubt me?'

Faye raised her palms. 'No, it's just not something we've seen before. It's fascinating stuff, though we've all got enough on our plates without having to deal with deadly barley fields on top of everything else.'

'Larry's field was once part of the wood, wasn't it?' Miss Charlotte asked.

Mrs Teach nodded. 'All of his farm was. Most farms around here were until Henry the Eighth came along and chopped up the trees to build warships. Why?'

'I think we can assume the wood's reach extends beyond the current boundary, then,' Miss Charlotte

319

mused. 'I think the wood, in its own inimitable way, came to my aid.'

'You're saying the wood hates Nazis?' Faye perked up for a moment, excited at the prospect of a new ally. Then her shoulders dropped. 'No, hang on. Last summer, I was chased through the wood by Harry Aston when he was turned into a demonic dog by Otto.' She took a breath and briefly reflected on how strange her life had become in the past year or so. 'He was a card-carrying Nazi. The wood didn't do me any favours then, so why should it now?'

Mrs Teach looked around them with a sly smile. 'But what's changed since then, Faye? What happened at Christmas?'

'Sid!' Faye's eyes lit up. 'Bobby said the woodwose ripped the head off a Nazi that was about to do him in. Sid was at Dunkirk, so he's got more reason than most to hate the Nazis. *He's* on our side.'

Miss Charlotte shook her head. 'I'm not sure he thinks in those terms. But he is the guardian of the wood and wants only what is best for it, and, like all right-thinking folk, he knows that the Nazis are a very bad thing indeed.'

Faye turned in a circle, hoping in vain that she might spot Sid. 'We could ask him? With him on our side, and the wood, and all the villagers . . . That's a lot of power.'

Mrs Teach wasn't convinced. 'If you recall our last encounter with him, he's hardly the chatty type.'

'I think the best way to ensure his co-operation is to demonstrate our good intent,' Miss Charlotte said.

'The sun has yet to rise, but today is Beltane. We should observe the old rituals this May Day. We shall have a celebration. We'll choose a May Queen and King.'

'That would be you and Bertie,' Mrs Teach added as an aside.

Faye's head briefly went numb. 'W-what?'

'We may not have a church, Faye, but if you're May Queen and King, you can still be wed. We can do it here in the wood.'

'No,' Miss Charlotte objected. 'We'll do it properly. We'll make an oatcake. And we'll need blindfolds. A May Queen should be chosen in accordance with the ritual.'

'Er, yes …' Faye began, though her addled brain failed to provide any further words upon which to build an argument. 'What she said.'

'Is everything all tickety-boo, Faye?' Mrs Teach tilted her head. 'You do still wish to marry Bertie, don't you?'

Faye's shoulders stiffened and she flexed her fingers.

'Oh dear,' Miss Charlotte said in a flat tone accompanied by a heavy and unsurprised eyelid. 'What went wrong?'

'Nothing went wrong,' Faye blurted. 'Bertie and I just had this long chat about how we were going to wait till after the war. It was painful and heartbreaking. There were tears and everything.'

'You didn't look very sad to me,' Miss Charlotte recalled. 'If anything, you were getting ahead of yourselves and about to consummate the marriage.'

'Faye Bright!' Mrs Teach gasped in shock.

'We were making up!' Faye protested.

'I'll say. You'll find no condemnation from me, Faye.'
Miss Charlotte winked her one good eye. 'Good luck
to you.'

Faye's specs were misting at the edges and her cheeks
burned. 'But this *isn't* a wedding, right? It's Beltane.'

'Correct,' Miss Charlotte replied. 'One with all the
Beltane trimmings. And one in which all the villagers here
will have a role to play. We need a May Queen and King.'

'And Nine Worthies to join them.' Mrs Teach bobbed
up and down in excitement. 'A parade led by the
Morris Men.'

'Ugh.' Faye pulled a face. 'Really?'

'They are essential for this to work,' Miss
Charlotte said.

'A Beltane celebration will bring the villagers together,' Mrs Teach said. 'And we will honour the wood
with the blessing of love, and become stronger and
closer to it.'

Miss Charlotte spread her arms wide. 'We make sure
Otto knows all about it. He is lured into the wood, and
our friend the woodwose does the rest.'

'Splendid plan,' Mrs Teach agreed.

'You make it sound so easy,' Faye said.

'Oh no, it'll be gruelling and dangerous and not
without pain and sacrifice, but it's the only hope we
have.' Miss Charlotte whipped out the oatcake she
had taken from Bertie. 'Right. Let's start with a little
nibble, shall we?'

Petunia appeared before them, pointing back to the
clearing. 'The villagers,' she said. 'They're leaving.'

ENDURING TRADITION

Faye hurried after Petunia and Harold the budgie – one floating, the other flying – back to the clearing with the hollow oak. It was the dead of night, but few were sleeping. Most of the villagers were huddled in disgruntled little cliques as they gathered their things together.

Mr Loaf already had his fiddle case tucked under his arm and was making for the village when Faye and Petunia arrived.

'Please stay!' Bertie was pleading with the village undertaker, but Mr Loaf simply stepped around him.

'I'm sorry, Bertie, but I've had enough of lurking about in the damp and dank woods. I'm off to Ramsgate. Goodbye.'

'Mr Loaf!' Bertie called after him, shuffling about as the others gathered their possessions, too.

'Let him go, Bertie,' Mrs Teach said as Mr Loaf scurried away, soon lost in the gloom of the wood. She clasped her hands together and stepped into the centre of the clearing. 'Good people of Woodville, if I might have your attention for a moment.'

There were few who would defy Mrs Teach at the best of times, but to see her flanked by Faye and Miss Charlotte was to encounter a triptych they didn't dare ignore. Some later whispered that they had seen the ghost of a girl by their sides, and a few had to be convinced that the budgie sitting on Miss Charlotte's shoulder was real.

Faye noted that the fire in the clearing had gone out. Her father and Doris were staring at the cooling embers with unblinking eyes. Bertie slumped down next to them.

'It will be some time before the sun rises, but today is May Day,' Mrs Teach began, raising her hands to the sky. 'We will greet the dawn with our celebrations for Beltane.'

'What have we got to celebrate?' Edith Palmer asked, her voice quiet as she cradled Reverend Jacobs' head in her lap. 'We've lost everything.'

'You said you were making plans.' Captain Marshall got to his feet, joined by Mr Baxter and Mr Hodgson. 'Is this it? Some sort of party?'

'Not just any party,' Miss Charlotte said, Harold fluttering from one of her shoulders to the other. 'A ceremony in which the Morris Men of Woodville shall play a crucial role.'

'Will we indeed?' Captain Marshall raised his chin. He may have been defeated in combat, but with his Morris Men he was still very much in command. 'And what if we refuse to join in with your little shindig? These people are in no mood for frivolity. Where will they sleep tomorrow night? What can be done about the enemy in the village?'

'Tell me, Captain Marshall,' Mrs Teach said, smiling sweetly, 'why do you perform these dances every year?'

Captain Marshall straightened his back. 'It's an enduring tradition.'

'Indeed, but what inspired that tradition in the first place?' Mrs Teach persisted. 'What are the roots of your dance?'

Captain Marshall and Mr Baxter all but fell over one another like eager schoolboys to be first to answer.

'Morris dancing dates back to the Moors of Morocco. They wore bells on their legs as they danced,' Captain Marshall declared. 'And that's why we blacken our faces.'

'Wrong,' Miss Charlotte said with a snort.

'Well, let's call that an interesting theory, shall we?' Mrs Teach added in a more conciliatory tone.

Mr Baxter raised a finger. 'Actually, I heard it was because the Morris Men got up to such terrible mischief, like stealing deer, that they disguised themselves with painted faces to evade arrest and—'

'Wrong again,' Miss Charlotte said, exhaling wearily.

Mr Baxter lowered his finger and Mr Hodgson stepped forwards in his summer frock with an eager grin. 'I thought it all came from the Latin. "Moris" means "custom", so—'

'Mr Aitch, since when were you a Morris Man and

not a bell-ringer?' Disappointment tugged at Faye's heart. The tower captain consorting with Morris Men didn't sit well with her.

Mr Hodgson flexed his lips and shrugged, palms up. 'Can't I be both?'

Faye hummed in reply. 'You just like joining in, don't you, Mr Aitch?'

He smiled and glanced at Captain Marshall, who nodded. 'And it's an enduring tradition,' Mr Hodgson said.

'Fair enough.' Faye sighed, then addressed all the Morris Men. 'So, let me get this straight. You do all these dances, practising every spare minute to get them right, performing them every year without fail, yet none of you can agree on why you do it?'

'Well . . .' Captain Marshall glanced at his colleagues. 'It's—'

'If any of you use the words "enduring" or "tradition" again, I shall be very cross.'

Mr Baxter folded his arms and considered. 'We do it for the company . . . the cider . . .' This got approving murmurs from the other Morris Men, who gathered behind him. Bobby Newton with his hoodening horse. Henry Mogg, whom Faye had once kicked in the shins at school. Cecil Sutton, who had tried to kiss her when they were ten. Come to think of it, she might have kicked him in the shins, too.

'And because we like it,' Mr Baxter concluded.

'That's a good enough reason to do anything, I suppose,' Faye said, turning to Mrs Teach and Miss

Charlotte. 'But I suspect you need to dig a little deeper.'

'Indeed,' Mrs Teach agreed, gesturing to their black rag coats and bowler hats. 'I'm fascinated by the change of costume.'

Miss Charlotte stepped forwards, plucking Mr Baxter's bowler from his head and inspecting its feathers and ribbons. 'Yes, it's a definite improvement on the usual straw hats and hankies.'

Captain Marshall self-consciously adjusted his own bowler. 'We thought we'd perform the Border Morris today. It's a more . . .' He pursed his lips and searched for the right word. ' . . .*primitive* style, with the sticks striking.'

'And we growl and shout,' Mr Baxter said as Miss Charlotte popped his bowler back onto his head. 'And we run at each other and slam our chests together.'

'And we got a bit fed up with the hankies,' Bobby said.

Faye smiled. 'So much for enduring tradition.'

'At the risk of sounding a bit . . . odd,' Mr Baxter began.

'Dressed as you are, I think you're entitled to be as odd as you like.' Faye gave him a wink.

'Once we started the Border Morris . . .' Mr Baxter's eyes edged to his companions as if he was preparing to reveal a shameful secret. 'There was something about it that just felt . . . right.'

This was greeted with nods of jangling agreement from the other Morris Men.

'Now we're getting somewhere,' Mrs Teach said.

'In truth, no one really knows why the Morris Men dance. Only that they must,' Miss Charlotte said. 'That feeling you experience when dancing is one that has been felt by humanity since the dance began. Before the deer thieves, before the Moors, before any stories that you have been told. It doesn't matter what you wear, and as for painting your faces ... Well, we'll come to that in a minute. But you can take it from me that you will play a pivotal role in a ritual that will banish evil from the village. So, I ask you again: will you join us?'

Captain Marshall gaped and turned to his company. Bobby was the first to raise his stick. The others followed suit, and they came together with an almighty *clack*.

Footsteps sounded from behind them, and Faye spun on her heel to find Mr Loaf arriving from the opposite direction in which he'd set off, his fiddle case still tucked under his arm. He flared his nostrils in befuddlement.

'I could have sworn ...' He looked behind him. 'I thought I'd ... Which way ...? Oh ...'

'Mr Loaf, welcome back.' Mrs Teach steered him towards his fellow Morris Men. 'You're just in time. Captain Marshall has just vowed to join our Beltane celebrations. We'll need your fiddle.'

'D-did I?' Captain Marshall asked.

'Yes, you did,' Mrs Teach confirmed. 'It's an enduring tradition.'

'That's all settled, then,' Miss Charlotte declared, taking out Bertie's oatcake and holding it at arm's length. 'Now we must choose a May Queen.'

Blood Magic

Otto's ruddy skin was blistered and scabbed. Red-raw and tender to the touch, it was only marginally less painful than the scalding sensation in his veins. He lay on his back, staring at the ceiling of the Green Man pub's dingy cellar. He had needed darkness and solitude, and he had been certain of getting both in the depths of this burned-out drinking hole.

That was the trouble with this dark magic. Oh, it gifted the most extraordinary power – what Otto had achieved in the last few days hadn't been attempted in centuries – but the practitioner paid a heavy toll. He ached to the marrow in his bones. It was consuming him from within. He had known this from the start, and it was a price he was willing to pay, but he needed more time if he was to deliver his final humiliation to Faye Bright.

Time, and blood. But that available to him was stale and weak. The villagers had all fled and the pickings were slim. Otto reached across the aether to summon the Kriegsmarine, but his light was gone, as was Mrs Wallace's. No great loss. Fortunately, Otto still had two of his undead helpers at hand. The Luftwaffe gunner and pilot had served their purpose and were spent forces. The pilot had been beheaded. Again. And the gunner was riddled with bullets, had holes in his palms and could barely stand. Otto had brought them down into the pub's cellar, where he'd had them hang ropes over the timbers in the ceiling. Then he'd snuffed out their lives. With great physical effort, he'd attached the ropes to their ankles, hoisted them into the air, made deep cuts in their arteries with a knife he'd found in the kitchen and drained them of what little blood remained in their bodies. The blood ritual was arduous and had taken hours. It should have replenished Otto's strength, but the contents of the pair's veins were curdled like milk left in the sun, and weak as American beer.

Time had passed slowly in the cellar as Otto recovered. Some of his strength had returned, but even sitting up required much gasping and trembling. He reminded himself that he was in the sanctuary of a powerful witch. There had to be something within these walls that would aid his recovery.

Stumbling, Otto emerged from the cellar hatch into the remains of the saloon bar. The crashed Rolls-Royce had destroyed much of the pub's facade and the subsequent fire had caused considerable damage, but thanks to the rain and the skills of its fourteenth-century builders, the pub remained remarkably intact.

He staggered into the hall behind the bar, then up the stairs. Faye's bedroom was a sparse affair. A small single bed, a wardrobe with few clothes, a shelf of tawdry fiction by the likes of Agatha Christie and Dashiell Hammett. No grimoires, no spell or ritual books, no scrying mirrors, vials of blood, knives or magical tools of any kind. How could this waif of a girl even call herself a witch?

Otto noticed a framed photograph on the bedside cabinet. He assumed it had to be Faye's parents. Otto had never met Kathryn Wynter – why would he have? After all, she had been merely an insignificant village witch, little more than a midwife – but somehow this woman of no importance had birthed a freakishly powerful practitioner of magic who had thwarted Otto's most ambitious plans. It was a mystery, to be sure. Faye Bright should have followed her mother's example of curing minor ailments, practising midwifery and living a bland and quiet life with her limping lover. But the foolish girl had to intervene and cause trouble. Otto knew her type. It was in her nature. In a way, he thanked her for it. The challenges she provided him only strengthened his resolve. He made a mental note to express his gratitude in the moments before he took her life.

He looked around the pathetic little room once more. There was nothing in here that could help his return to strength. He would need fresh blood. Perhaps he could lure some of the villagers from the wood. The girl's father or her lover, perhaps? Anyone would do, but to hurt Faye would only add to the vigour of his recovery. Her compassion was her weakness.

Dogs barked in the pre-dawn gloom outside. For a moment, Otto wondered if their blood might be enough to speed his recuperation, but as the barking intensified, he realised that he was not alone in the village. He peered out of Faye's bedroom window. Approaching from opposite ends of the Wode Road were two figures in ridiculous crimson robes.

Druids of the Black Sun.

Now this was surprising. Otto had known that his magical activity would create ripples on the aether that might draw attention from those who knew to observe, but he had never expected this extraordinary move.

Then he recalled Gunther's final words after the slaughter on the Focke-Wulf. How the Black Sun would find him, no matter what.

Hitler was far from convinced by the Black Sun. For all their pomp and swagger, they had proven to be notoriously unreliable and slapdash. Otto had been tasked with knocking them into shape, but the organisation was fragmented into pathetic little cliques and infighting was rife. They were more interested in getting one up on each other than obeying orders, and so Hitler used them sparingly. And yet this pair stalked the cobbled streets of Woodville. None of the Black Sun could fly like Otto, so they must have either been parachuted in or come by sea. He saw that each carried a knife. So, they weren't here to take him back to Hohenzollern Castle. They meant to kill him. The Führer had revoked his stay of execution.

Otto's bones ached, his arteries pulsed agonisingly, his head throbbed and he was so very tired. He couldn't defeat these two in a face-to-face confrontation. But he had been in worse situations than this in the past. He was a survivor. He was patient.

The Black Sun's ranks were riddled with fervent Nazis. Despite Hitler's low opinion of them, they hung on his every utterance. True believers in the cause. In other words, morons. Most came from wealthy families and had grown up rich, spoiled and lazy. They were often bored in their youth and dabbled in the dark arts until it got them into trouble. A few blackmail threats and soon they were acolytes of the Black Sun, convinced it was their true calling when, in fact, they were little more than magical cannon fodder. Lambs to the slaughter. And Otto was very much in need of their slaughter.

He took a hand mirror from Faye's bedside cabinet before moving stealthily downstairs to the pub's kitchen, where he snatched up a candle and some matches. Then he hurried as fast as his aching bones would carry him back down into the cellar. He needed to lose himself in the darkness and silence. He sat on the dusty floorboards and lit the candle, placing it at his feet. Then he smashed the mirror, selecting a pair of triangular shards and holding them over the flame, reciting a Mayan curse until the heat burned the tips of his fingers. Then he lay back and placed the shards over his eyes, the mirrored glass facing him.

In his mind's eye, Otto could see the village. He was moving freely around it. Without some kind of token from his would-be assassins, Otto could not speak with them via mirrors and glass, but he didn't need to. To begin with, he recalled the terrified faces of the villagers as they fled his inferno. Otto projected those faces onto the shards of glass littered across the village.

The Black Sun assassins spun on their heels as they caught glimpses of anguished faces in splintered shop windows and the shattered glass of houses up and down the Wode Road.

The barking of the unseen dogs intensified as Otto now projected the faces of the Kriegsmarine, the pilot and the gunner onto the glass. Now he could hear the Black Sun assassins running after these phantoms. Otto chuckled to himself in the pub cellar as he saw them dart in and out of buildings, chasing shadows and finding nothing. They began accusing one another of stupidity, and there was much shoving and more threats in German.

Otto smiled. This was almost too easy. Time to reel them in. The pair had reconvened outside the pub, so Otto projected his face onto the mirror behind the bar. It took them a while to notice. One jabbed the other in the ribs, then pointed as Otto's face ducked out of sight.

They ran into the pub, puzzling at the Rolls-Royce parked where a wall, windows and door used to be, then stopped, drawing their black-bladed knives. The taller one led the way, moving into the hall, then up the stairs. The shorter one explored the kitchen, then returned to the bar, only then noticing the hatch to the cellar behind it.

It was as the taller one returned from upstairs that Otto used the very last of his power to conjure a glamour so that both men saw each other as him. They cried out, clashing in a frenzy of stabbing blades. In moments, they lay bleeding out on the floor of the Green Man.

Otto crawled from the cellar, a sick grin on his face as he took their knives.

'Thank you, gentlemen,' he said, his voice a frail whisper. 'Let's not waste any blood, hmm? I need every drop.'

He took a deep breath before taking the first assassin by the ankles and dragging him into the cellar where the ropes and Otto's own knife waited for him.

'Yes, Black Sun blood,' he muttered with relish. 'Very rich, very strong. Once I'm done with you, I'll be more powerful than ever.'

The May Queen

Bertie shadowed the witches through the wood. He was cautious, of course, and he knew enough of glamours and the wood to understand that he couldn't wholly rely on his eyes. But there was no mistaking the imprints left by Miss Charlotte's motorcycle boots in the wet soil.

Bertie's stride could look ungainly at times, but in this wood he moved as silently as the mist. Rabbit hunting with his father as a young boy had taught him stealth, stillness and patience.

Sadly, Bertie could not say the same for his mind. Terrible thoughts clamoured for his attention, creating a racket of anxiety that drove the lad to distraction. Out of the corner of his eye, he caught a flicker of a bird on the wing. He paused, hunkered down and waited.

Nothing. It was nothing. He was on the move again.

Bertie knew all about Beltane from his Granny Joan. She had told him how she had been crowned May Queen in Woodville when she was a girl, but some busybody in the church had called the Beltane celebrations 'a heathen thing' and had them banned until the end of the Great War. Granny Joan being Granny Joan, she had wanted to know more, and she had later taken great delight in terrifying young Bertie with stories of May Queens being sacrificed to Baal, or Beil, or Belenos or something. Bertie didn't recall all the details, but he knew for certain that this was no silly village parade. It was a real ritual that, if recent experience was anything to go by, would have dark, terrifying and bloody consequences. Most of all, he knew that he couldn't let Faye face death again. Not after all she had been through. Besides, they had a wedding planned for the summer of 1960.

Distant voices tickled Bertie's keen ears. He had found the witches. They had left the wood and were standing in a fallow field by a hawthorn tree. The tree was in blossom, boasting countless white flowers, as if an artist had whipped their paintbrush across its branches.

Bertie remained crouched behind a hedgerow that ran along the border of the field. He watched as Miss Charlotte took his oatcake from her biking jacket and held it high. She spoke a few words to the rising sun, but Bertie was too far away to hear what she was saying. He moved crab-like behind the hedgerow until he came to a gap.

Miss Charlotte had stopped talking. She carefully broke the oatcake into thirds.

Mrs Teach took a small black velvet pouch from her

handbag. Carefully untying it, she tipped it over and shook ash onto one of the sections of oatcake. Bertie had seen her collecting the ash from the fire in the clearing with the hollow oak. That's when he'd known they were up to something and decided to track them.

Each witch took a piece of oatcake and placed it around the hawthorn tree, like three points of a compass.

Granny Joan had told Bertie about this tradition, too. They were going to dance, and when they stopped, whoever was closest to the oatcake covered in ash would be crowned the May Queen.

All three covered their eyes with scarves provided by Mrs Teach from her seemingly bottomless handbag. Once the scarves were tied in place, they clapped their hands in a steady rhythm. As they stood and clapped, the air around them shifted and a kind of heat haze rose from the ground. It blended and bent the first rays of daylight. Bertie blinked to find the ghostly school-children dancing in a circle around the hawthorn tree. Three boys and three girls in school uniforms. He couldn't be sure, but their faces and hands looked less burned and bloody than when he had seen them the other night. They began to sing, and the three witches danced with them around the tree.

> 'You must wake and call me early, call me
>   early, mother dear,
> To-morrow'll be the happiest time of all the
>   glad new-year,

Of all the glad new-year, mother, the mad-
    dest, merriest day;
For I'm to be Queen o' the May, mother,
    I'm to be Queen o' the May.'

Granny Joan had read that poem to Bertie every May Day. It was by Tennyson, though Bertie much preferred his 'Charge of the Light Brigade'.

Bertie had never seen Faye or the witches dance like this before. They were carefree as they skipped and spun. Mrs Teach's handbag whirled away. Miss Charlotte's white hair caught the light of the rising sun, and Faye wore a blissful smile as she turned, turned, turned.

'I sleep so sound all night, mother, that I
    shall never wake,
If you do not call me loud when the day
    begins to break;
But I must gather knots of flowers and
    buds, and garlands gay;
For I'm to be Queen o' the May, mother,
    I'm to be Queen o' the May.'

From his vantage point in the hedgerow, Bertie tried to recall how many verses this poem had and how long he would need to do what must be done. Five. There were five verses, he was sure of it.

'Little Effie shall go with me to-morrow to
 the green,
And you'll be there, too, mother, to see me
 made the Queen;
For the shepherd lads on every side'll come
 from far away;
And I'm to be Queen o' the May, mother,
 I'm to be Queen o' the May.'

Now Bertie was second-guessing himself. If he moved
the oatcake with the ash, there was a chance that he
would put it in the wrong place and be the cause of Faye
becoming May Queen. He thought about removing
the piece entirely, but then he would incur the wrath
of the witches, and he definitely did not want that.
Terrence's advice to not interfere with witchy stuff
echoed in Bertie's mind. But Bertie could not let Faye
be sacrificed.

'The night-winds come and go, mother,
 upon the meadow-grass,
And the happy stars above them seem to
 brighten as they pass;
There will not be a drop of rain the whole
 of the livelong day;
And I'm to be Queen o' the May, mother,
 I'm to be Queen o' the May.'

Determined, Bertie held his breath as he rose from
his crouch and stepped out from the protection of the

hedgerow. The ghostly children took no notice of him as he silently slipped between Mrs Teach and Miss Charlotte as they danced. He had to time this perfectly. This was the final verse.

> 'All the valley, mother'll be fresh and green
>   and still,
> And the cowslip and the crowfoot are over
>   all the hill,
> And the rivulet in the flowery dale'll mer-
>   rily glance and play,
> For I'm to be Queen o' the May, mother,
>   I'm to be Queen o' the May.'

The singing ended, the dancers stopped. And, wouldn't you know it, Faye's feet were pointed at the piece of oatcake covered in ash. Like a card sharp in a Western, Bertie switched it with the one closest to Miss Charlotte. Now all he had to do was limp back to the hedgerow before—

'Bertie Butterworth!' Mrs Teach spotted him first.

Miss Charlotte glared at him. 'What are you doing, boy?'

Faye shook her head. 'Oh, Bertie, no.'

Bertie took a step back, passing through one of the ghostly schoolchildren – the girl with the mousy hair in a ponytail – and shivering. He was still deciding if he should apologise, confess or give a defiant speech when Faye turned her ire on him.

'You switched the oatcakes, Bertie! Why?'

Bertie raised a finger. 'Yes, but I have a perfectly good reason.'

'He's not fibbing.' Petunia floated into sight to join the other ghostly children. 'But his aura has changed in a way that suggests he's hiding something.'

'No, no, I'm not, but—'

Harold the budgie whizzed by in a familiar flash of blue and green and landed on Miss Charlotte's shoulder, whispering in her ear.

'He's been following us through the wood,' she repeated.

'That's rather sneaky, Bertie,' Mrs Teach said as she clasped her handbag in front of her. 'I would have thought better of you.'

Bertie raised his palms. 'Yes, I've been sneaky and followed you, and yes, I switched the oatcake, but that's because I know how this ends,' he said, with more defiance than he'd been expecting. 'The May Queen is sacrificed to Baal, or Belenos, or someone, and ... and I won't let it happen to you, Faye. I don't want you to die.'

'You placed the oatcake at my feet.' Miss Charlotte's chill voice made Bertie's shoulders tense. 'You're perfectly happy for me to perish, I see.'

'You're different,' Bertie said, flapping a hand up and down at her. 'You're going to live for ever, clearly.'

'I bloody hope not,' Miss Charlotte muttered.

'Hasn't Faye given enough? She ...' The words caught in Bertie's throat. 'She's not some corn dolly. She's real, and she can't come back and—'

Faye drew him into an embrace, whispering into his ear. 'Can't I?'

'What?'

'You've just given me an idea, Bertie Butterworth.' She pulled back, holding him at arm's length. She smiled, a cunning glint in her eyes. 'I know what needs to be done. I've been having these visions. The village on fire, me waking up all covered in dirt, that hawthorn tree there . . .'

She gestured to the nearby tree. Bertie's mind whirled. This was making less and less sense with each word Faye uttered.

'And the Corn Bride wearing my mother's wedding dress.'

'Your mother's dress?' Bertie frowned. 'How can you be sure it's hers?'

'I can't,' Faye said, glancing at Mrs Teach. 'But I have a feeling. Mum can't speak to me the way Petunia does. I think she sent these children to find me. She gave the Corn Bride her dress. It all makes sense to me now. I know what I must do, Bertie.'

Bertie felt dizzy and there were spots on the edge of his vision. 'What?' he asked, knowing perfectly well that he wouldn't like the answer. 'What must you do?'

Faye broke away from him and snatched up the slice of oatcake covered in ash. She broke it in two. 'I'm to be Queen o' the May.'

The white flowers of the hawthorn tree silently glowed a dazzling white. A ripple of the air and the

Corn Bride was with them, standing before the tree with her head tipped to one side. She raised her straw hand and pointed at Faye.

'No!' Bertie lunged forwards, but Miss Charlotte grabbed him by the collar and pulled him into a tight hold.

Bertie watched helplessly as myriad white petals fluttered from the hawthorn tree. As they turned in the air, they burned like golden embers, swirling around Faye until their light became so bright that he had to shut his eyes tight.

A sudden warmth brushed his cheeks, his ears popped and a smell that reminded him of summer bonfires tickled his nostrils.

Miss Charlotte released her hold on him and he opened his eyes.

The Corn Bride was gone. All that remained of her was a pile of straw by the roots of the hawthorn tree.

Faye was wearing the Corn Bride's ivory wedding dress.

'Oh no,' Bertie whimpered.

Faye enjoyed a brief moment of astonishment at finding herself in a wedding dress complete with a crown of summer flowers. 'It's beautiful,' she murmured. Then she clapped her hands.

'Everyone gather up the straw from the Corn Bride!' she said, and Bertie and the witches did as their queen commanded. 'Don't miss a single sliver.'

As they did so, the ghostly children sang:

'Here we go gathering nuts in May,
Nuts in May, nuts in May,
Here we go gathering nuts in May,
On a cold and frosty morning.'

Bertie stood, embracing an armful of straw stems. 'We need a sack or a—'

'In here, Bertie,' Mrs Teach said, offering the black velvet pouch she had carried the ash in. It somehow expanded to accommodate all the straw. In just a few minutes, the remains of the Corn Bride had been stuffed into the velvet bag.

'I need you to keep that safe, Bertie,' Faye told him. 'Don't let it out of your sight.'

'I will, but . . . why?'

Faye hesitated before raising herself up. 'Your Queen commands it.'

Bertie shook his head. 'Not good enough, Your Majesty. I'll need more than that.' He turned to Petunia. 'Is she lying? What's she really thinking?'

'I'm not a mind reader,' Petunia protested, 'but she's certainly holding something back.'

'Indeed,' Mrs Teach agreed. 'Come on, young lady, what are you up to?'

Faye raised her palms. 'I've got a plan, but if I tell you, you'll all think I'm barmy.'

'That ship left port a long time ago,' Miss Charlotte said.

Faye clenched her hands into fists and growled, the tendons in her neck springing taut. 'Can't I ask you lot to just trust me for once? Please? I know what to do. I know how to beat Otto. But if I tell you now, I'm pretty sure none of you lot will let me do it, and we'll all be back where we started, and then he wins.'

Bertie stepped forward. 'But I don't want you to die.'

'Bertie, my love.' Faye took his hands and they stood together, face to face, Faye in her wedding gown, Bertie suddenly feeling very underdressed. 'I have no intention of dying today.'

'What's this?' The tips of Bertie's fingers brushed against something hard at the bottom of Faye's fourth finger on her left hand. He glanced down and the light caught the glint of gold.

'Oh.' Faye slipped her hand from his and turned it over, gazing open-mouthed at the gold band on her wedding finger. She was as surprised to see it as Bertie was. 'It was my mum's. Dad said I could have it, and I kept in a pocket of my dungarees. I'd completely forgotten it was there. It must have found my ring finger when I changed.'

Bertie's heart thumped and his mind scrambled to tell her that he had a ring, too, but as if Faye could sense he was going to blurt it out, she took his hands in hers and gently squeezed.

'I am the May Queen,' she said, drawing him closer, 'and I choose you for my May King. You can protect me. How does that sound?'

Bertie's cheeks warmed. His wedding ring felt heavy in his pocket, and he tried not to think of the eyes of the other witches and ghosts staring at him. 'Sounds . . . a bit like a wedding.'

347

Faye straightened her back. 'Hmm. Does it? Well, don't be getting any ideas, Bertie Butterworth.' She kissed him on the cheek. 'We will have a wedding one day, and we'll do it all properly. Just not today.' She released his hands, pushed her specs up her nose and turned to Mrs Teach and Miss Charlotte. 'We're ready. What's next?'

Bertie reeled, as though he had just stepped off one of the more dizzying attractions at Margate's Dreamland.

'We have our May Queen and King,' Mrs Teach began.

Miss Charlotte smiled at the pair of them, though Bertie felt like it was the kind of smile that sheep got from the farmer just before they were taken to the slaughterhouse. 'We just need our Nine Worthies,' she finished.

THE NINE WORTHIES

Miss Charlotte led the way back to the hollow oak, Mrs Teach one step behind her. Faye walked hand in hand with Bertie, hitching up her wedding dress as they stepped through the morning dew. She was in no hurry. She knew what was coming and she wanted these moments to last for as long as possible.

Bertie had fashioned the velvet bag containing the Corn Bride's straw into a knapsack. He'd attached it to a stick that he rested on his shoulder, giving him the cheery disposition of a young Dick Whittington.

'You two,' Miss Charlotte snapped. 'Keep up. We don't have long.'

Faye gently squeezed Bertie's hand and they picked up the pace.

Mrs Teach glanced around. 'Where's Petunia?'

'I sent her ahead to recce the village,' Miss Charlotte said. 'She and Harold will report back before we set off.'

'Harold's the budgie?' Bertie asked.

'He is, and before you ask: yes, I can hear his voice, and no, I don't know how or why.' Miss Charlotte ducked under the branch of a rowan tree, heavy with red berries. 'I find it best not to question these things.'

'Fair enough.' Bertie chuckled. 'It says something that Miss Charlotte hearing a budgie's voice in her head isn't the strangest thing I've come across today.'

'The day is young, Bertie.' Faye nodded ahead. 'What about this lot?'

They arrived at the hollow oak, where the villagers were taking turns to leap over the flames of a fire in the centre of the clearing. It was an old Beltane ritual. One that had been followed for laughs in May Day celebrations in the past, but which was now being performed with a new and serious resolve.

Mrs Pritchett was up next. She might have been the second-oldest woman in Woodville after Miss Charlotte, but she was fearless as she bunched up her skirts and hopped over the flames.

'Excellent.' Miss Charlotte turned to Terrence. 'Is that everyone?'

He nodded. 'We've all had a few goes, just to be sure.'

'Splendid. Mrs Teach, bring forth the ash.'

Mrs Teach stood before the hollow oak. 'Form a line, come along, spit-spot,' she commanded, before pointing at Captain Marshall. 'You first, Captain.'

The captain, like all the villagers, was exhausted to the point where he no longer questioned what the witches requested of him, no matter how strange. Faye reflected that this was exactly how Miss Charlotte and Mrs Teach preferred it.

'Close your eyes, please,' Mrs Teach ordered him, and he did as he was told. She bent to scoop a palmful of ash from the fire. It should have burned, but she whispered something to the ashes and they cooled to the grey of rain clouds. She smeared them across the captain's eyes and the bridge of his nose.

Faye stifled a laugh. She couldn't decide if the dark stripe across his face gave him the look of a seasoned warrior or a slightly startled badger.

'If you get any in your eyes, just blink it away. Do not wash it off,' Mrs Teach told him as she steered him to one side. 'Next!'

One by one, the villagers had their faces daubed with the ashes as Miss Charlotte paced around the fire in her tan biking leathers. 'You might be asking: why the ash on our faces? A not unreasonable question. It's something we've often done in the past on May Day. All part of the jolly japes, along with the dancing and singing and cider.'

Despite the early hour, this got some approving murmurs and licking of lips from the assembled villagers.

'Earlier our Morris Men were talking of painting their faces, and they spoke of Moors and disguises. You're welcome to believe that if you wish, gentlemen, but I can tell you that painting your face with ash from a Beltane fire will give you something much more potent.' Miss Charlotte waited until she knew she had the ear of everyone in the clearing. 'Protection,' she continued, clasping her hands behind her back. 'Today, we face an old enemy. We will return home, and we are bringing the May Queen with us.' She gestured to Faye, who bobbed a little curtsey. 'She can reclaim Woodville for us, but she cannot do it alone.'

A few villagers, not least Faye's father, were staring at her new wedding dress and wondering just where she had got it from, but they were all too baffled to ask.

'Our May Queen has chosen her May King.' Miss Charlotte extended a hand to Bertie, who dipped his head in an uncertain nod. 'And now she needs her Nine Worthies.' She left a little gap for a reaction. What she received were blank faces.

'It's not something we've ever done, dear,' Mrs Teach informed her as she brushed ash onto Mr Hodgson's face. A few particles landed on his frock. 'Not in living memory, at least.' Mrs Teach cleared her throat and raised her voice to address the villagers. 'The Nine Worthies represent chivalry and honour and must protect the May Queen on her journey home. Faye, darling, it is up to you to choose. Now, it used to be that you had to include three good pagans, three Christians and three Jews, but I suspect that you'll struggle to find such an eclectic mix in our little village, so take free rein as you select your Worthies. Oh, but you can't have Bertie. He's already May King.'

'Righto,' Faye said, pressing a finger to her chin.

'Oh, and you can't have either myself or Miss Charlotte.' Mrs Teach smiled. 'We shall be otherwise occupied.'

'Anyone else I can't have?'

'The Morris Men,' Miss Charlotte added. 'They'll be busy.'

'Oh yes,' Mrs Teach agreed. 'I think that's it.'

'How long do I have to think about it?'

Miss Charlotte looked up through the canopy where the branches swirled in the morning breeze against a brightening sky. 'Sun's up,' she said. 'You've got until all the villagers have ash on their faces, so . . .'

'Twenty minutes?' Mrs Teach suggested.

'Good. Bertie, you're with me.' Faye grabbed the lad by the crook of the elbow, leading him into the wood and out of sight of the clearing.

'W-where are we going?' he asked as he struggled to keep up with her, gripping his knapsack of Corn Bride straw. 'You have to choose the Nine Worthies, so—'

'I know exactly who I'm choosing,' Faye said, spinning Bertie around and taking both of his hands. 'I think I do, anyway. But I wanted some time alone with you.'

'Oh.' Bertie's cheeks were doing that thing where all his individual freckles blushed into one big freckle. 'What for?'

Faye took a breath as she wondered where to begin. 'Whatever happens next, Bertie, I'll be going away for some time. Most likely back to my training, or maybe even on a mission, but I won't be back for God knows how long.'

'I know. That's why you didn't want a wedding.'

'That's why I don't want a wedding *yet*, Bertie.

We will get married. But since I put this dress on, I thought—'

'I've got my ring!' Bertie blurted, rummaging in his pocket. 'I meant to tell you earlier, but the other witches were there and I wasn't sure if it would be bad luck or just foolish to show it, but ... look.'

Faye gasped as he rested it in his palm. 'Oh, Bertie, that's beautiful. Where did you get that?'

'My dad made it for me.' Bertie's smile lit up his face, and Faye had an overwhelming urge to kiss him.

So she did, clasping her hands on his cheeks and pressing hard. When she pulled away, her glasses were steamy.

'It's made of Spitfires,' Bertie said in a whisper, when he got his breath back.

Faye slipped the ring onto Bertie's finger. 'This is my promise to you, Bertie Butterworth. I shall always love you. I shall always be true to you. Even though the Official Secrets Act means there'll be some things I can't share, but, y'know ...'

Bertie, grinning like a loon, nodded.

'Bertie, as far as I'm concerned, we are married.'

'I love you, Faye Bright.'

'And I love you, too, Bertie Butterworth.'

Faye and Bertie spent the remainder of their allotted twenty minutes in that isolated spot in the wood. Faye decided to tell him her plan, as barmy as it sounded, because she trusted him more than anyone. What else happened there is between them, the wood and a rather startled nuthatch.

℘

They returned to the clearing on time, their faces flushed and their hair unkempt. Bertie's eyes were like saucers. He gripped his knapsack stick with white knuckles.

Terrence frowned. Miss Charlotte smirked.

Mrs Teach narrowed her eyes at them. 'What have you two been up—'

'I have chosen the Nine Worthies!' Faye announced at the top of her voice, ceasing all other conversations, especially those about what she and Bertie might have been doing in the woods. 'It was a long and—' She glanced at Bertie '—exhausting deliberation.'

Bertie's cheeks reddened. His eyes remained in their widened configuration.

'To begin with, I choose my father, Terrence Bright. There's no man who has protected me for longer, or better.'

Terrence gave her a wink.

'And it's only right that he's joined by Doris Finch, who, along with my father, will reclaim the Green Man pub.'

Doris bunched her fists and nodded.

'Next, I choose Mr Gilbert and Mr Brewer. These two gents have repeatedly proven their bravery in the Home Guard, and I love them dearly.'

The couple gave Faye a bow of their heads.

'Mrs Pritchett is one of our oldest residents, and the village is hers more than any other's here. I would be honoured if she would join us.'

Mrs Pritchett's pair of Yorkshire terriers yapped in approval as she lit a cigarette. 'Pleasure's mine, Faye.'

'Reverend Jacobs is the spiritual soul of our village, and he's been helped through some dark days by Edith Palmer, and so I choose them to join me.'

The Reverend and Edith sat side by side on a fallen log. Timothy had some colour back in his cheeks and Edith looked like she could wrestle a bear.

'And finally, I choose Miss Gordon, a fellow bell-ringer, and not least because she was sensible enough to bring a bow and arrow with her.'

Miss Gordon proudly raised her bow high.

'And those are my Nine Worthies—'

'That's eight,' Miss Charlotte said.

'Oh,' Faye said, immediately thinking of Constable Muldoon or Mr Paine, but then she noticed a movement in the shadows of the wood. 'Then I choose him.'

She pointed beyond the clearing and all heads turned to see what she had seen.

The woodwose stood by the hollow oak, his club resting on his shoulder.

KEEP BUGGERING ON

They came with the rising sun. A parade of villagers snaking through the wood, which, for once, did not play games with them. Not with the woodwose leading from the front.

Faye and Bertie, May Queen and King, were next, flanked by their Nine Worthies and the witches. Bertie had his stick and knapsack over his shoulder and wore a crown of bluebells. They were followed by the Morris Men, who danced and clacked their sticks in time with Mr Loaf's fiddle, Henry Mogg's melodeon, Finlay Motspur's tambourine and the drums of the Roberts twins. Bobby Newton hopped about under the sackcloth of his hoodening horse, back bent as he showed the way for the remaining villagers. Dozens of them came, many of whom had gathered up fallen branches and struck them in time with the Morris Men. It was an eerie sound that sent foxes running for cover and birds spiralling into the sky.

All had protective ash smeared in stripes across their

faces. Faye and Bertie carried a flaming torch each. Mrs Teach had surprised everyone with her ability to whip up fabric wicks out of spare rags plucked from the Morris Men's Border costumes, popping them on oak branches and lighting them with the flame from the fire by the hollow oak.

Faye expected trouble, and it didn't take long to kick off.

The first attack came from the front. The ghost of a headless Luftwaffe pilot rushed directly at them, arms outstretched.

The woodwose twirled his club like a cricket bat and brought it swinging through the pilot's transparent torso. The thing vanished in a swirl of ectoplasmic mist.

'That was him!' Bobby said, peering out from under his hoodening cloak, his voice tight with fear. 'That's the pilot who attacked me earlier. I mean, he had a head back then. At least, until that hairy fella ripped it off.'

Faye tensed, gripping Bertie's hand. This was just the beginning.

'Everyone be at the ready,' she called to the villagers. 'Just remember that these are spirits. They can't harm you. You'll be safe.'

Her last few words were interrupted by a squeak from Mr Loaf's fiddle. Faye glanced back to find him batting his instrument at a ghostly wraith that enveloped him in a roiling mist. He curled into a ball and wailed, kicking his legs like a child. The shapeless entity plunged a tendril into his mouth and he began to choke. So much for Faye's assurances of safety.

'Faye, we should help him,' Bertie said.

Faye shook her head. 'We can't move beyond the protection of the Nine Worthies, Bertie. That's exactly what Otto is trying to do with these attacks. To play on our sympathies and draw us out.'

As poor Mr Loaf thrashed about, his fellow Morris Men faltered.

'No! Don't stop!' Miss Charlotte clapped a rhythm. 'Your dance will protect him.'

Captain Marshall nodded at his men and they resumed their Border Morris with renewed vigour.

The wraith, clearly no enthusiast of Morris dancing, gave an unholy moan and expelled itself from Mr Loaf's trachea, spiralling into nothing in the gloom.

Bobby helped Mr Loaf to his feet. The addled funeral director staggered about, clutching at his neck.

'No time for that,' Miss Charlotte insisted. 'Play, man. Play like your life depends on it!'

'Which it most certainly does,' Mrs Teach muttered.

Mr Loaf rested his fiddle on his shoulder and, even as he gasped to refill his lungs, resumed drawing the bow across the strings, summoning something musical enough for the Morris Men to dance to. Henry Mogg's melodeon joined in, accompanied by the shambolic percussion section of Messrs Motspur and Roberts.

'Stand and deliver!' bellowed a voice from ahead.

'Oh, blimey. What now?' Faye craned her head around the woodwose to see a spectral highwayman blocking the path. He was flanked by his gang – a handful of thugs armed to the teeth with pistols and swords.

The woodwose raced at the group, swinging his club and despatching a pair of them immediately. The others ducked around him and came at the Worthies, firing their pistols. But the Morris Men played through them, their wild Border Morris dancing and aggressive clacking sticks turning the robbers into ectoplasmic mist.

'Faye, what the sodding hell is going on?' Terrence gestured at the lighter-than-air droplets evaporating around them.

'Otto's trying to scare us,' Faye said.

'It's bloody working,' her father replied, edging closer to Doris, whose stern face was both petrified and determined. It was a look that many of the villagers had developed out of necessity over the course of the war.

'Brace yourself, Terrence.' Mrs Teach made a fist. 'From what we've seen so far, I suspect Otto is resurrecting the spirits of those souls who have perished in these woods. And these trees have seen quite a bit of bloodshed over the years.'

Mrs Teach wasn't wrong. Roundhead cavalry from the Civil War charged them next, ghostly steeds thundering from the rear.

The woodwose vaulted about the parade, banishing as many Cromwellians as he could, but their numbers were overwhelming. Soon, they were mingling with the long tail of terrified villagers who cowered beneath the kicking hooves of the phantom cavalry.

Milly Baxter broke away from the pack, hands flailing as she dashed into the labyrinth of trees.

'Milly, no!' Faye cried. 'Come back!'

More ghostly warriors charged at them. Normans in chain mail, Saxons with axes, Norse berserkers with wild eyes and banshee screams. A cohort of Roman legionaries outflanked them, accompanied by a pair of battle elephants topped with little castles. Miss Gordon loosed arrows at them, but they passed straight through.

The soldiers' supernatural weapons couldn't harm anyone, but the villagers were too preoccupied with being terrified out of their minds to notice.

'We've got to keep together, we've got to keep moving, we've got to keep ...' Faye faltered. No one was listening.

Thankfully, Faye's May King had a rallying cry.

'We've got to keep buggering on!' Bertie hollered, raising a fist. 'Keep buggering on!'

'Good one, Bertie,' Terrence said, then cupped his hands around his mouth. 'Keep buggering on!'

Faye and the witches picked up the chant. Mr Loaf played along with his fiddle, Henry Mogg's melodeon picked up the tune, Finlay Motspur and the Roberts twins found a rhythm they could agree on, the Morris Men danced in time and soon every villager was bellowing, 'Keep buggering on! Keep buggering on!'

The woodwose continued to swipe at the spirit warriors, as did the Morris Men with their sticks. Even Milly Baxter came haring back with a fallen branch and gave a Viking what for. She inspired the other villagers to strike back and it wasn't long before the air was thick with evaporating ectoplasm and dozens of voices chanting, 'Keep buggering on!' in harmony.

Faye felt two inches taller and had never been more proud of her friends and neighbours as they made the wood theirs once more.

But they would need to reclaim their homes next, and she suspected it wouldn't be so simple.

Otto's Change of Heart

The villagers crossed the old Roman bridge and found themselves at the foot of the Wode Road.

The music from Mr Loaf's fiddle stopped, the Roberts twins ceased their drumming and the Morris Men ended their merry dance.

The scene was one of mournful devastation. Few homes or shops had any windows left intact, doors were framed by streaks of smoke like black weeds crawling up the walls and fragments of roof tiles littered the cobbles like shrapnel.

The facade of the Green Man was still pierced by Otto's Rolls-Royce, like a dagger in the heart of the village. But the old oak beams kept the building standing.

The morning air was sweet, and tendrils of steam gently rose from the puddles left by last night's rain. Faye heard little gasps and whispers. The strength and unity she had felt from her fellow villagers on their parade was fading fast.

'Faye.' Petunia was suddenly at her side, making her jump. Faye wondered who else could see the ghostly girl as she leaned close and whispered, 'Otto is in the church. He's doing something rather unexpected.'

'Unexpected how?' Faye asked.

'He's ... rebuilding it.'

'What?' Faye turned to Petunia, who could only shrug. Faye raised her flaming torch. 'This way, everyone!'

Flanked by the woodwose, Petunia, Bertie and the witches, Faye marched up the Wode Road.

Saint Irene's Church was a gutted, smouldering shell. The roof was gone, though a few beams reached for the morning sun like blackened fingers. Grey tears of melted lead dripped from the warped windows. The walls still stood, but the old Kentish ragstone was stained with soot and ash.

Reverend Jacobs gave a pained sob and fell to his knees, crossing himself and praying for strength. Edith crouched by his side, embracing and comforting him.

Faye kept on, ducking under the leaning lychgate, opening the church's blackened oak door and stepping inside.

The first thing that caught her eye were two swifts darting about in a beam of light, swooping low over the fallen pews, then spiralling above the altar.

Then she saw him. Otto sat before a fallen brass cross in the centre of a pentagram. The five-pointed star was painted in what looked to Faye like blood.

Otto's eyes were closed, his legs crossed and his palms raised to the sky. Beads of sweat clustered on his bald head. His skin had a pinkish hue, and it was covered in flaky patches and pocks from scabs, as if he had been burned recently.

Around him, fragments of stone rose from the piles of rubble, drifted through the air and settled on the walls, slotting perfectly into cracks and fissures like pieces of a giant puzzle.

'He really is.' Miss Charlotte's voice was hushed in disbelief as she stood by Faye. 'He's rebuilding the bloody church.'

Mrs Teach wrinkled her brow. 'What's he playing at?'

Others joined them, filing in through the oak door, gasping at the terrible damage, then becoming deathly silent when their eyes fell on the old Druid in the tweed suit surrounded by floating fragments of stone and glass.

Otto opened his eyes, and the whites glowed like the midsummer sun.

'Ah, Faye Bright. In person, at last,' he said, trying to sound cheerful, though she could hear the strain in his voice, laced with hatred. 'It's been too long. Dover, wasn't it?'

Faye nodded, trying her best not to be unnerved by his glowing eyes. 'Last time I saw you, your arm was on fire.'

Otto chuckled, then noticed they weren't alone. 'You've brought some friends and . . .' He gasped when he saw the woodwose, then dipped his head in respect. '*Der Wilde Mann. Willkommen.*'

To Faye's surprise, the woodwose returned the nod.

'We have men like him in Bavaria,' Otto explained. 'Such a shame you'll never visit Naila. Quite beautiful. They worship his kind there, you know.' He surveyed the other villagers gathered behind Faye. 'What a splendid gathering on what promises to be a beautiful Beltane.'

Faye summoned every inch of bravery she possessed. 'It was supposed to be my wedding day, Otto. But you can't just let other people be happy, can you? Ruining my wedding is one thing – I suppose you're entitled to your revenge – but to destroy the homes and livelihoods of the people of Woodville is despicable. You deserve what's coming to you, sunshine.'

Otto, to Faye's surprise, nodded gravely. 'It's true, I have done terrible things to … Oh, hello.' He brightened when he noticed Petunia floating behind the witches. 'A pleasure to see you, little girl. Petunia, wasn't it?'

Petunia folded her arms and scowled in the way that only young girls can.

'Out of pain, I hope?' Otto enquired sincerely. 'Free to do as you wish now, hmm? Good.' He smiled at Faye, his eyes still glowing. 'I do so enjoy a happy ending. I like your dress, by the way. You were saying?'

Faye shifted, suddenly uncomfortable in her wedding dress. She missed her dungarees and jacket. At least she had kept her comfy boots on. 'Normally, I'd order you to leave this place and never return,' she told Otto, 'but I have this nagging feeling that you'll just keep coming back for more, so I'm going to end this now.'

Otto pouted. 'That sounds rather final.'

'It's meant to be.'

'I understand.' Otto slowly shook his head as fragments of stone continued to drift through the air and slot into place in the walls around them. 'A desire for vengeance is powerful, Faye, I know. But something quite astonishing happened to me last night. I . . . I had a revelation. Two men came for me. Druids from the Order of the Black Sun. Oh . . .' Otto winced and gestured to Terrence. 'I apologise in advance for the bloody mess that you will find in your cellar. Now, where was I?'

Mrs Teach gripped her handbag. 'Some nonsense about a revelation,' she said. 'Now do please get on with it.'

'I say we kill him now,' muttered Miss Charlotte.

Otto's glowing eyes widened. 'Yes, a revelation! In defeating these two assassins, I discovered a strength that I never knew was possible. A power so strong that it satisfied every shallow craving I have ever had. And it made me realise that I can use this power to make the world a better place.'

Miss Charlotte leaned closer to Faye. 'I'm serious. This is how every crackpot tyrant starts. I can wring his neck right now.'

'Something tells me it'll take more than a broken neck to stop him.' Faye stepped forwards, raising her voice. 'Otto, you can't expect any of us to believe you for a second, surely?'

'Of course you have your doubts. As would I. Which is why I'm demonstrating my good intentions by rebuilding your church.' Otto angled his head, speaking over Faye's shoulder to the villagers. 'Your whole village, in fact. Soon it will be as good as new.'

Murmurs rippled through the crowd. There wasn't a single person among them who hadn't lost something in Otto's inferno.

'I will even rebuild your bell tower, Faye.' Otto smiled and it gave Faye the shivers. 'You can have bells on your wedding day. My gift to you.'

The murmurs took on a more positive tone. Faye looked about her. The villagers were nodding. In the time she had been talking with Otto, a whole section of the church roof had been replaced. It was as though he was turning back time.

'F-Faye.' Reverend Jacobs stepped over the rubble, aided by Edith. 'Perhaps we could exercise a degree of clemency, hmm? "Forgetting those things which are behind, and reaching forth unto those things which are before, I press towards the mark." Philippians, chapter three, verse—'

'Actually, Reverend, I'm going to take a lesson from the Book of Faye, chapter one, verse one. I'll take this old Nazi – who, I would remind you, possessed your mind while he pretended to be a demon – and kick his arse from here into next week.'

'Please, Faye.' The Reverend clasped his hands

together. 'The church ...' He turned to the villagers. 'Can we find it in our hearts to forgive this man?'

Faye took a breath and closed her eyes. She didn't want to see who said what, but there was no mistaking the words as the villagers debated.

'Maybe he's not so bad after all?'

'He doesn't look like a Nazi. Would a Nazi wear a nice tweed suit?'

'He's rebuilding our church. I say leave him to it.'

She opened her eyes and bunched her fists, very much a bride looking for a fight. She beckoned the witches closer.

'Miss Charlotte, Mrs Teach, I think it's time we showed them who he really is. And who we are.'

'Indeed.' Mrs Teach inclined her head. 'And who are we, exactly?'

'Witches,' Miss Charlotte said.

'Yes, but we're also their friends and neighbours,' Faye said. 'And I am their May Queen – a Corn Bride – and that comes with a certain responsibility.'

Charlotte frowned. 'Faye, I'm not sure you know what you're saying.'

Bertie's eyes darted from witch to witch. 'What do you mean, Faye? What responsibility?'

Faye's heart twisted to see his open mouth and wide eyes. She wanted to make love to him, and kiss him and assure him that everything would be all right, but she couldn't lie to him. He had every right to be worried. He knew what she was planning. She could see the panic in his eyes.

'Faye?' he asked again, his voice cracking.

She didn't answer. Faye wanted to reassure Bertie, but the odds were there was a good chance that Faye would be dead within the next five minutes.

MIRROR, MIRROR

Bertie had been told there would be moments in his life that would change him. A lot of the pilots who came into the pub spoke of those tiny decisions, made in a split-second, that had saved their lives. Bertie himself had survived all kinds of scrapes in the last year or so that had emboldened him. But after what he and Faye had just done in the woods, well ... It was an eye-opener, let's just leave it at that. He'd thought he'd loved her before, but now he loved her more than life itself. He knew she would be going away soon – there was no avoiding her duty – but she would eventually return, and they could do ... *that* again. Bertie was no witch or warlock, but he knew magic when he saw it.

But before any of this could happen, they had to be rid of Otto.

Bertie gripped his flaming torch in one hand and the stick of his knapsack in the other as he stood by Faye, ready to leap to her defence. Not that she was fazed by the Bavarian Druid with his glowing eyes and floating bits of ragstone. It was the villagers who were turning against her now.

Reverend Jacobs was desperate to restore his church. Milly Baxter and Betty Marshall were backing him up with sniping remarks, which was no surprise. But even the more sympathetic villagers – Mr Loaf the undertaker, Mr Paine from the newsagent's, Mrs Yorke from the bakery – were all murmuring their doubts. If this Otto fellow could rebuild the village, why not let him do it?

What Bertie knew, and they didn't, was that Otto was a conniving bastard. He was ready to alert the villagers to this, but he had also learned his lesson about interfering. He now knew when to hold back and let Faye do her thing.

'Folks, I understand your concerns,' Faye said, turning to the villagers. 'Who wouldn't want to give him a chance to make everything as it was, eh? But let me show you who you're dealing with here.'

Holding her torch in one hand, Faye bent her knees and crouched in her ivory wedding dress to snatch up a shard of glass. She stood and held it over her head, turning it so that it caught the brightening sunlight. 'Can everyone pick up a little bit of glass like this? Mind your fingers. Don't cut yourselves. That's it.'

Bertie tucked the knapsack under his arm and crouched to pick up his own shard of glass. About half the villagers did the same. The other half remained standing with their arms folded.

'The May Queen calls upon her Nine Worthies to

protect her!' Faye cried, and Bertie and the witches found themselves surrounded by the Worthies. Terrence caught his eye and gave him a wink, though Bertie could sense the fear in him. In all of them. Even the woodwose, who stood ready by Faye's side.

Otto remained sitting cross-legged as he continued to reconstruct the church that he had destroyed. In his tweed suit he looked like an ordinary fellow who might read the papers while smoking a pipe and wearing his favourite slippers. Apart from the glowing eyes and floating debris, of course.

Faye held her shard over the flame of her torch. The light of the fire danced in the glass of her spectacles. Bertie was overcome with the urge to hold her tight and protect her, but her steely resolve kept him at bay.

'Candle magic and mirror magic,' she said, loud enough for all to hear. 'Some of the first rituals I ever learned. I remember this one from my mother's book.' She glanced at Mrs Teach and Miss Charlotte, who did not flinch at the mention of the book they had burned, the one that had meant so much to Faye as the last connection to her mother. 'This flame is from our Beltane fire. It protects us and gives us power.'

Bertie wondered why her glass wasn't cracking in the intense heat. Instead, its surface turned a shining green, then purple, then black.

The same was happening to the shard of glass that he held. Every villager who had a shard of glass saw the same thing. Green glass, then purple, then black, then a mirror.

'Folks.' Faye raised her mirrored glass for all to see. 'Aim your mirror at Otto and look at the reflection.'

Bertie did so, along with many other villagers. A few cried out, dropping their mirrors. The church echoed with the tinkling of broken glass.

Bertie couldn't look away from the ghastly sight.

In the mirror, Otto crouched over Bertie's prone body, a bloody hole in the lad's chest. He plunged a hand inside, wrenching out Bertie's still-beating heart. Otto's skin was bright red, blistered and scabbed, and his eyes glowed white again as he bit down on the heart, shaking his head vigorously as he tore a lump loose, blood dribbling from the corners of his mouth. As Otto chewed, he made a sound like someone squeezing a wet sponge.

Bertie felt bile rising in his gullet and had to take a few sharp breaths to keep it down. Around him, he could hear other villagers doing the same.

'That's who Otto really is,' Faye cried.

Those without mirrors rushed to see what disgusted their neighbours so. There followed more glass tinkling as mirrors were dropped or batted away in horror.

'He did this with the men who came to kill him. It's what gives him strength. While you lot sit back and wait for him to rebuild the village, he'll come to you in the night and feast on your hearts, one by one.'

Bertie's ears popped as every piece of floating debris dropped to the church's stone floor in what sounded like the world's shortest round of applause. He looked up from his glass to find Otto standing. His eyes were no longer glowing, and he was smiling. Not a friendly smile. More of a *You're-all-going-to-die* smile.

Faye tossed her glass away and held her torch with both hands. 'They see you for who you really are now, Otto.'

'Do you think I care? I know what I am. I came to terms with that centuries ago. I can see the hatred in your eyes. All of you. There is no one on this tawdry planet who loathes me more than I do.' He pressed a hand to his chest whimsically. 'And that loathing gives me strength.'

'Doesn't have to be like that.' Faye tilted her head. 'You ever thought of being nice to people?'

Otto's surprised laugh made Bertie wonder if this was actually the first time anyone had ever suggested this to the Druid. Otto pursed his lips, considering the idea.

'And what would be the point of that? This is all there is. The hate, intolerance, cruelty, spite. It was here long before you feeble creatures ever existed and it will remain for an eternity after you have turned to dust. Darkness and oblivion and pain. It is this ultimate truth that gives me my strength. We come from darkness, we return to darkness. Embrace the brutal honesty of it, Faye. It's liberating.'

Bertie's skin crawled as the bleak truth of Otto's words took hold of him, but Faye simply sighed.

'I feel sorry for you, Otto, I really do.'

'Spare me your platitudes.'

'No, it's true.' Faye said, stepping out of the protective circle of the Nine Worthies.

Bertie instinctively moved forwards, but the touch of Miss Charlotte's hand on his shoulder paralysed him. He couldn't be sure if it was magic or his own fear, but his legs were as heavy as anchors.

'There's a lot of darkness about, especially now,' Faye continued as she closed in on Otto. 'No rationing of pain and sorrow for us. And I reckon you're right that it'll always be a fact of life. But ask yourself this, Otto: is it worth fighting for? Is the reward you get worth the aggro?' She glanced at his scalded skin before giving a little shrug. 'Me? I go looking for the light. It might only be tiny and difficult to find, but there's always a flame somewhere. A flickering candle in the dark. And it endures. It grows.'

Otto brushed the air with his hand. A breeze blasted between them, snuffing out Faye's torch. 'Yes, but it never lasts, child.'

Faye tossed the smouldering torch away and surged forwards, gripping Otto's rough and blistered hands. He tried to pull away, his head shaking, his brow furrowed.

'W-what are you doing?'

'Just a little test, Otto.' Faye smiled and called over her shoulder. 'Captain!'

On cue, Captain Marshall and his set of dancers burst into action. The Roberts twins banged their drums, Finlay Motspur whacked his tambourine, the dancers' sticks clacked in time with Mr Loaf's fiddle and Henry Mogg's melodeon as they danced a Border Morris around Faye and Otto.

The ghostly children joined them, dancing and singing,

> *'Little fly upon the wall,*
> *Ain't you got no clothes at all?*
> *Ain't you got no blouse or skirt?*
> *Ain't you got no shimmy shirt?'*

Bertie felt a strange warmth wash over him. Something about the dance and the music and the sunlight blossomed a new hope inside him. Things were going to be good after all. He had to squint as Faye's ivory wedding dress began to glow.

'The Corn Bride died today, Otto,' Faye told him.

Beads of sweat dripped down Otto's forehead. Both of them were glowing as Faye held his hands tight.

'And this dress wasn't all she gave me.'

White flames erupted around them. Otto and Faye threw back their heads and gritted their teeth.

'Faye!' Bertie cried, but still he could not move his legs. He could barely turn his head to find Terrence, also frozen, with Mrs Teach resting a hand on his shoulder. She looked on, unblinking, jaw set, as the heat intensified.

⁊

Faye has never known pain like it. Every atom of her is on fire. It's like the sun has fallen on her.

You think you can defeat me, child?

Otto's voice comes to her through the roar of the torment.

It's not about the fight, Otto. It's about who lasts longest. We're both hurting, but you need to ask yourself what will keep you going through the pain? What's your reward at the end of this? Darkness? Oblivion?

And you?

Otto's words become distorted moans as his flesh blackens.

What is your reward, girl?

Faye turns, even though her blistered skin cries out in protest. She looks to her father. To Mrs Teach and Miss Charlotte. And to her Bertie. And she gives Otto her answer.

Love. Love will see me through.

She grits her teeth. Turns back to him.

And besides, I'm not a girl.

She loosens one hand, shows him her mirror, angling it so that he can see who she really is in the reflection. A blank face of straw. Now Otto knows what she is doing. But it's too late, and he screams. Centuries of hate and bitterness have led to this moment, and he is finally defeated. The burning in his blood washes over him. The flesh slides off both of their bones. Otto gargles his last as his eyes melt and shrink in their sockets and his brain is cooked in his skull. Faye's glasses crack and melt.

Another voice comes to her.

I'm so proud of you, poppet. I love you.

Love you, too, Mum.

Then darkness.

ALL GOOD CHILDREN . . .

June, 1941

One, two, three, four, five, six, seven,
All good children go to heaven;
When they die their sin's forgiven.

One, two, three, four, five, six, seven,
All good children go to heaven:
A penny by the water,
Tuppence by the sea,
Threepence by the railway,
Out goes she!

TRADITIONAL CHILDREN'S RHYME

They had a funeral for Faye, but there had been nothing
to bury. Not even ashes. She and Otto had been inciner-
ated in a flash of light.

Bertie had been lost in the fog of grief ever since. He woke, brushed his teeth, got dressed and managed all the usual functions of life, but food was little more than a stodge that caught in his throat, drink burned his gullet and birdsong was an irritant.

Terrence was a shadow of his former self. His lined face remained uncreased by smiles or laughter. He simply looked baffled, as if unable to grasp what he had witnessed.

Every day, all day, Bertie worked with Terrence, rebuilding the Green Man in silence. If it hadn't been for the patience and kindness of Doris, the pair of them would have wasted away. What made it all the more heartbreaking was that, in the tradition of these strange events in Woodville, the villagers eventually forgot what had really happened. They spoke of a devastating fire, a demolished church, half-remembered memories of an air raid and that strange night they spent in the wood. But they never mentioned Otto. And, since the funeral, no one had mentioned Faye.

Almost a year to the day since the crow folk came to Woodville, the village returned to some semblance of normality.

Petunia took it upon herself to return the ghostly schoolchildren back to where Faye had found them in the tunnels of Oxford Circus underground station. When they embarked on their journey, they were rosy-cheeked and full of cheer. Any sign of their Blitz trauma was gone. When Petunia returned, she said they'd run into the darkness singing an old rhyme about good children going to heaven.

Harold the budgie was adopted by Miss Charlotte, who welcomed him to her lodgings above the antique shop. Her room appeared to have been completely unaffected by the fire, though truthfully it was difficult to tell.

And for a while, that was the end of it.

⚥

Towards the middle of June, Miss Charlotte and Mrs Teach came to the pub. The pair had remained silent on the subject of Faye's death and the strange events that had led up to it. Bertie couldn't help but resent their lack of sympathy, but he knew better than to publicly scold a witch.

Terrence was plastering the ceiling of the saloon bar and Bertie was holding his stepladder steady when they arrived. They stood framed by the scaffold that propped up the new ceiling, the pear-shaped Mrs Teach gripping her handbag, the slender Miss Charlotte sporting a new crimson eye patch to match her coat. There was none of the old small talk or banter. Mrs Teach got straight to the point.

'Miss Charlotte and I have become aware of a curious coincidence, and we have a feeling that it may be—' Mrs Teach folded her lips as she thought '—significant.'

Terrence wiped his brow and slowly clambered down the stepladder. His once cheery voice was drained of all its joy. 'Mrs Teach, with all due respect—'

'We're having the same dream,' Miss Charlotte interrupted, 'and we wondered if you might be having a similar experience?'

Bertie stepped aside as Terrence reached the bottom of the ladder. They exchanged a short and guilty look.

'What sort of dreams?' Terrence asked.

'The ghostly children came singing to me,' Miss Charlotte said.

There was a brief pause before Mrs Teach nudged Miss Charlotte, who rolled her eyes and – to Bertie's astonishment – began to sing.

'*Two little witches, walking all day. One named Charlotte, one named Faye.*' She waved herself into silence. 'You get the idea.'

Bertie's heart flipped. Terrence gave a little gasp.

'The Reverend Jacobs reports having heard this one in his sleep,' Mrs Teach said, before clearing her throat and reciting,

> '*Pious Parson, pious people,*
> *Sold the bells to build a steeple.*
> *A very fine trick of the Woodville people,*
> *To sell their bells and build no steeple.*'

'And what about you, Mrs Teach?' Bertie asked. 'Have they sung to you?'

Mrs Teach hesitated. 'I have had my sleep interrupted these past three nights with a rousing rendition of "*A wise old owl sat on an oak; the more she saw, the less she spoke; the less she spoke, the more she heard; why aren't we all like that wise old bird?"'* She cleared her throat. 'Frankly, I'm offended.'

'And you, Bertie?' Miss Charlotte pinned him with her one good eye.

Dreams are strange things. If anyone had asked Bertie over breakfast about his dreams, he would not have been able to recall a single thing, but now all the mischief and joy in the children's voices came rushing back to him.

> *'Rosy apple, lemon and pear,*
> *Bunch of roses she shall wear,*
> *Gold and silver by her side,*
> *I know Faye shall be my bride.'*

Bertie looked up, only then realising he had been singing aloud. His eyes stung, and his cheeks were wet with tears.

Terrence rested a hand on his shoulder and squeezed. 'I had a song, too,' he said. 'It's one that Kathryn would sing to Faye when she was a baby:

> *"Your baby has gone down the plughole,*
> *Your baby has gone down the plug.*
> *The poor little thing was so skinny and thin,*
> *She should have been bathed in a jug.*
> *Your baby is perfectly happy,*
> *She won't need a bath anymore,*
> *She's floating away down the drainpipe,*
> *Not lost but gone before ..."'*

Terrence sniffed and rubbed his jaw. Bertie couldn't be sure if the older man was about to laugh or cry.

'All of us have been revisited by those little scamps,' Mrs Teach said. 'I think someone is trying to convey a message to us. Either the spirit of Faye, or her mother.'

'Only one way to know for sure.' Miss Charlotte opened her palm to reveal a cluster of strange old coins to Bertie and Terrence. 'Ever heard of corpse coins?' she asked.

Soon, doors and windows were closed, candles were lit and all four of them lay on the floor of the saloon bar with obolus coins over their eyes. Bertie, Terrence, Mrs Teach and Miss Charlotte shared a vision . . .

⌀

Faye awakes naked by the hawthorn tree. Her specs are gone, melted in the moment she passed through the aether. She is gasping for air, her hands are trembling, clods of soil spill from her body and the only noises from her are wordless, hoarse cries of fear.

Someone rushes to her side and wraps a blanket around her. Words are spoken. Old words with such power that the mind knows not to host them for too long, for fear of causing the listener to lose their sanity.

Faye's skin glows. A ripple passes through the air. Crows clap their wings as they scatter to find somewhere less dangerously magical.

Faye's hands stop shaking; her breathing calms.

'Blimmin' 'eck. It worked.'

'*Of course it did.*'

Faye looks up into the brown eyes of Vera Fivetrees, High Witch of the British Empire.

'*Welcome back, child.*'

Behind Vera is a two-seater Spitfire, painted black. A young pilot, the same woman who flew Vera here last summer, sits in the rear bubble.

'*Ginny will fly you to London,*' *Vera explains.*

'*What about you?*'

'*I'll take the train. Don't worry about me. And you ...*' *Vera turns directly to those watching.* '*No one can know. Understand?*'

'*Yes, Mrs Fivetrees,*' *comes Bertie's voice.*

'*We promise,*' *Terrence says.*

They stand on either side of Faye. Bertie has his arms wrapped around her over the blanket.

'*This isn't a childish promise, boys. You are both bound by the Official Secrets Act. Tell anyone and you're off to jail, or worse!*' *Vera Fivetrees warns them.*

Terrence hands Faye a bag. '*There's a change of clothes, your spare specs and a toothbrush, and ...*' *He looks to Bertie.*

'*Don't forget this.*' *Bertie opens his palm, revealing a small gold band.*

Faye wraps the blanket tighter around her as she looks down at the ring. She smiles sadly, then folds his hand closed. '*You look after it, Bertie. I'll be back before you know it.*' *She kisses him so fiercely that she almost drops her blanket. Terrence and Vera have to look away.*

The Spitfire's engine growls, flames burst from its exhausts and the props spin.

'I have to go.' Faye hugs her father, and kisses both him and Bertie again before running to the fighter plane. They watch as it takes off and is chased by the rising sun.

﹠

Bertie was the first to rise, gasping for air as the obolus coins fell from his eyes, clattering to the floor. Terrence was next, and the pair did their best to evade the glares of the two witches.

Mrs Teach was the first to unleash her outrage, rising to her feet. 'You both knew about this? You knew Faye was alive all this time?'

Bertie helped Terrence get to his feet. The pair made quite a performance of it, in the vain hope that they could avoid the inevitable ear-bashing. All they could do was shrug apologetically.

That didn't stop Mrs Teach from fuming. 'There was a funeral! You both looked so grief-stricken!'

'Well, we do miss her,' Terrence said.

'And Vera Fivetrees said we had to have a funeral just in case any spies were watching,' Bertie added.

'You clever little stags,' Miss Charlotte said, baring her teeth in an unsettling smile. 'I never knew you two had it in you.'

'Why didn't you tell us?' Mrs Teach demanded.

'Faye told us not to,' Bertie said.

'And you heard Vera,' Terrence cut in. 'We don't want to be breaking the Official Secrets Act, do we?'

Mrs Teach made fists. 'I'll be breaking a lot more than that, I can tell you.'

Miss Charlotte rested a hand on her fellow witch's shoulder. 'Philomena, I think these boys have a point. They were under no obligation to tell us, so ...' She broke off, thinking for a moment. 'Had Faye been planning this all along?'

Bertie shrugged. 'You know when she said she had a barmy plan? *That's* when she knew what to do. Even then, she didn't tell me everything. She made me memorise a special telephone number and said I should call Vera or Bellamy as soon as I could, then give them the Corn Bride's straw. So I cycled up to Hayward Lodge – I'd heard their telephone was still working, y'see – and made the call.'

'Vera turned up at the pub gone midnight,' Terrence said. 'That's when I found out about all this. I was half-mad with grief, then this witch from Grenada tells me the spirit of my daughter is in a sack of straw. Well, who was I to argue with that?'

'Vera spent all night making a huge corn doll from the straw. It was as big as me.' Bertie demonstrated by raising a hand as high as his head. 'And then we buried it in the field with the hawthorn tree. As the sun rose, Vera did her magic and Faye was ... well, reborn.'

Terrence nodded solemnly. 'We dug her out of the soil like a King Edward potato.'

'And you saw the rest,' Bertie said, ending their story.

'And she left us no letter? No word?' Mrs Teach

asked, and the pair shook their heads. 'That's gratitude for you.'

'That's war, Mrs Teach,' Bertie said, with as much defiance as he could muster.

Mrs Teach opened her mouth to protest, but Bertie raised his hand.

'Faye has a job to do. And if that means we have to pretend that she's ... not here, then so be it. She talked about being the light in the dark, and I reckon that's what we all need to be.'

The witches shared a look, and nodded.

Mrs Teach cleared her throat and spoke calmly. 'If you say so, Bertie.'

'I do,' he replied, his mouth dry. 'What do you say, Mr Bright?'

Bertie looked at Terrence, who was staring at the motes of dust gently drifting through a beam of sunlight. This was a man who had lost a daughter, found her again, and now had to let her go and continue pretending she was dead. How could a man endure such turmoil?

'Me?' Terrence blinked, smiled and slapped his thighs. 'I say we should put the kettle on.'

EPILOGUE

Somewhere beneath the Thames, a young woman in an ATS uniform is led through a long tunnel to a room that you won't find on any blueprints.

Some say that's because it was constructed in complete secrecy for a sinister purpose. Others reckon it's because it was once a broom cupboard.

The soldier accompanying the young woman raps a knuckle on the door.

'Enter!' a voice replies from the other side.

The soldier opens the door, allowing the young woman to step inside and, after a brief assessment, quickly determine that this was indeed once a broom cupboard. And a small one at that.

A man with a neatly trimmed beard, dressed in a tweed suit, sits behind a tiny desk that's host to several teetering piles of folders and paperwork. It takes some considerable gymnastic effort on his part to rise and shuffle around them.

'Am I delighted to see you?' Bellamy Dumonde

asks, before answering his own question. 'I most certainly am.'

He shakes the young woman's hand vigorously, then steps back, bumping into the table and creating an avalanche of paper that cascades to the floor.

'Oh, blinkin' flip, Belly,' says Faye Bright with a chuckle.

Bellamy flexes his lips into a smile and gestures around the tiny room. 'Such is the glamour of His Majesty's Secret Service, Agent Wynter. Let's get on with it, shall we? There's a war to win, you know.'

THE END

THE WITCHES OF WOODVILLE ...
MIGHT RETURN?

ACKNOWLEDGEMENTS

To my editor Georgie and the gang at Simon & Schuster UK.

My agent Ed Wilson and all at Johnson & Alcock.

Special thanks to Julian Barr and Ian W Sainsbury for once again casting their eyes over my dirty laundry.

A big thank you to Steve Austen and the Wantsum Morris Men for checking my Morris dancer bits. Any errors are my own.

And finally, my gratitude to everyone who's read these books, and especially you, that gorgeous nerd who reads the acknowledgements. I like you best.

JOIN THE WOODVILLE VILLAGE LIBRARY AND GET FREE STORIES

Head Librarian, Araminta Cranberry, welcomes all applications to join the village library. There you will find free stories featuring secret histories of Mrs Teach and Miss Charlotte, a tale from ancient Britain with a cameo from Julius Caesar, a full-colour comic book and a recipe for Jam Roly Poly, with more to come ...

Simply sign up for the Woodville Village Newsletter here:

https://witchesofwoodville.com/#library